THE GODDESS IS FIERCE

JB TREPAGNIER

THE GODDESS IS FIERCE

We have a witness, but they have no memories and could actually be the murderer.

Sol is a big, beautiful teddy bear. It's hard to believe he's capable of murdering witches. And Azren doesn't know what his motive could be any better than he does. It doesn't make sense, but there's no one else it could be unless they are just really good at hiding.

We can get all of Sol's memories back and hopefully exonerate him. We just have to locate a very tricky raven who likes to speak in riddles. No problem, right?

GEORGE

I wasn't prepared for what came out of Azren's mouth. Sol being a god wasn't what shocked me. Sol being *that* god, is what did it. We learned about Baldur in history. He was my Uncle Loki's kin and the one family member he refused to talk about when we asked.

Because Loki was the one who was responsible for his death. All he would ever say about Baldur was that he had deep regrets about it. Baldur wasn't involved with hurting Loki's kids at all and had always been kind to him. Loki picked him because it would hurt everyone who *was* involved the most.

From what I learned in history, Baldur was a beloved god associated with light who was supersensitive and had a bit of foresight. He started dreaming about his death, so his mother Frigg basically tried to figure out what his weakness was. She asked everything if it could kill him, but she forgot to ask the mistletoe.

They all assumed he didn't have one, since they

thought they ruled out everything. They thought he was a different kind of god, so they would throw weapons at him and celebrate they didn't harm him. But Loki was in the background, hurt about his kids and plotting.

He fashioned a spear out of mistletoe and brought it to one of these parties. Loki gave the spear to Baldur's blind brother Hod and guided his arm as he threw it. The spear pierced Baldur's heart and instantly killed him. Baldur's family hunted Loki and got their revenge by chaining him in a cave while snake venom dripped onto his face.

Loki and Odin had made their peace about the whole thing, but all Loki would ever say about it to me was that he wished he had done the whole thing differently, because Baldur didn't deserve what he did.

And he probably didn't. I didn't know Sol all that well, but I never got vibes off him that he was capable of murdering witches like that, even with his magic being totally gone.

But finding out he was Baldur changed all that.

I didn't know Baldur. Everything I'd ever been told about him was that he was a gentle god. I knew enough to know that when his family was hurting Loki's kids, Baldur wasn't involved in that. But he'd also been murdered and spent a ton of time in the Aether.

My dad went there willingly after he got tired of mortals until my mom was tricked into forcing him back into his vessel. There were a lot of gods hanging out there right now because they were tired of being alive. I was still kind of shaky on the whole thing, but I thought it was different if you went there willingly versus if you were murdered and forced there.

Baldur didn't remember anything. The guy in front of me seemed pretty broken up at the idea he could have brutally murdered all those witches. It looked like he still hadn't even processed finding out who the fuck he was. The Baldur I learned about in history class wasn't capable of that, but he wasn't that god anymore.

I looked to Azren for answers. I knew Azren didn't know every single god, but maybe they knew Baldur. I got my answer when Azren pulled him into a massive hug. Baldur looked stunned and just gave him a bro pat on the back.

"You know me?"

"A long time ago. After you died, I tried to make a deal with your parents to get you back, but it was beyond my skill unless I brought you back, mortal. To restore you *exactly* as you were, we needed your vessel. None of us have the skill to build one of those, so we had to wait for the Fates to do it.

"You've been dead thousands of years. Your mother, Frigg, is in Asgard and your father, Odin, has been hanging out on this realm just in case you came back to either place. They would have felt it if you came back with your magic. If you had your magic and memories, you could have sought them out. You've been here this whole time?"

"Here and around. This is kind of a lot to process. I didn't exactly go to any type of school. The only thing I know about the gods is what I read from books and then later when the internet was available. I only really read about the ones who created anything because I was trying to figure out if someone made me and messed up. Would Baldur have killed those witches?"

"Absolutely not. You used to be kind, gentle, and beloved. I can't tell you if that changed while you were in the Aether. Most gods that died didn't take so long to come back."

"Can we get his memories back?" Matilda asked.

"Maybe not what happened after, but who he was before he died?"

"First things first," Azren said. "I need to find his father. Stay here with him. I'll be back."

Azren disappeared in a cloud of smoke. I'd met Odin before when I was younger. He scared me at first. Odin was massive, with a waist-length beard and one eye. My mom realized I was being a little asshole about it and pulled me aside.

I put on my big girl panties and went back into the room. Odin ended up being great. He loved kids. Michael was six and Matilda and I were five. Odin had the *best* stories. We kept begging for more until we were falling asleep on his couch. He kept telling them until we were out.

Now that I was older, I realized Odin always had this profound sadness about him. I always thought he isolated himself in his villa away from his family because he was eccentric, like the other gods I'd met, and had some big reason that wasn't explained to me.

It had been his son this entire time. He'd been waiting for Baldur this entire time and Baldur had been here with no memories or magic. Baldur looked terrified at the idea of meeting his dad. I didn't *know* if he was the one doing this, but I still felt bad for him.

"I've met your dad. We'd stay with him if we'd vacation in France. He's intense, but he's brilliant and really good with kids. I imagine he was a great dad. You were born like me instead of created, and your parents weren't weird about that like some of the other gods. Like, they can *choose* not to have kids, but do it anyway and treat them like garbage. Your parents weren't like that."

"It's honestly a lot. What if I came back broken?"

Azren would fix it, but I knew exactly what Baldur

needed right now. We could stew on theories if he would ever get his magic and memories back and if he was the one who killed all those witches, or we could talk about anything else.

Who was Baldur *right now?* He was a god before, but he'd been living on Earth for a few hundred years with no memories or magic. I'm sure there were big parts of him that were still the same even without his memories, and there were parts that were new because of his experiences.

I needed to distract him and get to know him. He was a born god, *just like me.* And there was one person I knew who was also a part of this that had the ability to set everyone at ease, even Baldur.

I needed West.

WEST

This was like, the second time we had a roommate intervention with Church because of George. The first time, I didn't join in because he didn't do anything wrong. I mean, yeah, I thought he should just go talk to her instead of creeping in trees, but that girl was special. You didn't want to make a dumbass of yourself on the first impression and ruin it. Church nearly did because he was creeping in trees instead of *talking* to her, but she was just insanely cool like that.

We were having the second intervention because he legitimately was being a dumbass this time. The dude found out his girl was a god and ran instead of immediately falling on his knees and worshipping her. I mean, she would have *hated* that, but not as much as it would have hurt her the way he actually reacted.

"She could have kept her secret and let one of the other gods heal me, but I would have been in pain much longer. Fuck, Drake. If that was just your hair, I *never* want to experience your venom. I didn't think anything could hurt worse than when that Earth ball exploded near my face and I lost my hearing, but that was so much worse."

Yeah, I didn't want to think about that. Oscar was my brother, and Drake was becoming a pretty good friend. He was my boyfriend in law now. If there hadn't been a god in the room, Oscar could have been permanently disfigured. And Drake had been violated when Kaylee stole his hair. He'd been paranoid about that this entire time.

Church was the only one of us angry about her secret, but I think Oscar and Ren would have been, too, if they found out she kept it while Oscar was in pain like that. I'd known her secret this entire time and the reason she was keeping it, but I might have felt some things, too, if she watched Oscar suffer when she could fix it.

"I *hate* that if someone was going to make a potion with my hair, they had to use it on people I care about."

"What's the deal, anyway?" Ren asked. "She's still the same person. You knew she was insanely powerful. We've been around enough gods to have figured out that she feels exactly like them. George wasn't faking it when she was nervous about having sex with us for the first time or when West got her on her back in magical combat. The *only* thing that's changed about her is that you know she's not a witch now."

It was that part for me. I figured it out, and I wasn't the smartest person in the room ever. If I was, you should probably worry about the room. We'd been around enough gods to know they were mostly like regular people, just a lot more powerful. And George was still young enough to be kind of awkward. I loved that about her.

"It's not that she's a god. It's because—"

We didn't get to finish our intervention because my

phone went off. It was our girlfriend, and she needed us at Azren's cabin. She said it was an emergency and with everything going on, Church was going to have to wait. Or he could nut up and come with us.

"Look, bro, she asked for us, and with everything going on, we should be there for her. You can stay here and pout, or you can get over it and come."

"She's got Azren. What does she need me for?"

Was Church fucking serious? She'd had Azren this entire time. Pretty sure she had Church and me first. Why was that a problem now?

"Yeah, she's got Azren, dickhead. She still asked for us. George has been a god this entire time, and she still picked us. Get over it," Ren snapped.

"I *know* it doesn't make sense. I just need time. Go without me."

Bethany had mostly left Church's nuts alone since we got back from Yule break. She must have gotten over him calling the ghosts dicks. The ghosts might not be willing to tell George and Azren who was doing this, but they knew they were working together to stop the murders. If you got to know George and didn't get petty about how powerful she was, she was a great girl.

Bethany must have been feeling pretty protective of George because she chose that moment to fly out of the floor and assault Church's sack again.

Honestly, he had it coming that time.

REN

George didn't come get us for a little celestial travel. I *was not* athletic, like my boyfriend, girlfriend, and some of the other men she was dating. That said, I could totally walk my adorable three tails across campus to Azren's cabin. I'd barely even had time to show off my new tail because we were trying to talk sense into Church. But tomorrow, *everything* was going to be about my new tail.

We left Church on his bed, cupping his balls. I honestly felt bad about the full-frontal assault to his nuts when he just insulted the ghosts, but he kinda had it coming this time. I was guessing if *we* couldn't talk sense into him, getting his nuts punched by a spirit until he realized George being a god didn't matter was a pretty good lesson.

We started off towards Azren's cabin when I saw that fucking bear shifter again. It felt good stealing his shoes. Especially when he pitched such a tantrum about it. But he was being a turd again, and he was sporting even more expensive sneakers on his feet. Still, George needed us and I could ignore him. At least, I planned on it until he got right up in our business.

"Bro, what's it like to fuck a god? Does her pussy make you lucky?"

Rude. I used the new fire powers I got with my new tail to set those ridiculous sneakers on fire right as West punched him right in the face. A lot of people just assumed West was this easygoing lion because he was always goofing off, but West was the Spanish Inquisition if you pissed him off. That fucking bear shifter was trying to stop his nose from bleeding and put out the fire on his new shoes.

We just left him there and kept going. West clapped me on the back.

"Can I tell you that I adore the fact that you've used your new fire powers to light two bitches up?"

"He's going to try to get me expelled," I moaned.

It felt really good and this time, he knew it was me, but that fucker was also a legacy student. If the board didn't want to kiss his stupid ass, they definitely wanted to keep his stupid parents happy. Oscar just chuckled.

"Did you miss everything after George healed me and you got your new tail? Gabriel Morningstar is the new headmaster and Church's grandfather is running the board. Something tells me there are going to be some big changes when it comes to legacy students. You didn't burn him alive, and he started it. You were well within academy rules." Oscar said.

He was probably right. I was a little shocked when we got to Azren's cabin. Azren was gone, but there was someone else sitting on his sofa. The big guy blushed when he saw Oscar and me.

He delivered our luggage to our dorm room and we both immediately wanted to know where he came from. We thought it was a little strange that the snobs in charge of hiring put a guy with a big gaping hole where his magic should be anywhere near this campus, but we didn't care about that.

The maintenance guy was utterly gorgeous. Oscar wasn't as small as I was, but he wasn't as big as West. The maintenance guy was *massive* and looked like he could fling us both around the bedroom just right. I'm sure a ton of students on this campus treated him like garbage, but Oscar and I saw a big, giant, hot man and our dicks overrode our brains.

We kind of hit on him and found out he was also a little shy, so we apologized. I mean, we got vibes that he was a little fluid with his sexuality, but I guess we came on a little strong. I didn't really know why he was here.

"Guys, you might know the maintenance guy as Sol, but this is actually Baldur. He came back from the dead with no memories or magic. Azren is fetching his dad, Odin, so we can figure out how to get those back."

Oh, my shit. Me and my dick. I hit on a *god* and made him uncomfortable. I'd been around Azren a good bit. Azren would probably be into it if I hit on them, and I was still terrified to do it. George was different. I hit on her before I knew she was a god and now that I'd gotten to know her, I knew she was totally into me.

I cleared my throat.

"Sorry for suggesting you throw us around naked at the moon orgy when we first met. My boyfriend and I thought you were insanely hot, but we had no idea you were a god."

George started giggling. So did West. I was definitely getting revenge on West for laughing at me.

"Oh, I wasn't mad about it," Baldur said. "It was flattering. I make most supernaturals uncomfortable, so I've never been invited to a moon orgy before. And the two of you were actually serious instead of fucking with me like all the students here. I'm not a virgin, but I actually didn't know what to say, so I didn't say anything."

Oh, thank shit. He wasn't going to get his god mojo back and then beat my ass.

"So, we could still do the moon orgy if George is also into it?" I said, wagging my eyebrows.

She looked like she was definitely thinking about it. Baldur was absolutely beautiful. George probably would if she got to know him and decided he should be a part of our group.

"I'm going to need all of you to be a little less thirsty because Baldur here could be the serial killer butchering witches," Mags said.

Any fantasies I was having about god sandwiches instantly left my head. Damn. I usually had impeccable taste in partners. I mean, Oscar and George were completely perfect.

"We don't *know* that," George said. "All we know is that it's happening now, and it happened in the past while he was here and he had blackouts during the murders. There's no other evidence."

Oscar and I were looking at her like she was insane. That was some pretty damning evidence. West was her ride or die. If she wanted to get crazy with her god powers, he'd be egging her on and helping her hide the evidence.

"We're all late to the party, but I'm guessing you mean lots of blood," West said.

Fucking West. He liked to pretend he was pretty, and that was all there was to him. West might have barely passed high school and had no chance of getting into college, but that didn't mean he was stupid. The only reason he didn't do well in high school was because he just didn't like it, so he didn't bother.

He was actually smart as hell. He figured out George's secret long before the rest of us, and he was totally right. We were all at the crime scene. It was brutal and bloody. There was no way in fuck anyone did that without getting blood on themselves, even a god.

"None of my clothes were missing like I got rid of them because of the blood. I never woke up with blood on me, either."

"Even with my magic, I'm not self-cleaning. If I had blood on me, I'd have to take a shower. It's not a god thing that we can murder anyone without getting dirty. He doesn't have his magic, anyway. I don't know if that means he can be injured.

"My dad, Balthazar, is really into serial-killer documentaries. I used to watch them with him sometimes. My other dad, Felix, is really into forensic shows and I watched those with him, too. Knives get slippery when they get bloody. Hands get cut. Can you get cut, Baldur?"

"I've never been sick that I remember, but I've needed stitches several times with the jobs I've had to take. I never had any wounds when someone got murdered. If it was me, I should. I can't imagine someone is going to just lay there and let someone hurt them. I should have bruises and scratches."

That was the thing. There were *no* defensive wounds on the bodies. It was like they *did* just lie there and let it happen. And their memories were tampered with. That took magic and right now, he had none. We could all feel it.

There was the possibility he could have found some

kind of potion on the dark web to do all that. It would have been much harder before the internet and this had been going on for a while. He would have had to have gotten his hands on a seriously dark grimoire and the chances of him even getting close enough to a dark witch to look at their grimoire when he felt like that were pretty slim. He was pretty, but most witches were going to care more about that gaping hole where his magic would be and wouldn't teach him, either.

"I agree with George. He might have been here, but I don't think he did it," Oscar said.

"Of course, you do," Mags said. "You're all in love with her and dick stupid."

"You know I have a healthy level of suspicion, and I'm not ruling out it *could* be him, but you saw all that blood. He would have gotten some on him."

"Unless he keeps a duffle bag of serial killer clothes stashed somewhere and only his blackout brain knows the location. He could shower and change into his regular clothes before he wakes up and never knows."

"Dude, you are *dark*. I dig it," West said.

Mags just glared at him.

"I'm George's familiar, so I'm supposed to be looking out for her, but I *will* put a curse on your dick that takes her longer than five minutes to heal off of you if you talk to me like that again."

West needed to watch it because we were *all* terrified of Matilda and Mags. Dick curses aside. Matilda and her group were fiercely protective of each other. Matilda *and* Mina would fuck us up for talking to their girlfriend in a certain way.

"What do you think is taking so long?" Baldur asked.

"Do you think my father doesn't want to see me because I came back defective?"

"No. Azren is brilliant, and Odin sacrificed an eye for knowledge. I don't know anything about resurrected gods, but something tells me a step got missed. They just need to figure out what it was and everything will be fine. Oh, my shit. I need to text Freya. She'll want to see you, too. I'm guessing you're not ready to talk to Loki yet, but I know he feels terrible about killing you."

Oh, fuck. I didn't know if Baldur killed those witches, but I'd met Loki. He had few regrets. If we put the two of them together in the same room, someone might end up dead again. And from what I understood, Freya was staying with Loki and his family.

But George had already sent that text. There was a swarm of daisies in the air. I was guessing that was Freya.

I really liked Loki, but I hoped she left him at home.

BALDUR

My father still hadn't come. Azren had been gone a while. I didn't remember anything about being his son, and I was trying to think back about everything I'd read about Odin. I knew he was intense. They called him the All Father. He had been the leader of all the other gods in that family. Odin had other sons that were written about way more often than Baldur was.

I believed Azren when they said that was who I was, but Baldur had been dead thousands of years. Odin might not give a shit anymore. They might have all moved on.

I couldn't *remember* the woman who appeared in a swirl of daisies. I knew she was Freya because George said she texted her. But there was something familiar about her, even though I couldn't remember ever seeing her face before. Seeing her again was comforting. She was abso-lutely stunning, but I wasn't drawn to her like that. I *needed* to touch her, but I didn't think I should.

"Baldur?" she whispered, tears springing to her eyes.

I stood, but I didn't make a move. Freya did, though. She moved like lightning and wrapped me up in a huge hug. Supernaturals avoided touching me. The two sitting in this room that wanted me to throw them around at the moon orgy were literally the first that ever wanted to. Now, I had a beautiful god hugging me so hard, it was a little hard to breathe.

"How? I've been on this campus numerous times as a mortal, as both a student and a teacher. I might not have *felt* you since your magic isn't there, but I'd recognize your stupid face anywhere. You were one of the first to welcome me when I got to Asgard and you used to love pranking me. Loki didn't tell me what he was planning or I would have talked him out of it. We were all devastated and then you didn't come back right away."

"Something kept drawing me here. It was even stronger this last time. It's pretty intense now."

"I'm guessing it was whatever god is doing this. There used to be a time when we were all over this realm. You probably came back in the United States and felt the only god on this realm, so you came to the Academy of the Profane for help. The reason the pull felt so much stronger lately is that the God of Chaos and Loki ended up in Profane and they both sired god children.

"You were drawn to the closest god because they were meant to *help* you. You just happened to be drawn to a psycho serial killer who left me their trophies for some reason."

"Hello? He's been dead a *long* time. The two of you knew each other from before. He could have been drawn to *you* and left you those hearts," Mags said.

The witch didn't trust me. I didn't blame her. I didn't

trust me either because there was a lot I didn't remember. I felt drawn to Freya. If something in me went dark during the blackouts and I had trophies and clothes hidden somewhere, I could have left that on her doorstep.

"You'd have to know Baldur. Things were much different when people were actively worshipping us. It was a lot more violent. People didn't negotiate or ask. If someone wanted your shit, they killed you and took it. You had to be strong enough to defend your things, so even the people who *shouldn't* know how to fight were warriors. A lot of the gods encouraged it and asked for more blood in the form of sacrifice.

"Baldur was a God of Light. He was so fucking kind and gentle, it was almost like he was born into the wrong family. He was against all the sacrifice and violence. You'd think that meant no one liked him, but it was no secret he was Odin's favorite. We all loved him. Even Loki loved him. Loki only picked him because it would hurt the most and he didn't think Baldur would stay dead this long. I *know* Baldur. He has the same look in his eyes now as he did the last time I saw him. He's not capable of this."

I appreciated her vote of confidence. She would have known me better than Azren did any better than anyone in this room. But that was all from before. I clearly came back wrong. It wasn't just the blackouts. I knew they were all trying to figure out a motive.

Sitting here now, I was okay with it and didn't intend to do anything about it. But what if when I blacked out, there was a deep, dark part of me that wanted revenge for how the supernatural community treated me for something I couldn't help?

GEORGE

Seriously, where was Azren? Baldur didn't know any of us and he didn't remember Freya. I was eighteen and in college now, but sometimes, I just really needed my mom and my dads. I probably always would. I didn't know if Odin was going to trigger some mass influx of memories, but I knew the two of them needed to see each other.

My mom was smart. She had an entire library of knowledge at her fingertips. So were my dads. Azren was a scholar who was older than the universe, and Odin sacrificed an eye for knowledge. If *anyone* could figure out how to help Baldur, it was those two.

I trusted Mags. We grew up together, and she taught me a lot of magic and wisdom from the first time she was alive. Freya had also mentored me a lot when she was Minerva Krauss. I believed Freya when she said Baldur wasn't capable of slaughtering witches. I got vibes from him that he was a big teddy bear who had been beaten down since he got back.

I also wasn't discounting Mags's suspicions. She also made a damned good point about him hiding clothes. I hadn't brought this up, but gods were only vulnerable when we wanted to be. If he didn't remember he was supposed to be a god, then yeah, he might get cut and need stitches. If Baldur was remembering he was a god during his blackouts, then he could just choose for the knife not to cut him if his hand slipped.

"Where the fuck are Azren and Odin?" I muttered.

"Probably getting what they need to help Baldur," Freya said. "It was different for me because Azren put me in a mortal vessel and I *chose* to leave my primary one, but I do have a little experience with this. I didn't have my memories either. I didn't start getting flashes of them until the magic in my mortal body had been awakened. I needed some extra help because my body was mortal. We need to get Baldur his magic back and his memories will come."

"I'm just a stupid lion, but maybe it's different for him since he's not in a mortal body. Maybe he won't get his magic back until he remembers he's supposed to have it."

I *hated* when West tried to say he wasn't smart because he was quite intelligent. West was goofy and loveable, but he often said things that were spot on. Honestly, he could be completely right about this. Freya gave him an appraising look.

"You're definitely all lion, but not even remotely stupid. Maybe a little choosy with how you applied yourself in school and you didn't have the right teacher to motivate you, but you and stupid don't belong in the same sentence. I like you for George and you could be perfectly right about this."

West puffed up his chest and tossed his mane over his shoulder. He didn't know all of Freya's mortal iterations, but he knew she was my mentor when I was younger, and everyone knew she taught Odin magic. When I talked about her with them, I talked about what an amazing teacher she was and how much she loved it.

We could all tell West he wasn't stupid, but it meant a *lot* more coming from Freya because she had a long history of being a teacher. I knew how Freya got her memories back and West's suggestion made a lot of sense. Gods had our main power and a lot of powers we all shared. Honestly, we hadn't even scratched the surface of what all we could do with our shared powers. A lot of us could do more with our main powers, too.

Baldur's magic being missing because he didn't know he was supposed to have it made a ton of sense. Just telling him wasn't going to do it. He had to *feel* it.

"How do you give a god his memories back?" Drake asked. "It would fix a ton of problems and maybe answer some questions in the now if I could remember who killed my parents. I was there, but I was just a baby. I'm pretty sure whoever killed my parents is doing this."

Baldur's face fell and his shoulders slumped.

"I'm sorry. I don't remember."

"I honestly don't think it was you. I don't think it's you doing this. The reaper that came for my parents adopted me. She spoke to my parents before she reaped them. They didn't see who did it, but they felt how powerful they were. My parents were Basilisks.

"No offense, but you don't *feel* like the other gods I know. My parents wouldn't have said they felt someone insanely powerful. They would have said they felt someone with a hole where their magic should be. And if you've had stitches before, then my parents could have bitten you. Basilisk venom might not kill you, but if it got in your bloodstream, it would have hurt enough for them to get us away."

"Basilisk venom hurts like a bitch," Oscar said.

"I watched it eat away at Oscar's skin, and that was just a potion made from Drake's hair. Directly from their fangs is supposed to be even worse," Ren said.

It was. And I didn't know enough about the state of Baldur now to know if Basilisk venom would hurt him. It wouldn't kill this vessel. Only mistletoe could do that, but without his magic, it might hurt like fuck.

"There's an easy way to get Baldur's memories back, but locating her is tricky. Odin created two ravens—Huginn and Muninn. They represented thought and memory. Azren would visit Odin and give him my new name and where they dropped my essence. Odin would find Muninn and tell her. Around my eighteenth birthday, she'd always find me and help me remember who I was.

"Muninn is a raven shifter, so she's tricky. She always made me work for it and gave me all these riddles. Everyone's sexuality was a little fluid back then, even if we weren't as fluid as Loki. Sometimes, I ended up in some pretty repressed families in an era where humans were *very* prudish and she would only give me my memories back by kissing me."

Freya meant when she was Minerva Krauss. Her father was a misogynistic racist who was upset about the fact that his wife never gave him a son and disowned her for getting an independent study at the Academy of the Profane because he thought it made him look bad. She was also mated to three werewolves that she had to keep a secret because the color of their skin was darker than hers.

I'd never kissed Baldur. I didn't even know if he wanted me to. Ren and Oscar seemed into the idea, but I hadn't talked to West and I wasn't all that sure if Church had broken up with me or not. I really needed to talk to him, but I needed to be doing this before any other witches died. I didn't know if Baldur came back from the Aether a little crazy and was slaughtering witches, but I didn't really like the idea of another woman kissing him.

Which was stupid because I hardly knew anything about him. It was just this *feeling*.

"So, we just need to get a kinky, tricky raven to kiss him, and that'll fix him?" West asked.

"In theory. This is more Azren's domain, and Muninn is Odin's creation. Odin is an animal lover. He used to have this huge sanctuary on Asgard. When Loki and Odin *really* sat down and talked after everything went down with Baldur and Odin heard out all of Loki's grievances, he gave his pets free range to come and go from the sanctuary.

"Odin saw an eight-legged horse who could travel between realms and run that fast and he wanted it, but Sleipnir was more than a horse and Loki's son. Huginn and Muninn can also travel between realms, but they used to only be able to do that under Odin's orders.

"Huginn and Muninn are more similar to Sleipnir than his other animals. When Loki made him see what he did to Sleipnir, he let the ravens come and go as they please. He can contact them when he needs to, but they are harder to locate when they are off realm. If I had to guess, Odin wants his son to remember him, so he's trying to find Muninn."

That made sense. Freya knew Odin much better than I did. Loki and Odin made their peace and Sleipnir had forgiven him for keeping him as a pet, but they both preferred to live in the present than the past, so they didn't talk about that time very much.

"So, I just need to kiss Muninn and I'll be fixed?" Baldur asked.

"Probably not. Muninn is older than you. She's known you since you were a baby. She might find that inappropriate. Muninn always kissed *me* because I was an adult when I met her and I think she was a little mad because I turned down a threesome with her and Huginn back in the day because they weren't my type. I think I hurt both their feelings because I'd literally just traded an orgy with the dwarves for a really pretty necklace, but they weren't my type."

"Back then, nearly everyone wanted Freya. She had the looks, the power, and the personality. Freya broke a lot of hearts. *I* didn't want her like that because I love Frigg, but I'm afraid Huginn and Muninn had a little crush," Odin said, strolling in from the kitchen.

"Now, where is my son?"

BALDUR

I had been searching for these answers for so long, but now that I had them, I wasn't sure I was ready for them. I guess I should have known my parents would be out there somewhere since I'd been alive this long without ever aging. Being a god *never* crossed my mind, so I just assumed they were dead like everyone else I'd met.

But that was my father standing in front of me with tears in his eye. I just stared, trying to see what we had in common. We were both insanely tall, but we didn't look alike at all. He had a long beard he kept in a neat braid and I preferred to be clean shaven, but he was also dark-haired with olive skin and I was very blond with tan skin. The only thing we had in common were our eyes and every single god in this room had silver eyes.

"I missed you, boy. You've been gone so long; I've almost forgotten how much you look like your mother."

That answered that, but I couldn't remember her either.

I didn't read much on Baldur when I was trying to figure out if a god had created me and spectacularly fucked up, but I knew I had brothers, too.

"I'm sorry. I can't remember *anything*. I feel drawn to you and Freya, but I couldn't tell you why."

"That's easily fixable. Huginn and Muninn are on a walkabout in a different realm. You don't remember, but I did that a lot. It was always refreshing, enlightening, and I always learned something new. They'll be traveling in raven form and might only shift if they are comfortable where they are. I sent them a message, but when it's traveling across realms like this, it takes a few days to get to them.

"They'll come right away when they get it. They prefer being ravens for the most part because they think gods and mortals are annoying, but you were always different. They loved to shift and tell you stories when you were a baby. You were the most loved out of all of us."

Freya said that, too. Loki still murdered me. I probably knew more about why he did that now than I did before, but I still didn't understand it because I didn't remember what kind of relationship I had with Loki before all this.

I didn't remember anything about Odin, but he knew me. He'd sired and raised me. He must have been able to read me, even now.

"Loki loved you, too. He's always been brilliant in a way that scared the rest of us because he's a trickster. We never held it against him that he was born from the giants because they shunned him and he was never as violent as they were. He snuck back to the realm he was born on and took up with a particularly violent giant.

"Angrboda treated him like garbage, but she was his first love and he thought he was rebelling against both his families. We didn't know she bore him three children until she got tired of them and dumped them on Asgard for him to care for.

"Loki adored those kids and I'm not proud of this, but we let our dislike of giants get the better of us. We were worried Loki's intelligence and Angrboda's violence paired with the magic those kids were given were going to end up destroying our realm.

"*We* struck first and killed his kids. If Loki had gotten his revenge by going after someone who directly hurt his kids, we would have understood eventually. He never usually resorted to violence. Not when he could fuck someone up without it.

"Loki's mind doesn't work like that. He was hurt, and he wanted everyone to feel what he was feeling. At the time, he didn't know you were the one who tried to talk everyone out of hurting those kids. Loki knew hurting you would devastate all of Asgard the way he was devastated, so he bided his time until he could make it happen.

"And honestly, we made it easy for him. You've always had a touch of foresight. Your mom freaked out when you told her you had been dreaming about your death, so we were the ones who found out your weakness for him. It was a completely different time, and you *hated* the game we played where we threw things at you to prove they wouldn't hurt you. It gave him the opening to use the mistletoe on you. *None* of this would have happened to you if not for your family. Loki would have had no reason. Loki hated killing as much as you did. Loki was the one who engineered your death, but it was our fault he did it. I'm so sorry. I've waited all this time to apologize."

The stories I'd read about that went a little differently and they all said Loki killed Baldur because he was just a bad person. Honestly, none of this meant anything until I could *remember.*

"The lion had a theory and I think he's spot on," Freya said. "Baldur's magic is missing because he can't remember he's supposed to have it. We don't even know half of what we are capable of. Any time we've tried to learn and press those limits, we've generally learned there are none. I didn't start remembering until I got my magic when I was in mortal bodies. It makes a lot of sense."

"You came up with that?" Azren asked. "It's actually brilliant. You probably should have been a student here."

The lion just smirked.

"I'm allergic to authority and homework, but thanks."

"I'm going to need someone to babysit me until Muninn can get my memories back. Someone capable of stopping me if I have a blackout and want to murder a witch."

Just then, there was a knock on the door and Azren let Gabriel Morningstar in. I'd always liked him. He had a kind word for me most days and after I found out he was George and Matilda's dad, I wasn't all that shocked.

The potions lab and the Dark Arts theatre were the worst classrooms to clean up, and I'd been doing it under several different professors. They got pretty gross from the exploding potions and the blood and gore from Dark Magic. *Some* professors ended their classes a little early and had the students clean up their mistakes. Others just left it for me and the rest of maintenance to clean up.

Gabriel never did. And I could hear some of his students in the hallway complaining about it. He was going to make an incredible headmaster, but I was pretty sure he was here to kick me off campus and fire me.

"Azren texted me. Hi, Sol. Or I guess I should call you Baldur now. Congrats on getting your answers. It must be a relief. I'm going to be moving you from the staff cabin you're staying in to one of the ones we had back in the day when entire families worked here. There are more bedrooms than the one you're in. Odin can take one and Freya can take the other if she likes. They can see about jogging some memories while we wait for Huginn and Muninn to get the message."

"Shouldn't you be banning me from campus? It could be me."

Gabriel just smirked at me.

"I *could* until we know more, but we've got your daddy and a war goddess here to stop you and they've both known you since you were a baby. I'm guessing they know any tricks you might pull during a blackout to stop you if it's you who's doing this. Besides, if it's a god we don't know about, I need as many of you on campus as I can. They don't seem afraid of Azren like every other god I've heard about, but Azren can't be everywhere at once and they know that.

"If they decide to be ballsy with this many gods on campus, we might be able to catch them. Besides, Azren warned all the students what to look out for from what we know about their victims. We'll probably get a heads up and if Muninn is here, we might be able to get the memories back of the potential victim and protect them before they can get murdered. You need to be with your family and my kids need to be in bed because both of them are really shitty about getting up early and that's not fair to Mags."

Even with everything going on, I smiled to myself when George and Matilda sulked when their daddy told them to go to bed. George was a god, and I knew Matilda was getting a reputation for beating everyone's asses in magical combat. It was adorable, the two strongest supernaturals at the Academy of the Profane just got sent to bed by their dad.

And, apparently, I was going to have to get used to being roommates with my very powerful father until I got my memories back.

CHURCH

This was so fucking stupid. I wanted to be with my hive. I knew damned well it was *me* that was being an idiot, too. I couldn't even go for a walk to clear my head because Bethany was pissed at me again and getting nut punched hurt. I was alone in my dorm room trying to find something to watch while they were all out with my girlfriend.

I knew she had a big secret. It tasted *amazing* and gave me this huge power boost when I was near her. It shouldn't have even been a huge shocker that she was a god. She felt like a witch until she took her necklace off, but she also gave off the same kind of power as her dad and Azren did, which witches *didn't* do.

I gave up trying to find something to watch and tried to go to sleep. I was *dying* to know what she needed them for and I was killing myself inside that I couldn't watch her with Azren just yet and be there with them.

I couldn't sleep either. I was still trying when my roommates got home. They were all pissed at me and tried to 'intervention' me *again* so I couldn't exactly ask what went down without being an even bigger asshole than I already was.

I felt a pillow smack me in the face pretty hard. It smelled like West's expensive hair products.

"I know you're faking, dildo face."

Ah, fuck. He gave me that nickname during our first moon orgy with George. He called me that on purpose.

"I'm an eighteen-year-old energy vampire. We're allowed five minutes to be stupid and dramatic over a girl."

"We know vampires tend to get dramatic and stupid, but not this time," Ren said. "Not over that particular girl."

Before I could even say anything, I was surrounded by purple smoke and the scent of lavender and marshmallows. I felt this really hard yank and the next thing I knew, I wasn't in my bed anymore. When I looked around, I was at our moon orgy spot and George was standing there in these adorable pajamas that shouldn't be sexy.

She waved her hand and a thick blanket and pillows appeared on the ground. She saw me shiver since it was still cold outside and I was just in sweatpants and no shirt. George gave me an appraising glance and then conjured me a coat. When I joined her on the blanket, a steaming mug of hot chocolate appeared in my hands. That was a pretty handy trick.

"Sorry, I couldn't sleep without talking to you. I hate that you're mad at me. I need to explain why I lied."

George told me about the necklace and that the other gods could have hurt her when she was younger. She said they still might because of the magic she was born with. I wasn't mad she lied about being a god. I'd known she had a big fat juicy secret as soon as I walked into the same room as her on the first day of class.

"George, I've always known you had a secret and I'm not upset because of what you are. We're not really your coven, are we? Gods don't do that. Most of the gods we study about in school marry other gods and are monogamous."

That was what I was upset about. I was petrified we were all just some stupid college fling and when we all graduated, she was just going to ghost us to fuck off with Azren. Drake and I were both rare and powerful supernaturals. Most supernaturals would have loved to collect us for their group, but I couldn't compete with the God of Death.

George just shrugged

"Yeah, some gods marry other gods and act like monogamy is the only way, but they are also serial cheaters. Every god is different. Lilith has been devoted to Samael for millennia, but my dad and my uncle joined my mom's coven. Gods might not do covens like witches, but I *thought* I was in West's pride, Oscar's coven, and *your* hive. Unless you've changed your mind about having me."

"Fuck no. But wouldn't you rather be monogamous with the god everyone fears?"

"No, and Azren doesn't expect me to either. My dad and my uncle love being a part of my mom and aunt's covens. I adore the shit out of my big family. I grew up having five dads around and that's the kind of family I want. I don't particularly want it with a group of gods when I already have it with all of you."

Yeah, vampires could be stupid and dramatic, but I'd already done that. I seriously didn't need her to kiss my ass and beg to be in my hive. I *wanted* her there. My mind was settled.

"I guess I was kind of a dumbass, huh?"

"In all fairness, I intended to tell you all *much* differently. Kaylee kind of took that away from me when she hurt Oscar. And she did the one thing Drake has been worried about this entire time. If my dad hadn't come to calm Matilda and me down, Kaylee would be dead."

I hadn't really thought about it like that. I was pissed Oscar got hurt and Drake had been violated, but really George had been, too. It was a massive secret. I didn't know anything about gods who were going to come out of the woodworks because she was born and not made or would get mad about her magic. I *did* know every ass kisser at the Academy of the Profane was going to be drawn to her magnificent ass now. Oh, shit. We were going to be beating up legacy students left and right.

"I'm sorry. After she threw a forbidden potion at Oscar in front of the entire dining hall, I don't think anyone would have been upset if you smote her or Matilda ate her."

"The Paranormal Investigation Bureau might take it the wrong way. *My* dad would be proud of me and Balthazar would probably fist bump me, but my mom and the rest of my dads only want us permanently maiming someone if it's going to stop them from killing someone."

"What happened earlier tonight? I *wanted* to go, but I had a lapse in sanity and was jealous of Azren."

"Snuggle with me. I *need* my Church hugs."

I laid on my back and opened my arms. Yeah, I got stupid, but it was kind of nice that my girlfriend was this powerful god and she needed me to hold her. I wrapped my arms around her and kissed the top of her head as she nuzzled my chest with her cheek.

What she told me was an even bigger shocker than finding out my girlfriend was a god. I only remembered the maintenance guy who brought our luggage because it was the first time I'd met Oscar and Ren and the first thing out of their mouth when he set our luggage down was to suggest he get a little rough with them at the moon orgy.

I noticed the big gaping hole where his magic was supposed to be, but I noticed this big, beautiful mother-fucker was embarrassed as fuck at getting invited to a moon orgy more. George told me he said that was the first time he'd been invited, which was also shocking. There were plenty of thirsty supernaturals that weren't Ren and Oscar who should have wanted to hit that before this.

It seemed like the gods had this handled. I was just happy things were okay with George and me again. I squeezed her and played with her hair.

"Was this our first fight?" I asked.

"I think so. It was pretty minor as far as fights go."

"Bethany didn't think so. She assaulted my nuts again."

I groaned when George slithered like a Basilisk so that she was straddling me. She started grinding against my dick and she was giving me bedroom eyes.

"Poor baby. Want me to make it feel better?"

It was freezing cold outside and I couldn't think of a better reason to get naked and warm myself up.

GEORGE

Mother fuck. It was cold outside. There was still snow everywhere. Maybe I should have kidnapped Church somewhere warmer if I was going to get him naked. I was just hoping we weren't broken up, but I should have known we'd eventually get naked if we weren't.

Our breaths were coming out in puffs. I'd been hiding for so long, I'd almost forgotten I could do something about this. Especially when it started snowing on us. I waved my hand and put a heated dome over us and let it warm up. My guys were different. Oscar had a regular body temperature, but West and Ren ran hot because of their animal counterparts. Church had a heartbeat and didn't feel like a corpse, but he was always cooler to the touch, especially since he didn't feed off of blood.

"That's kind of badass," Church said, playing with my hair. "What else can you do?"

"I have all the regular god powers. I can conjure

anything, travel where I want without walking, and shapeshifting, but there's still a *lot* about shapeshifting I still need to learn. I can, apparently, mimic any kind of magical creature I'm near. West wants me to figure out how to turn into a lion so we can do lion things. Ren said if I can figure out the Kitsune thing, I'm not allowed to get nine tails before him. That's still a ways off."

I could technically do the energy vampire thing, too. This was the part that could be too much for Church. He said he wasn't mad I was a god and just needed to be reassured this wasn't just a college fling for me. But me being a god *and* doing what he could do? Church was rare. He was probably one of only a few of his kind on this entire realm. Church could have some big opinions about me having all these god powers *and* his, too, when I was around him.

"So, like, if *I'm* an energy vampire and you go all energy vampire, does that mean we have a greater chance of making a little energy vampire baby?"

"I'm not sure, but you aren't knocking me up tonight, sir. We are only freshmen and I still want to travel more. That's totally not what I expected you to say, by the way."

"You're adorable. I didn't mean *tonight*. I meant later. West wants ten kids, by the way, and he's not picky if they are his cubs."

I moaned.

"I want a lot of kids, but if West wants ten, he's going to have to figure out how to make the MPREG fiction in my mom's library a reality."

"I'm not up to date on the various kinds of smut the Library of the Profane carries."

"Don't tell my mom that, or she's going to give you a reading list. Are we warm enough to get naked now?"

"Yeah. And it's actually kind of romantic that the snow

is falling all around us, but not getting *on* us and we have all these comfy pillows and blankets. That hot chocolate was delicious, by the way."

"It's the Hell version. Bram used to make it for us when we were kids. There's a certain spice they add you can only get there. But right now, we are wearing entirely too many clothes."

Honestly, I hadn't really tested the range of my mimic powers. Some of the things I could do, I wasn't sure if it was because I was a god or I just shared a house with witches and warlocks. Disappearing our clothes was a known witch trick, but if I could conjure clothes, I *should* be able to get rid of them, too, if I was too far away from a witch.

It was going to totally *suck* if my vampire boyfriend just got over the fact that I was a god, then I snapped my fingers, and all our clothes stayed on. Was that like erectile dysfunction for girl gods? I couldn't exactly pray to a god this was going to work. My dad was kind of insane. If he thought I needed him right now, he'd appear and shit would get awkward. Church would never get his pants back and my dad would probably try to give me a pep talk.

I just snapped my fingers and hoped for the best. I breathed a small sigh of relief when our clothes disappeared and reappeared folded on the blanket next to us. Church used his vampire speed to flip me on my back. He surprised me, but even if I knew it was coming, I would have let him.

Church braced himself on his elbows and gave me a fangy grin. His fangs weren't as big as Belladonna's or a vampire who fed off blood, but they were respectable fangs that could rip flesh or do the whole kinky thing when he bit me. He dragged those sexy things down my neck.

"Aren't you invincible? How did I bite this long, perfect neck before?"

"Because I wanted you to. And I'm kindly requesting you do it again."

Church moved down and was nibbling on my nipples.

"You don't have to ask twice. Could you god-mojo me and make me bite you?"

"Church, no. Everyone was created with free will. Most gods consider it high maintenance to control people. I don't think we even know how."

"What if the god doing this has figured that out?"

I groaned.

"That's an Azren theory, not 'your girlfriend's boob was just in your mouth' theory. Can we have that conversation when we have a god who is much older and smarter than me with us and we aren't horny?"

"Yes, ma'am."

Church used his vampire speed and strength to flip me again so I was on top of him.

"I changed my mind," Church said. "I want to get topped by my insanely powerful girlfriend. I think it would be hot as shit. Just don't break my dick. I *think* Bethany is going to leave it alone now that I've made it right with you."

I gripped Church's cock and slid down.

"I can't *make* a ghost do anything they don't want to do. If I could, they would have told us who is doing this long before anyone died. But me telling her to lay off your dick holds more weight than anyone else on campus. I'm really fond of this cock. I've got *big* plans for it and not just at moon orgies. You hear that, Bethany?" I yelled. "Hands off my boyfriend's dick. I'm only eighteen and this is my first serious relationship. I don't know if I'm the crazy possessive type. I might be!"

"That was fucking hot," Church growled, gripping my hips as I rode him.

Church wanted to be topped, but he also wasn't a passive vampire and I loved that about him. Church sat up so he could be more of an active participant and have better access to my neck. He cupped my ass so he could bounce me on his cock and started nibbling on my collarbone. When he changed the angle by sitting up, it increased the pleasure because of the way he was hitting my clit now.

I just flung my head back and rode Church while I stared at the sky. There wasn't a full moon out tonight, but the sky was clear. Snow was falling all around the dome I erected around us.

"I'm close," I gasped.

Church wrapped his arms around me so tightly and bounced me even harder on his cock. Don't ask me how he timed this just right. As I was about to explode, Church sunk his fangs into my neck and every star in the sky lit up as I came. I squeezed him tight as I shuddered. Church was always intense. As we came down, he nipped at the tip of my nose.

"I guess I figured out why it's so explosive when you come and I taste your blood," he chuckled.

"Come back to my dorm and sleep in my bed?" I asked, playing with his hair.

Honestly, this had all been a lot, and I just needed a distraction.

"Are Matilda and Mags going to eat me or curse my dick?"

"No. They'll figure out we've made up and be fine with it."

"Then, yes. I'd love to."

AZREN

Gabriel showed Baldur and Odin to their new home. He just needed to tell Freya which one it was as she'd been on this campus a good bit as a mortal. Freya wanted to be close to Baldur, but she stayed behind with me since she knew Odin needed to be with him more.

"I feel terrible. Do you think he was here while I was? He wouldn't have remembered me, especially in a mortal body, but I *would* have recognized him. It's been thousands of years since I've seen Baldur, but I watched that boy grow into a man. He's also a big boy, even for a god."

That he was. He was also a God of Light. Even without his magic and being beaten down by mortals for so long, he was still radiant, even if he didn't have his signature glow.

"Every time he was here before, people died. If they were targeting special witches, they would have gone after you. I don't think he was here when you were. He *was* here when I was. I'm not a snob. I wouldn't overlook a janitor. I don't know all the gods, but I knew Baldur because I was friends with Loki. I should have found him before George brought him to me."

"I think he was looking for a god to help him, but he didn't remember you, so he just saw the scary God of Death. He found George instead. I think the big guy has a crush."

And I could tell George was interested but conflicted because he could be a murderer. George had a *lot* more in common with Baldur than she did with me. They were both born gods who were beloved by their families. If he didn't come back a killer, I could see the two of them together. There was just one tiny problem.

"When Baldur gets his memories back, he's going to remember his wife," I pointed out.

"If they are both into each other, he's going to need her when he gets his memories back. Nanna moved on pretty hard when he didn't come back right away. I haven't been back to Asgard in a long time, but she's been gone even longer. She wanted to lose herself in another god, but no one in Asgard would do that to Baldur because we knew he'd eventually come back. Last I heard, she found another God of Light from a different god family and replaced him. Odin and Frigg still talk every day. They'd know if she ever came home, but they were pretty mad she left, and Baldur was their favorite. I don't think either of them would be itching for a reunion."

I sighed. Poor Baldur. I wasn't as close with him as I was with Loki and Freya, but he'd been about peace and light during a time when nearly everyone was solving their problems with violence. He was ahead of his time and for all the preaching he tried to give his family, they didn't really start considering his words until they really sat down with Loki and found out *why* he killed Baldur.

"I hate that for him," I said. "Baldur has been through a lot. If either of us knew what Loki was planning, we would have talked him out of it or at least redirected him towards someone who was actually guilty. I can't imagine what he went through for that long in the Aether just stewing about it and then to come back with no memories and get treated the way he probably did by supernaturals? When he gets his memories back, he going to remember Nanna and have to hear she replaced him like that."

"I don't think the murders were Baldur. His light is gone, but it also isn't."

I actually understood that. Gods all had golden auras, but light gods always glowed brighter. Baldur didn't have either right now and was grappling with the fact that he could be a serial killer. He still had the same look in his eyes and came to me for help, even if he didn't remember me and thought I might kill him. Anyone else in that situation would have left, but Baldur did the right thing.

"How long does it usually take for Huginn and Muninn to come when they are on a walkabout? I'd always visit Odin to tell him where I was putting you so Muninn could visit when you turned eighteen. I knew she always made it to you because you never died, but I had no idea they were so hard to get in contact with."

"I haven't been home in a while, but it was only ever a few days, depending on how far away they are. And you'd better spill, mister. You forget I was created with multiple powers and domains. And one of those was that even though you were trying to hide it, I picked up vibes between you and George."

I started laughing. After everything that just went down in my cabin, I couldn't stop. I couldn't hide my scent on her from certain supernaturals, but it could be explained away by my private lessons with her for the most part. The people close to her figured it out because they knew her the best.

We hadn't told Reyson yet. He wouldn't figure it out until we did. We weren't brothers, but we were created at the same time and pooled our magic with the others to make the universe. We all bonded on our new playground figuring out our powers. Her dad was one of my oldest friends.

He was also the God of Chaos. He was rarely rational, and it was impossible to figure out how he was going to react in any situation. And I said that as someone who had known him our entire lives. Reyson could either be very happy about this or he could keep trying to beat my ass until his wife calmed him down. Ripley Bell was the *only* person I'd known since the universe had been created who could rein in the God of Chaos.

And then there was Freya. I hadn't known her as long, but she was a dear friend. Freya was the god of many things. Love and sex were two of them. George and I were probably broadcasting *all kinds* of shit to Freya that we could have kept a secret if we were around her alone.

"Sorry," I said, wiping the tears from my eyes. "I was so worried about everything I forgot about your superpowers. I'm crazy about her. I was just supposed to be teaching her and helping her with her powers, but she's amazing. She punched me in the face, Freya."

Freya cocked an eyebrow at me.

"I don't kink shame, but I think you're good for each other."

"I'm not—It's not—It was never a kink thing. I don't

ask her to hit me. I'm older than the universe. In my long life, everyone has been too scared of me to get properly angry with me or hit me. Then this furious eighteen-year-old god storms into my office because she's mad at me and breaks my nose. She was glorious, and she's not scared of me. She treats me like everyone else."

"Her daddy might change his mind about hitting you when he finds out," Freya hooted.

"I know," I moaned. "How did Loki take it when you told him Baldur was back?"

"I didn't. I had to see it for myself first. I was planning on going back to Ravyn's cottage to break the news before I started staying with Baldur and Odin. He needs to know, but he *has* to stay away until Baldur is ready to see him. I do need to get back there. It's getting late."

Freya disappeared in a shower of daisies. I usually operated off a few hours of sleep, but Freya liked her beauty rest. I'd been sleeping alone for a long time, but now that I'd spent the night with George, I wanted to do it again.

I didn't particularly want to sleep alone in this cabin anymore.

DRAKE

Church never came back after George appeared in our dorm room in a cloud of purple smoke to kidnap him. We were taking bets if they were just having a *really* long makeup sex session or he was a dick to her and she smote him. Or Bethany was creeping and *saw* him be an ass to her and dick punched him so hard, he died. Matilda could have eaten him or Michael could have flown him to a roof somewhere and left him to freeze in the snow.

Our girlfriend was a god, but she had some pretty powerful siblings. I knew there were other realms with Hellhounds and angels, but there weren't that many in this one. They could fuck us up just as easily as George could.

We were joking about it, but we were kind of worried about Church. George didn't strike me as the smiting type of god, but she caused a whole weather disturbance, and she *might* have when Kaylee hurt Oscar. Her dad was the *only* thing that calmed her down and I had a feeling her family had a lot of experience with that. I doubted Professor Morningstar was there when she kidnapped Church.

Last night was honestly *a lot*. She had to reveal her secret before she was ready to and then we found out the maintenance guy was a god without magic who might be killing witches. I couldn't say I wouldn't kill someone who was supposed to care about me but was being an asshole for something I couldn't help under those circumstances. I couldn't wave my hand and kill someone like she could, but a small nick of my fangs could do the job.

I liked Church. He was a good friend, and he always treated her well. I was hoping he kept that vibe after he found out her secret and they were just off somewhere fucking like bunnies.

I went down to the dining hall for breakfast. West usually got there early to fix her latte and Church grabbed her breakfast. Ren usually had something stolen in his pockets and Oscar would pass her a new drawing. He was doing some kind of comic with her as an anime superhero and he'd give her a new page every day.

None of them were here yet. I was kind of the odd man out in that I wasn't sharing a dorm with them. It would have been a bonding experience and their dorm room was great for four people, but it would have been crowded with five. I basically had my dorm to myself. My roommate was an incubus and everyone wanted a piece of him. I was pretty sure he was having a good night with entire dorm rooms most nights. I had the place to myself to play my violin.

Still, I could do this. It might be just me, but I was a part of this group. I didn't have super speed like Church, but I fixed George's latte and I'd been eating breakfast with everyone long enough to learn their preferred beverage. I made sure to get Matilda and Mags their lattes, too. They were her sister and her familiar, but they were my friends, too. I didn't know Mina or Belladonna as well, but I made an extra trip to get coffee for them, too.

I was just sitting down when Mina and Belladonna joined me with their food. They were looking around for Matilda and Mags because they were usually here by now. I didn't know how much they knew and I didn't know if it was my place to tell them. I cleared my throat. Mina just smirked at me.

"Don't worry. Our girlfriends filled us in while George was out with Church. Big shocker."

"Then Matilda came and slept in my bed and Mags went to sleep with Mina because George brought Church back to their dorm room and they said he breathes too loud in his sleep. Not snoring, just too loud for shifter ears. It probably wouldn't have irritated them as much if he wasn't a man."

I started laughing.

"We had some theories about Church's untimely demise for being a dick to a baby god who loves him, but I had no idea he was in danger for breathing too loud around lesbians."

"It's the *audacity*," Belladonna said, tossing her white hair over her shoulder.

"I don't think you can help that in your sleep. Especially when you are sleeping next to someone you love," I pointed out.

"There they are," Mina said, perking up.

George, Matilda, and Mags were strolling in the dining hall arm in arm. George was wearing the boys' uniform instead of the one the girls usually wore. Holy fuck. I was guessing she used her magic to tailor it a bit because it fit her like a glove and showed off all of her curves. It almost wasn't fair. I was a good-looking guy, and I didn't look remotely that good in my uniform.

That was hot as shit. She was wearing her long, black hair down and had brushed out her curls so her hair fell in soft waves down her back. She'd played up her eyes with eyeliner and mascara so her silver eyes were popping. George was an utter goddess, and she was *mine.*

This asshole bear shifter whose shoes Ren bragged about stealing from jumped in front of her. He had a black eye, and he was walking kind of funny, but he stomped in front of *my* girlfriend like he even noticed her before she basically announced she was a god in front of the entire Academy of the Profane. This fuckhead had his chest puffed up like he was about to do a thing.

I *could* have gone over there and defended my girlfriend's honor, but she was out as a god now and could handle this herself. I leaned back in my chair and took a sip of my coffee.

"This isn't going to end well. Want to take bets on what she does to him?"

I might have a slight problem with wanting to bet on a lot of things.

"I'm not going to bet on what I *think* she's going to do. I went to high school with Eugene," Belladonna said. "What she *should* do is put some kind of god magic on him so all his body hair falls out and he's hairless every time he shifts. I'll bet naked bears look *weird.* It would knock him down a peg and he'd probably never leave his dorm until his hair grew back. That's a long time everyone would only have to deal with him in class. I'm a big fan of doing that to him."

Damn. That was brutal.

"You really don't like him, do you?"

"He was two years ahead of me. He decided I was going to be a conquest on my first day of high school. I *had* to put him in his place because my parents are racist and I had no interest in guys. He took it personally and tried to embarrass me. He's an idiot, but he's trainable. You just need to teach him a few times that you're stronger than him."

"Shh. I think he's about to embarrass himself," Mina said.

We all looked over. They were close enough that we could see and hear everything.

"Damn, girl. You're hot as fuck even if you seem to be confused over which uniform you're supposed to be wearing. Want to be my date at the next moon orgy? I can fuck you better than anyone you've invited before."

My coffee went down the wrong way and I started choking. Did he really just say that out loud? To a fucking *god?* Belladonna pounded me on the back.

"I don't know how trainable he is because if he's said that before, someone would have beat his ass or already figured out how to make him hairless."

Mina started savoring her toast like it was the best thing she'd ever eaten. Honestly, the bread and the butter weren't store bought. They made them both in the kitchen and they were pretty good. I knew she was also enjoying the scene right in front of us. There was a baby god, a Hellhound, and a hybrid all staring at Eugene like he was shit they just stepped in and I had a feeling if he hadn't learned his lesson before, he was about to.

George just cocked her head at him.

"Do you say shit like that to all women or did I happen to wake up incredibly unlucky this morning?"

"Oh, you woke up *incredibly* lucky because Eugene Gilroy noticed you in the dining hall last night and decided to make his move. You're probably the luckiest girl in the Academy of the Profane."

This was a fucking train wreck. I wished the other guys were here to witness this. West would probably have something hilarious to say.

"What happened to your eye and feet?" Mags asked. "You've got a healing potion for burns on your feet."

"Last night, some idiot lion punched me. I would have kicked his ass, but he was with a Kitsune who set my shoes on fire. I *demanded* they be expelled, but Professor Morningstar is an idiot who is soft on crime."

Everyone at my table started giggling because we knew exactly who punched him in the face and set his shoes on fire. We also knew if talking to her like that didn't piss her off, insulting her dad probably would.

"You know *Headmaster* Morningstar is our dad, right?" Matilda growled.

"I'll bet Hellhounds are *beasts* in bed. You should join us at the moon orgy, cutie. I've always had this fantasy about twins."

Oh, my shit. It just kept getting worse. If George didn't do something... He just pissed off four powerful lesbians who might seriously fuck him up. And it wasn't just these four. Basilisks were classified as shifters, so I had a lot of classes with Matilda. She was a *huge* flirt until she got with Mina and Belladonna. She still was, but it was mostly harmless now. Eugene could have every single lesbian, bisexual, and woman who had ever questioned her sexuality ready to beat his ass for talking to Matilda that way.

George waved her hand like Eugene was a pest. His whole body locked up, and he levitated eight feet in the air. The only thing he appeared to be able to move was his eyes to blink. Matilda's eyes were glowing amber and Mags looked like she was two seconds away from hexing the ever-living shit out of him. Mina and Belladonna were pissed, but they looked like they found this whole thing amusing.

I needed popcorn because now Michael and Dexter were here. Dexter already had his phone out filming everything. By now, he had a massive social media following and a history of epic videos where shitty people got knocked down a peg. Michael was pretty protective of his people. He'd threatened a few people because of his sister and beat the shit out of a guy for hurting Dexter.

Michael didn't look like he was about to go all avenging angel again. He looked like he found all this utterly hilarious.

"Have you been disrespecting women again, Eugene? Didn't you spend Yule break trying to heal the side effects from a hex a five-foot nothing witch without a lot of power gave you? You finally stopped leaking pus out your asshole and decided to try that shit with my baby sisters? A god and a Hellhound? Seriously?"

"I take it back. Pus out the butthole is *much* better than naked bears," Belladonna said.

"You're savage. I love it," I said.

"Shut up," Mina said. "This is the best movie I've seen in ages. It's got gods, angels, hot lesbians, and butthole pus."

"He mentioned twincest," Mags growled.

Even if Matilda wasn't a lesbian and I was scared she'd eat me, I had absolutely zero desire to have twins in my bed. Before I met George, I wouldn't have said no to two women, but twins were *weird*. Especially since I knew Eugene intended for them to kiss and touch each other. I didn't know what George had planned, but maybe anal leakage wasn't enough.

"This is all you, sweetie," Michael said. "I don't have to defend your honor so you don't blow the big god secret anymore. Do something big for my honey's social media followers. It makes him happy when he goes viral."

"Love you, baby," Dexter said, blowing Michael a kiss.

"I'm having a brain fart now that I don't have to hide. I don't *know* what to do."

Mags got giddy, and that didn't bode well for Eugene. She grabbed George and whispered in her ear and I swear to shit, my girlfriend let out this diabolical giggle. Mags and George both chanted something different at Eugene. Whatever spell that was hit him so hard, he flew across the room and crashed into a table.

Church, Ren, Oscar, and West were finally joining us in the dining hall. They came in right when a massive bear shifter was flying through the air. Oscar just sneered and stepped over him. Ren pretended to accidentally kick him in the face. West just tossed his mane over his shoulder and told him that's what he got for fucking with our girlfriend.

We all sat down and everyone started to eat. But I was the giddy one now. I mean, I was betting Mags and George just topped butthole pus with whatever they hit him with, so I had to ask.

"It was two hexes I taught George that no one really knows anymore. They are from a time when no one had TV and the printing press hadn't been invented yet, so only rich people could afford books. Everyone's entertainment was getting drunk at the pub or showing up to watch executions. Watching someone get drawn and quartered was essentially the same thing as the world dodgeball play-offs are now."

West gasped.

"You shut your mouth. Don't compare my precious dodgeball to that."

"Anyway, we hit him with *two* hexes from back then. I know how to break them and Minerva Krauss probably would have figured it out in a day, but she was also a genius. Modern witches are going to take *much* longer to break those hexes. Trust me, they are terrible. The menfolk tried to make them illegal back in my day."

"I hate him," Belladonna said. "Just tell me if it's worse than losing all his body hair when he shifts or leaking puss out of his butt?"

"Didn't you have a feud with him in high school?" Church asked. "I always thought it was because you didn't like shifters, but now you're dating one. I'm guessing there's more to the story than I initially thought."

"He tried more than just words with me. Eugene cornered me in the library and wouldn't take no for an answer. I didn't have my magic yet, so no super speed or strength to get away. One of the senior vampires was in there late. He wasn't eighteen yet either, but neither was Eugene. He was able to chase him off. I put him in his place twice after that, but I had to use my wits instead of anything vampire related."

"I'm sorry. I wish we'd been better friends in high school. I had magic. I could have helped."

"No, I get it. I was terrible in high school. My parents really wanted you in my hive and they kept pressuring me about it. I didn't want any of the men they kept pushing at me, so I pretended like I did and just acted like a vile bitch so none of you really wanted me."

"Well, I'm glad you stood up to your parents and are

with someone you care about because you're actually pretty cool," Church said.

"What did the bear do? He asked us to rate your performance at the moon orgies, so West hit him and I set his shoes on fire. I would hope he was a little more tactful addressing a god."

"He wasn't," Matilda said.

George filled the rest of the guys in on what happened before they got there. They were all pretty pissed.

"Guys, chill. I knew people were going to treat me differently when I took the necklace off. Eugene got gross about it, but this is going to happen again. I lost my virginity to a guy who was just using me because of my dad. He didn't even know *I* was a god. People are going to be trying to get close to me because of what they think I can do for them. A *lot* of them are going to try to get me at moon orgies, either because they think I'll fall for them or they just want bragging right. I can deal with it."

I sat back in my chair. I got her a little bit more. I understood she originally had the necklace for her safety, but I was pretty sure she kept it on so long because she just wanted to be treated like every other person.

I didn't need to say anything to her other guys. We needed to shield her from that as much as we could.

GEORGE

Almost everyone who didn't grow up with me seemed shocked about what went down in the dining hall with Eugene. Belladonna wasn't because she'd had a similar experience. Even Drake seemed surprised and he grew up with Azren. I was guessing Azren shielded him from a lot of the stuff that came with being a god.

My parents prepared me for this. My mom tried to teach me not to take it to heart. Most of my dads told me not to let it go to my head. My dad and my uncle told me to use it to my advantage. If I liked it the first time it happened, find a way to make it happen again on my terms. If I hated everything about it, make a giant show about it to deter other people from doing it.

Tossing Eugene around the dining hall was child's play. Mags had an arsenal of medieval hexes and curses that no one immediately knew how to curse in modern times and were so nasty, some of the men got together and tried to get them outlawed as dark magic. I was pretty sure I made a point, but I also knew there were going to be more people like him.

As we were walking to history, I was surprised at the number of students coming up to me to thank me for what I did to Eugene. It wasn't just freshmen, and it wasn't just women. He didn't proposition the men. He was a fucking bully and everyone was worried about retaliating because his dad was a judge.

I thought I was just making a point and deterring a few people, but I actually made a few friends. Most of them knew I was on the dodgeball team and that I was good at it. They would have come to cheer the team on, but now they had other reasons to root for me.

We took our seats in history. Kaylee was gone now. I would have thought most of her minions wouldn't want to be associated with her anymore after she threw an illegal potion at me in front of everyone and ended up getting it on Oscar. I mean, it made sense to me when I woke up, but gods weren't omnipotent and I'd been wrong before.

Paris jumped in front of me before I could get to my desk. Her hair was *wrecked.* She had to have spent hours and a ton of money at the salon getting it untangled after she mouthed off to Loki, but it was still damaged to all fuck. She probably should have just cut it short and let it grow back out. I was pretty sure Paris was one of those girls who thought short hair was just for lesbians. Pixie cuts were for everyone and were cute as fuck.

She looked like she wanted to start some shit with me. I sighed and made a motion with my hand for her to proceed. Paris was a stronger witch than Kaylee was. If she wasn't lazy, she could have easily graduated from the Academy of the Profane with honors. Paris didn't need to ass kiss Kaylee Krauss to graduate. She just needed to apply herself.

"You have a lot of nerve bullying Eugene, George. He's an awesome guy. He grew up with my cousin and came to every one of my birthday parties. Eugene can't help that he ate too much paste in kindergarten and it affected him as an adult."

I leaned forward and she clinched her fists like she was trying not to fling a hex at me.

"Based on the *numerous* people who came up to me on my way to class, Eugene is the bully and he has massive consent issues. A lot of the women who approached me have said he cornered them and the only reason he stopped was because they used their magic and made him or in the case of a fourteen-year-old vampire with no magic, another vampire came in and stopped him.

"From what I understand, most people are too afraid to fight back because of who his daddy is, but he's been hexed before. Well, my daddy outranks his daddy. *I* outrank him, too. Your boy tried the wrong thing with someone stronger than him and got put in his place. That's *exactly* how the supernatural world works. And it's something you should keep in mind because Kaylee forced me to reveal my secret *way* before I wanted to, so I'm not hiding anymore. How long were you in the salon after you pissed Loki off?"

Paris paled and ran her hand over her hair. She scurried to her desk. Honestly, Paris had one of those faces that would look adorable with a pixie cut, but she was too scared to do it. Her hair was probably just as important to her as West's was to him. I could tell that just from the look on her face when I brought up what Loki did.

I didn't need to make some big show of power to get Paris to back off. She'd already tangled with one god and lost. I just needed to threaten to finish the job he did on her hair.

Azren floated into the room, so I took my seat. It wasn't fair. I was just as much a god as Azren was, but I was nowhere near that ethereal or graceful. They sat on the edge of their desk and just stared at us. It was so nice having them back as our history teacher. I was guessing we could resume our private lessons, too, unless they were working with Baldur.

Loki wasn't here. Either someone decided he shouldn't be around college students after he fucked up Kaylee and Paris's hair or he just got bored with teaching and decided not to show up anymore.

"I have an announcement to make," Azren said. "Loki decided he didn't really want to teach anymore if magical corrections were going to be such a big deal when it's not for regular supernaturals. There are also two new gods on campus who will be teaching a class in a special kind of magic.

"They said it will come easier to witches, but *any* supernatural can do it. It's called Seidr and we have two experts to teach it. Odin will be teaching the beginner levels and *his* teacher, Freya will be teaching the advanced levels. It's a multifaceted form of magic that can do divination, healing, and illusions and it can be tapped into by anyone god-touched. Humans could do it if they dug down deep.

"If you're interested, there's a signup sheet in the dining hall. It'll be an additional class added to your workload, but it's completely worth it. Freya is an amazing teacher, and she taught it to me, too. Odin can be a little gruff, but he's a good teacher. If you think you're going to sign up for his class and try some of the things you do in my class because I have done nothing to you yet, just remember Thor was a little dick when he was a kid. He was this insanely powerful little asshole of a brute and Odin raised him into being a decent guy. Don't fuck with him. I heard about what happened in the dining hall. You should probably avoid pissing off any of the many gods that are now at the Academy of the Profane. The only reason any of us haven't seriously hurt you is because it's not really a fair fight."

I wanted to take that extra class so bad. Freya had taught me a little in addition to the rest of her knowledge, but to take a class at the Academy of the Profane with her as a professor would be amazing. Odin was probably a fantastic teacher, too.

Despite Azren's warning, Odin was great with kids and probably college students, too. When we were staying at his chateau when we were kids, Michael and I were wrestling and broke some insanely expensive antique. My mom was so mad and embarrassed, but Odin just laughed, waved his hand to fix it, and told her we were only going to be this age once.

Dexter's hand shot up and so did Drake's. Dexter was pretty much Azren's pet because he always asked Azren challenging questions or knew the answer when Azren asked us something. You wouldn't even know Drake and Azren were so close from history class. Azren never called on him and Drake never raised his hand, even though I was pretty sure Drake knew the answer. Azren called on Dexter first.

"Pixie magic is chaotic by nature. It can backfire if we don't learn to use it correctly. Could *I* take this new class?"

"Dexter, you're one of my best students, and when I was headmaster, pretty much all of your professors said the same about you. I think if *any* pixie can handle Seidr, it's you. Freya is also a close personal friend, and she's loving your social media right now."

She probably tuned in to his social media because he had several videos of people coming for me and losing, but she stayed because the rest of it was pretty awesome. His videos and posts were a mix of pixie shenanigans, social commentary, dodgeball, and he even roped my idiot brother into doing videos with him. Michael looked insanely happy, so those videos were my favorite. I didn't think *anything* embarrassed Dexter, but he blushed when Azren complimented him.

Azren nodded to Drake next.

"Is this going to make the witches more powerful?"

We were back to that. We'd come such a long way and then Kaylee broke into his dorm room and did the one thing he'd been paranoid about this entire time. And then she used the potion on people he cared about. Azren had known Drake longer than I had. They would know what to say in this situation.

"Maybe. Seidr would also give Basilisks a less fatal way to fight back. The divination portion could give you an idea if one of them is plotting against you. You'd have a form of magic to fight back with that only people who took this class would know about. You can't always get close enough to bite someone. This would also help you if you think someone is thinking about breaking into your dorm again. You should do it."

"Do we *have* to?" Paris asked. "Some of us are getting sick of the god invasion at the Academy of the Profane."

"No one is forcing you," Azren said, rolling their eyes. "You could totally decline an amazing opportunity to learn an old form of magic that would give you a leg up in the magical community, barely do any work at the best magical university in the country, and be content to be mediocre. Your last name will only get you so far in life."

Paris shrieked and stormed out of class. At the rate she kept flouncing out of history, she was going to flunk the class if her papers weren't any good. Before Azren could continue with their lecture someone came into the classroom after Paris slammed the door. He handed Azren a note and left. Azren gave it a glance.

"George, Headmaster Morningstar wants to see you in his office when you get a chance."

Was it still a big secret Gabriel was my dad? He went by Bell on all his legal paperwork, but everyone still called him Morningstar because of the whole angel connection. It was honestly kind of disrespectful to my mom, but she didn't mind or correct anyone, so the rest of us didn't.

I just nodded. I loved Gabriel and now that he was at his rightful place as headmaster, I could visit him on campus more often.

I wasn't sure what he wanted, but I was actually happy to get a summons from the headmaster.

GEORGE

Matilda, Mags, and I brought our lunch to my dad's office. He was buried under paperwork but smiled when he saw us. We also brought him a plate. Gabriel was the kind of guy who got caught up in his work and forgot to eat. My mom and dads constantly had to remind him.

"Hey, girls."

"I don't see lunch," Matilda said, putting her hands on her hips.

"You caught me. Lindsey left behind a mess. Azren tried to fix some of it, but they were more concerned with catching the killer. I'm having to go through all the strikes she ignored, probations that should have been enforced, and students who should have been expelled. Church Senior is helping me rewrite some school policies involving legacy students and we *cannot* let the one about deaths on campus stand. We also had to adjust for having a god as a student for the first time."

I groaned. Dexter wasn't the only student at the Academy of the Profane with a massive social media following. He was the only one who cared more about me than going viral to *ask* if he should post the video of what went down in the dining hall when I ended up taking my necklace off. Everyone posted their videos. If they didn't have a video, they made a text post about it.

Everyone knew I was a god by now. If they hadn't approached me in person, they were all over my social media. I was having random posts from when I was fifteen get thousands of likes and new comments. And I was an awkward little asshole at fifteen.

"Please don't tell me the Academy of the Profane is going to use this for publicity and plaster random photos of me from campus or dodgeball practice on their website or brochures."

"Honestly? A lot of them want to. If Church Senior wasn't in charge and I wasn't headmaster, they probably would. The rest of the board is salivating that a god is attending the Academy of the Profane, but Church Senior was a teacher and then headmaster. He's well aware you're a god, but he's also smart enough to acknowledge you're also an eighteen-year-old girl.

"He's going to add additional security to campus. There's going to be agents from the Paranormal Investigation Bureau patrolling. It's not just so nosy paparazzi don't crash and interrupt your studies. The board *should* have ordered it when the first student got butchered each time it happened. They couldn't do much to stop a god, but they might *see* something and report it to all the gods that are crashing here now."

I nodded. From what I knew about my boyfriend's grandfather, he was a hard-ass, but he was also a decent guy. My mom and aunt were terrified of him when they were students. They said he had been supportive and nurturing, but they had been so scared one of the guys they put in their place was going to complain and they'd get in trouble.

After they graduated, they found out a lot of those guys *did* complain, Church did his due diligence and investigated, then told the guys they had it coming and not to bother him again. He never brought it up to my mom and aunt because he thought they didn't do anything wrong and it wasn't needed. If my secret *had* to be out, Church Senior being board president was going to be a good thing.

"You let Baldur stay on campus," Mags said. "That's the only decision you've made so far that I'm questioning."

"Because I don't think it's him. Back when my family was being shunned, my choices were essentially to work with humans or clean up some things for bad people. I never did anything illegal, and I never helped them get away with anything. It was more when they were playing around with dark magic they shouldn't be touching and it backfired on them.

"Those people all have a certain look and feel about them. I'm sure you know what I'm talking about, Mags. If you dig really deep beyond what he's giving off with his magic missing, Baldur doesn't feel like that. Even if he can't remember what happened during his blackouts, that kind of thing sticks to a person.

"Witches and warlocks in particular are in tune to that kind of thing. We might not *know* what that feeling is until we've been around bad people and can put our finger on it. Baldur is awkward to be around because of his missing magic, but I've had more interactions with him than anyone in this room when we all thought he was just Sol in maintenance. He doesn't *feel* like he's ever done anything dark. You'll feel it, too, if you spend more time around him. He needs help and when he gets his memories back, he could tell us who did this."

Mags nodded and finally looked a little settled. Odin, Freya, and Azren could all tell her Baldur wouldn't have done this before he died, but that was thousands of years ago, and he didn't even remember that person. There was one thing Mags *could* trust—a witch or warlock's intuition and especially Gabriel when it came to dark magic. Honestly, it settled *my* mind, too, because I felt drawn to Baldur and I didn't want it to be him.

"You aren't eating," Matilda said. "I'm going to tell Mom."

Gabriel probably would have worked through lunch, came home light headed, and then Mom would have fussed at him right before my dad fed him. Gabriel was doing more talking than eating because there was a lot to say, but honestly, he was capable of doing both.

"Sorry. Don't tell your mom. There's just a lot to say and you need to get to class after this. About why I called for you. I had a meeting with Church Senior and Azren. Since you're the first and will probably be the only god to attend here, there's not really a curriculum for you.

"You've been surrounded by a mixed bag of supernaturals your entire life, but we never knew your big power was to mimic, so we only ever gave you a solid background in witchcraft because we thought you could use it to pretend to be a witch for as long as you wanted.

"You're already way more advanced than most of the freshmen witching classes and you don't really need potions as a god. You *do* need help learning how to use your mimic powers and you've always struggled with shapeshifting. Azren said gods can shapeshift into any kind of supernatural or animal, but they can't use their powers and they don't have the same senses. You can technically tap into all of that.

"We've decided to pull you out of some of your intro witch classes you either don't need or I know we've already taught you. I'm going to be moving you into intro classes for shifters, vampires, and Fae because it's all things you haven't learned and need to. I thought it would be poetic justice to put you into intro to flying since you could sprout wings and do it if you wanted to, but Azren insisted getting revenge for all those times your brother flew you up in the air and tried to drop you wasn't worth it because you'd never need to fly since you can portal."

I didn't want to be in intro to flying. It would be insanely cool and I always told Michael he looked like an asshole walking around with his wings out all the time, but that was just me giving him a hard time. His wings were fucking gorgeous, and he was insanely proud of them. Yeah, he might have tried to drop me a few times when we were kids, but now his wings and my skills were kind of our thing on the dodgeball field. I didn't *need* to fly when I could portal and I had my big brother.

"That's actually kind of cool. And I do suck at shapeshifting. I could have class with Matilda, Church, Drake, and Ren and actually figure out *how* I've been mimicking witches."

"Azren is going to be working on that and your shapeshifting this semester. Your dad never cared about shapeshifting, so he never really pressed the limits like Azren and Loki have. You aren't a trickster like Loki's kid is, so it never clicked like it did with her when he tried to teach you."

"This is *so cool*," Matilda squealed. "You'll be in my shifting classes and once you figure it out, we can shift and chase that guy you hexed in the dining hall all over campus. Hellhound beats bear."

"And when you figure out the vampire thing, you can use the speed to give him wedgies. His ass and balls aren't going to recover until they figure out how to break those hexes."

"What happened in the dining hall?" Gabriel demanded.

"Some bear shifter named Eugene either wanted bragging rights or to elevate his station by joining my group and got gross about inviting me to the moon orgy. Then, he got grosser by suggesting Matilda join us. If he complained about getting punched and set on fire, it's because he also said something gross in front of my guys. He's nasty."

"Ah. He was in here complaining about getting assaulted, but I'm aware of how he talks about people and hadn't had time to look into the situation yet. I've found at least two complaints against Eugene so far that are serious enough to be strikes. Lindsey ignored them. If I find one more, he's gone. His last name won't save him. Church Senior is about to pull out the original charter Beatrix Halliwell wrote. A bunch of families are about to get pissed off that their kids are only getting into the Academy of the Profane if they have the test scores and not because of their last names. A world of opportunity is about to open up for countless students who *do* have the test scores, but the spaces were filled up by people who didn't."

Which was how it should be. Matilda, Michael, and I got in because we were related to Gabriel, but we didn't rely on that. We had some of the best test scores in our high school. Beatrix Halliwell founded all three Profane buildings on the site of the biggest supernatural massacre in this country to help *all* supernaturals. The library was open to everyone who didn't intend to use the contents for evil. The museum had always been available for anyone to visit. The academy was supposed to educate everyone with the test scores to get in and it slowly became something different.

Gabriel clapped his hands.

"Now, the three of you need to get to class. You can report back to your mom I ate lunch with you and didn't work through it now that I'm headmaster. George, I've emailed your new class schedule to you. You'll start tomorrow."

"I'm excited!" I squealed.

I was. Most of my classes were things my family had already taught me. I messed up in class when I was distracted, but I shouldn't have because it was stuff I already knew.

This was my chance to fuck up for real and have a true Academy of the Profane experience like my mom did because I was about to learn things I'd never done before.

OSCAR

So far, Azren and Zion were the only professors who didn't acknowledge George had just come out as a god. Azren already knew, and I knew they wouldn't because they wanted her to feel normal. Zion would have been just as shocked as everyone else. Zion and the internet were a terrible mix, and I was guessing he didn't use the internet at all, but people had literally been talking about it all day. Magical combat was my last class of the day. Zion would have heard about it in one of his earlier classes.

Zion Skinner didn't do a damned thing any of our other professors did all day. All of them kissed her ass and then they spent the rest of class expecting her to know the answer to everything. I knew the answer and had my hand up. A lot of students did, but the professors wouldn't call on us. When it came to the practical portion of class, she had to do it first.

It was uncomfortable as fuck and it wasn't even happening to me. I was grateful to Zion. He treated her just like he did before Yule break. Zion treated her just like the rest of us. Which was honestly kind of insulting in this endearing way. If one of us did anything amazing, he just told us it was passable and we might not die in a magic fight. Dude seriously said that to my girlfriend, a literal god.

We were all on the dodgeball field for practice before dinner. It was going to be a beast of a practice. It was still freezing cold out and the field was covered in snow. I was *really* hoping I didn't end up face first in that shit. I was trying to stretch and warm up while avoiding getting it on me. I was from California. I didn't *do* snow. West was going to have to rethink his whole naked thing because our first game was coming up.

I was watching George while we warmed up. We were late to breakfast because *all* of our families called. Ren's sister was stalking us on social media. She saw the video where George got outed. Hana immediately told her parents, who walked over and told my Abuela. My Abuela was close with West's moms, so she called them.

They all blew up our phone to ask if the video was real and we were seriously dating a god. My Abuela was signing like a mad woman on video chat telling me not to fuck this up because not only was this girl a god, but she *liked* her. My Abuela loved Ren, too, but she wanted grandbabies, preferably with someone I loved who was in my coven.

Then we all had to chat once Church came home to change. We decided we weren't going to treat her any differently. West said she didn't want that and the rest of the students were already going to do that. By the time we got to the dining hall, she was putting the beat-down on Eugene because he did. Then, I watched her getting treated differently by most of our professors. It was stupid. I was glad we could count on Azren and Zion to just be normal.

Zion was pacing, and he finally addressed us.

"We have a problem. Some little fucking pissant from Misty Vale got scared by the footage the cheerleaders have been posting of our practices. He knows we are going to beat their asses in two weeks. The sniveling little skid mark has raised a complaint over a video that went viral because our Team Witch isn't exactly a witch."

Mother fucker. What a whiner. George stood and bowed her head.

"Sorry," she mumbled. "I'll go."

"You sit your ass down," Zion growled. "I've been watching you play most of the semester and I've talked to your daddy. You haven't been using any more strength than any of the vampires and I haven't seen *anything* from you that I haven't seen on the field before. Your dad says you're a mimic, so you are actually *doing* witchcraft, just like the little asshole who doesn't want to go up against you.

"Your dad, your tutor, the board, and myself have all written a letter to the college dodgeball league in response to the letter I got. If you little ankle biters could raise a stink on that social media thing, that would be great. George *deserves* to play with this team. She's an amazing player, and she's supportive of this team."

Dexter already had his phone out of his sweatshirt pocket and the cheerleaders were spilling onto the field. West was coming down and so were the dodgeball fans who came out to watch every practice. Belladonna and Matilda were co-captains of the cheerleading squad, but they also had pretty big social media followings and the vampires ended up liking Belladonna *much* better once she got the stick out of her ass.

There were a ton of thirsty bitches just waiting for West to drop a shirtless selfie. Ren, Church, and I had decent followings, but nowhere near as big as the rest of our group. Matilda, Mags, Belladonna, and West had their phones out like they were ready to go to war.

"What do you need us to do?" Belladonna asked.

Matilda just tossed her hair over her shoulder and was furiously typing.

"You just leave it to me. Watch for my post and follow my lead."

Drake didn't really do social media. Most of his followers were back on the Netherworld. He wrapped George up in a huge hug because she probably needed one right now.

There was one thing I knew about Matilda Bell. Her twin sister *would* be on the dodgeball team when all was said and done.

GEORGE

I hadn't even thought someone might try to kick me off the dodgeball team when I took my necklace off. Everyone had my back. I knew the dodgeball team, and the cheerleaders did because they really liked me. The rest of them could have either wanted a favor or just knew I could help the team win because a lot of them had never spoken to me before.

After dinner, I just really needed to clear my head. I *wanted* to spend time with my guys, but I also wanted an hour to just take a walk in the snow. I promised I'd visit them when I got back. Honestly, I didn't put much stock in gods and their walkabouts, but sometimes, I just really wanted to go for a walk. Like, just a few miles away from my house, not wandering the globe and realms. It always cleared my head.

I found myself walking toward the staff cabins. I wasn't looking for Azren, though. I never walked to theirs. I always portalled so no one suspected we were together. Azren's cabin wasn't even in this direction. I was looking for Baldur and I didn't even know where he was staying.

Most of the cabins had these adorable porches out front. I found him sitting on a chair in front of one. I took the other chair.

"How are you doing?" he asked. "The students have been talking about you all day. The professors have been, too."

"How am *I* doing? How are *you* doing? I've known I was a god this entire time. My parents prepared me for taking off my necklace. I expected most of what happened today. You had no way of knowing any of this was going to happen when you asked me to bring you to Azren."

"No, but Azren could have said anything and I wouldn't have expected it. I can't really process being a god who got murdered and resurrected because I don't remember any of that. You might be used to being a god, but *I'm* used to being treated a certain way because I'm different. I'd rather talk about how you're feeling with everything. It's a big change for you. I was in the dining hall in the shadows when everything went down. I *know* you weren't intending on showing everyone what you were. That girl forced you to because she hurt your boyfriend. The potion she threw at you couldn't hurt you, but I would imagine what happened after did."

I didn't know what went on during Baldur's blackouts. He didn't either. I hadn't been around bad people like Gabriel had to feel what my dad said bad people gave off and Baldur didn't. But my mom *and* my dad always told me to trust my gut and right now, it was screaming Baldur didn't kill anyone.

Everyone who knew him before said he was a pacifist and embodied everything a light god should. He might not remember any of that, but I think literally everyone I knew would be blaming the person who killed them for the situation Baldur found himself in. Loki had a *lot* of guilt about killing him and probably would just stand there and let Baldur do what he wanted if Baldur wanted to beat his ass.

Baldur knew who killed him. He knew he was literally within walking distance of that person. He didn't walk over there and confront him. I'd seen him on campus doing his usual maintenance job and now he wanted to talk about *my* feelings. Baldur might not have the powers or memories of a God of Light, but that's totally what a God of Light would do. If he wasn't over there trying to beat my Uncle Loki's ass, he wasn't killing witches.

"It wasn't too bad," I said. "I only had it on because they weren't sure if one of the idiot gods who don't like those of us who were born instead of made were going to kidnap me until they could figure out my weakness. I kept it on because I didn't want people to treat me differently from my twin. Yeah, Kaylee *forced* me to take it off or let Oscar be hurt longer to keep it, but it was time. I might get kicked off the dodgeball team, but everything else was expected."

"Zion Skinner isn't going to let that happen," Baldur said. "He's always been kind to me. He saw me catch a glass that was falling off the table and told me it was unfortunate the league wouldn't let me play dodgeball because I had the reflexes for it. We've been friends since."

"Ha! I knew he was a big softy!"

Seriously. He was an unorthodox magical combat teacher. The dodgeball players *loved* his class. If we weren't sparring, he'd put us through the wringer until someone complained, and then they had to use their magic to *make* him let us stop. Zion rarely complimented us. If someone pulled off something amazing, he'd congratulate us for being passable and not embarrassing him by dying in a magic fight after we graduated.

But Zion was also supportive as shit and rarely said anything about it. The cheerleaders didn't know he helped Azren get the board to approve their team because he didn't want credit. I knew because Azren and I were together.

Anyone might have thought Zion was fighting to keep me on the dodgeball team because Michael and I together could win games, but I knew it was more than that. He carried on magical combat like it was any other day and he would have known I wasn't a witch because he had that letter. I usually loved it when *the* Zion Skinner acknowledged me in class, but it meant a lot he focused on everyone *but* me after my secret was out.

And now that I knew he had befriended Baldur when everyone thought he was just that guy in maintenance who felt weird to be around?

Total softy.

"Don't let him fool you. He loves teaching and coaching dodgeball. After he retired, the only options they gave him were doing commentary at games. They thought he was going to be insulting and they could profit from it if he caused a scandal. He knew that and he hated it. Zion wanted to coach, but they wouldn't hire him. He eats lunch with me when he can and all he talks about are his students and the dodgeball team."

Baldur had this little twinkle in his eye. I honestly had no idea Zion had befriended Baldur. I loved everything about that, and it seemed to mean a lot to Baldur because he probably didn't have a lot of those here. I mean, I *said* I was going to do it when he delivered our luggage and then I got wrapped up in everything and forgot about it until he approached me.

"Zion's secret is safe with me. Not his friendship with you, the whole actually liking us part."

Baldur was probably bigger than my dad, but he looked nervous as hell for a minute.

"Zion is one of the only friends I've ever had at the Academy of the Profane and I've been here several times over the last few hundred years. Do you think that's going to change if I tell him who I am and what I might have done?"

"You know him better than I do, but he didn't treat me any differently in class and the only reason he even acknowledged I'm a god at dodgeball practice was because some warlock at another school tried to get me kicked off the team because of it. I think he'll be happy for you that you figured out who you are.

"As for the murders, my dad has been around a lot of bad people. He said it leaves a mark behind you can feel. Even if you don't remember, he knows what it feels like. Gabriel said it's masked because your magic is missing, but you feel like a good person.

"And I don't think it's you either. I adore my Uncle Loki. He's an amazing dad and a supportive uncle. He's tried to help me with god stuff and he helped my sister's girlfriend fight her homophobic parents just because he adores my twin. We all know what he did to you. I'm not excusing him, but I know he was hurt and lashing out.

"If you walked across the lawn and beat the shit out of him, he would let you. He'd tell his whole family not to interfere, and they'd listen. I wouldn't *like* watching my Uncle Loki get the shit beaten out of him, but I'd get it if you did it and I wouldn't stop you if he told me not to. None of this would be happening if you hadn't been murdered. You haven't spoken a single bad word about my uncle. That's a

God of Light thing, even if you don't remember being one. The guy that is butchering witches would have gotten revenge if it was you.

"Maybe tell Zion who you are, but leave out the rest. The people who knew you before don't think it's you. Gabriel has been around the new you for years and *he* doesn't think it's you. I grew up with a lot of witches and warlocks *and* the god who created them. They are big on intuition, and *I* don't think you did it. Muninn is going to give your memories back and then you'll know that, too."

"Thanks, George. Is it weird I always seem to feel better when I'm near you?"

"Probably no weirder than me feeling drawn to you. When you get your memories back, we actually have a lot in common. We're both born gods with big families and loving parents. When we'd visit Odin on vacation, he'd always laugh at Michael and me and he say Michael always reminded him of the angel version of your brother Thor when he was younger. Michael and I were born with magic so we had to assert dominance by beating the crap out of each other when we were little. If we broke something expensive, my mom was always mortified, and Odin always said it reminded him of his kids. I think he was talking about you and Thor."

"I feel more comfortable with you than I do with Odin. He's trying, but he wanted to follow me all over campus and do all my duties with magic. The only thing he told me that made sense in all this was when he said I always used to like working with my hands and I used to do wood carvings. I actually still do that. I made you something. Stay here."

Baldur disappeared for a bit. He came back with a blanket and something in his hand. Baldur wrapped me in the blanket because it was still pretty cold outside. It smelled like him. Baldur smelled like bergamot and black tea. It was a cozy scent that drew me in. He looked like he was embarrassed about what he wanted to give me.

Baldur thrust his hand out. There was this gorgeous wood carving in his hand. It was an effigy of me kneeling next to a Hellhound. It was beautiful, and it meant so much to me that he included my twin in the carving. He looked like he was terrified I wasn't going to like it, but I loved it. Some guys didn't accept that my twin was such a major part of my life and didn't like that she was such a strong woman.

My twin came with me. Matilda and Baldur hadn't had that many interactions and what little they did have, she'd mostly sided with Mags that I should be a little more suspicious of him until he got his memories back. A lot of that had gone down right in front of Baldur and he still included her in the carving because he could tell how close we were and he didn't hold it against her.

And the big teddy bear looked like he would be devastated if I hated it. I jumped up and wrapped him in a huge hug. I'd honestly been wanting to do that for a while, and he looked like he needed it. The carving was perfect. With *everything* going on with him, he chose to make this for me.

He stood there like a tree for a bit before he finally hugged me back. Baldur's biceps were bigger than my thighs. He gave *amazing* hugs, and he squeezed me like no one had given him one in a long time. I didn't want him to let go, so I just craned my head up at him.

"It's beautiful. And it means a lot to me that you included my sister. I know Mags and Matilda have been suspicious, but they are trying to protect me, and they'll be *much* nicer."

Baldur's silver eyes bore into mine.

"Everything is kind of scary. Finding out the truth is a *lot*. I know Odin is my father and Freya watched me grow up, but I don't remember them. Why does it only feel better when I'm around *you?*"

"Probably the same reason I barely know you and don't know what happens during your blackouts, but I *really* want you to kiss me right now."

Baldur groaned.

"And I really want to kiss you, too, but not like this. For one, you need to talk to your guys and see if it's okay with them to be kissing me. Secondly, *if* they're okay with it, when I kiss you, it's going to be when I have my magic back and we're equals."

"I don't care about your magic."

"Oh, I know. I'm just wondering if there's a light-god trick I'm going to remember to make the kiss unforgettable. And I'm not an idiot. Those guys adore you and I'm pretty sure Azren does, too. If we're going to go further than kissing and I think we both want to, then you need to talk to them. I don't want to get my magic and memories back and just bring drama and tension with it."

I squeezed him and nuzzled his chest with my face.

"You might not have your magic or remember anything about being Baldur, but based on everything Freya and Odin said, there's a lot of the original you in there."

"I hope so."

Yeah, I had absolutely *no* evidence Baldur wasn't killing witches during his blackouts, but I could just *feel* he wasn't the one doing this.

WEST

I needed the boyfriends-in-law to take this dire situation *much* more seriously. George was taking a walk in this ball-shrinking-cold weather and we had *jobs* to do. Some horrible person tried to get my girlfriend kicked off the dodgeball team. We didn't just need to save her spot. No, this deserved some next-level retribution.

"Seriously, Oscar, why can't you give him magical crabs and treatment-resistant head lice? This guy came for our woman."

"For one, he's two states away from us. Secondly, you can't give someone magical crabs unless *you* have magical crabs and you sleep with them. Do you want me to cheat on George and Ren? I don't even have magical crabs."

"Well, I don't see *you* suggesting anything. Dexter just posted something. He's much better at this shit than the rest of you. I'll bet Dexter would give himself magical crabs and fuck this guy," I sulked, queuing up Dexter's post.

"Dexter is *totally* not giving himself a magical STD and cheating on Michael," Church said.

"Put the video on the TV," Ren said. "Dexter doesn't need to do whatever the fuck that idea was. He just needs pixie fuckery, glitter, and his phone."

Good point. We'd save the magical crabs thing as backup. Someone was going to have to take one for the team. The video queued up to Dexter and Michael in bed together. Dexter was reclining on Michael's naked chest and Michael had his wings wrapped around him. It was cozy and sexy. Dexter had set a whole-ass mood, so this was going to be epic. Michael was casually playing with Dexter's hair.

"So, it appears the Team Warlock at Misty Vale doesn't want to take on our Team Witch because she's really a god. She's a special kind of god who is playing dodgeball with witch magic. George Bell has a signature move with the Air Ball. That move isn't possible without her brother, my boyfriend, the hot guy sitting behind me. There's *also* never been an angel in the history of dodgeball. If you kick George off the team, she'd just teach her trick to the new Team Witch who could pull it off with Michael and we'd still kick their asses.

"Anyway, this particular warlock isn't worried about that. I'd like to show you something he doesn't want you to see. It's pretty fucking embarrassing and the real reason he's going after George Bell and not her brother. Pixie wings and angel wings are fundamentally different. Pixies are also built differently. We can't carry another person in the air, but we *can* use pixie dust to help them fly. It's wildly unpredictable and ill-advised unless you're fully trained. I can't tell if the pixie who agreed to this is just stupid or didn't like this fucker. Anyway, see for yourself."

The video cut to dodgeball practice at another school. Don't ask me how Dexter got his hands on this, but Dexter also worked in mysterious ways. Their team had obviously tried to copy George and Michael's trick with the Air Ball with a pixie and the Team Warlock. Michael was the only angel I knew, but you could tell from looking at them that pixie wings and angel wings were much different. They were both totally gorgeous, but Michael's were built to carry another person. Dexter's were like butterfly wings.

I didn't know pixies could make someone fly by dousing them with glitter because I'd never seen one do it, but that was this team's big plan. They took their places on the field and this pixie coated this dude with so much glitter, he looked like Edward Cullen on crack.

I could tell this wasn't going to end well, but this was riveting. Their coach released all four balls and when the pixie took to the air, the warlock did, too. George relied on Michael in the air because he'd been flying for a long time. This glittered chuckle fuck had never taken a flying class in his life and thought he could tame the Air Ball and fly on his own.

News at five. He could not. I'd watched George and Michael do this enough to know when the Air Ball knew someone was in the air trying to tame it, it started to fight back. George had to snag it pretty fast. This warlock had some balls. He thought he could easily accomplish what George and Michael had spent ages in front of the library perfecting in just one practice with a pixie.

I had this guy pegged, He probably went straight for the Earth Ball because it was easier and a tiny bit slower. The Air Ball was a different beast. He didn't immobilize it fast enough, and it sent a mini tornado at him. Since he got himself in the air with all the bravado of a dude with big-dick energy and nothing to back it up, the tornado snagged him. It was like a warlock washing machine for a bit and then he got flung far off the field like those old Looney Toons cartoons I used to watch with my pops when I was a kid.

I was about to comment when George appeared in our dorm room in a cloud of purple smoke that smelled like lavender and marshmallows. I pounced like the lion I was and sat down with her in my lap. I nuzzled her hair with my cheeks.

"Watch this shit. Play it again."

George watched the whole shit show go down with her mouth open. There had been a lot of fuckery since we all arrived at the Academy of the Profane, but we finally reached a level that rendered her speechless.

"That whole move isn't possible without my brother. I didn't even know I could sprout wings and fly myself until last semester, but even if I can *in theory* I don't know how and I also don't know how to fly. My dad is going to be changing my schedule so I won't just be taking classes with witches to figure out my magic, but flying isn't going to be one of them because I don't really need it. I might *eventually* learn, but that's going to be a ways off. I'm going to need Michael for that move for the next four years if they don't kick me off the team."

Ren started giggling.

"I'm pretty sure your brother and his boyfriend took care of that."

"My idiot brother may have also gotten himself kicked off the team!"

"He didn't," I said. "Some guys masturbate to naked women but sometimes I do it to dodgeball playbooks and the regulation manual. The *only* qualification for playing dodgeball is magic. Like, if you take up with a human, have two kids, and one has magic and one doesn't, the kid with magic can play dodgeball and the one without can't because it's not safe for them.

"They'd have to make a new rule that gods and angels can't play, but they'd have to say it's because it's not fair to everyone else. If they do that for you and Michael, it's going to kick open all kinds of nasty doors they don't want open. Someone can say vampire speed and strength isn't fair or pixies shouldn't play because the rest of them don't have wings. I'm pretty sure the letter to Zion was just them covering their bases to say they did something. Your brother and his boyfriend just pointed out you couldn't do what you did without an angel and shamed the other team for trying to get you banned because they couldn't pull it off when they tried to plagiarize it."

"You can't trademark dodgeball moves, West," George pointed out.

"You should! It's in poor taste."

"I don't think anyone is going to try to tame the Air Ball without an angel again," Ren giggled. "Dude got flung further than I've ever seen anyone in a dodgeball match before. It was almost like a movie special effect. It's probably going to take a healer ages to fix everything. He's probably out for the whole season."

"I could portal there and heal him. That would show everyone gods have good powers and I could talk to him about what my actual gifts are."

"Absolutely not," I said. "The dude is a victim of his own fuckery, and he tried to take dodgeball away from you. Hear me out. Portal to him and give him magical crabs. Gods can do that, right?"

"Without catching them myself and sleeping with him?"

"Nix that fucking plan. Absolutely not. I'll come up with something better than magical crabs."

"Conjuring living things is tricky, so I'm not sure I could conjure them."

"Damn. So, the treatment-resistant head lice are out, too. Someone needs to come up with something."

"Bro, Dexter just plastered him getting flung across the whole dodgeball field to the entire internet. He probably hit a tree and broke his ass. Why are you stuck on crabs and lice?" Drake asked.

"Because he probably broke his arms, too, and can't scratch," I said.

"That's actually a good idea," Church said. "Maybe we could hook him up with Paris. Belladonna was gossiping with me in one of our vampire classes that she was in the infirmary for a potion because she gets migraines and Paris was there getting a potion. Paris made the healer shut up real fast when she tried to tell her you put it on your vagina in front of Belladonna. Belladonna has been sitting on this information in case Paris decides to carry on Kaylee's feud. She thinks of you like a sister now because she's dating Matilda and Mags. Belladonna perfected the mean girl thing in high school because of her family and she'll drag it out again if she needs to."

That could also work. I could take one for the team and use my lion charm to flirt with Paris and make her think *I'd* go there if *she* went there.

"Guys, leave it," George said. "There's something I wanted to talk to you about."

Oh, fine. His ass was probably broken, Dexter embarrassed him, and I really didn't think George was getting kicked off the team. Yeah, he suffered, but had he suffered *enough* for trying to take something away from my girl-friend that she loved? I'd think about that later. Right now, she needed me to listen, and that's what good boyfriends did.

"So, I just intended on going for a walk, but I found myself looking for Baldur. I don't know why, but I'm drawn to him. I really don't think it's him killing witches. I need you to know we nearly kissed. I wanted him to, but he stopped and said he wouldn't until I talked to all of you, and he had his magic back."

Was that it? I mean, I was pretty sure she was going to go there if he wasn't a killer. I knew he was a god of Light and I was just a lion, but he was nearly as pretty as I was. And from what I learned in history, everyone loved Freya and she kept extolling his virtues before he died.

I saw it coming, and I was fine with it. I'd do *anything* to make her happy and if the other gods loved this guy, I prob-ably would, too. And he respected all of us enough to hold back until she talked to us first. He could have just gone there and told us to deal with it since he was a god.

I didn't think Ren and Oscar had a problem with it. They technically tried to hit that the first day they met him when we thought he was just the maintenance guy who felt weird to be around. I think Ren and Oscar were even cooler with it now that Baldur had told them the only reason he hadn't taken them up on it was that he was just shocked to be invited to his first moon orgy.

Church might be a problem. George and Church appar-ently made their peace for several hours in the snow and she saved his dick from more beatings from Bethany. Church's little tantrum was because he got slightly jealous that he wasn't as fabulous as Azren and thought she was going to fuck off with them. Adding Baldur might be a little much.

"George, honestly, I thought it was going to head there, but I need to tell you something you aren't going to like," Church said.

I swear to all fuck if Church got stupid about this, I'd punch him in the nuts myself. George braced herself like Church was about to tell her she could have Baldur or she could have him.

"I've been researching Baldur at the library between classes. I know you don't think it's him and the people who knew him before didn't, but I was looking for *anything*. There's not a lot about Baldur. I think he was young when he died. I have no problem with the two of you being together. I wasn't going to say anything unless you said for sure you had feelings, but what little I could find on Baldur was that he was married before he died. Please don't get too deep with him until he gets his memories back. I don't want to see you get hurt."

Yeah, George should know that, but I still wanted to give Church a nut punch for telling her that.

"Ugh. Thanks for telling me. We're both drawn to each other, but that's who he is now. I'm aware that could change when he remembers who he is. I should probably talk to Freya, too."

"I wish you could sleep in here with us. I had an amazing night's sleep in your dorm room the other night," Church said.

"The lesbians said you breathed too loud and probably would have beat your ass if George didn't like you," Drake laughed.

"I don't snore! Guys, honestly, we've been rooming together this entire time. You'd tell me if I snored right?"

Drake fell out laughing. Church was flipping out, and he definitely didn't snore. I would have purred up a storm if I got to sleep in her bed. Matilda probably would have eaten me.

"You don't snore. You breathed too loudly for a man in their dorm," Drake giggled.

"I don't get it."

Church looked utterly confused and now I was trying not to laugh, too. I was not under any grand impression that Matilda and Mags decided to talk to me in the first place because I was sitting with George.

"My sister likes all of you. She really does. Mags does, too. But they like you in the sense some people like other people's kids. You get to interact and have fun with them on your terms and at the end of the day, they go to their house and you go to yours. They adore spending time with you, but they don't want to live with you, even if it's just for the night. If they didn't get annoyed by your breathing, you would have moved too much and they would have gone to Belladonna and Mina's room. If I do that again with any of you, I'll have to talk to them first because it's their room, too."

I got it. This was *our* room, and we all wanted her here, but there wasn't space and we couldn't exactly push the beds together.

But they'd eventually graduate. We'd get our own place with a big, giant bed. Maybe Baldur would be with us, maybe he wouldn't, but we'd all pile into that bed and sleep the way a lion's pride was meant to.

I couldn't wait. I didn't have a single drop of foresight, but I knew this was going to work out.

And maybe I'd think up something better than magical crabs for that stupid warlock.

AZREN

I loved teaching, and I was motivated to fix whoever was murdering students at the Academy of the Profane. Especially since Baldur might be involved. I didn't kill Baldur, but I had a *lot* of guilt about his death. Loki was a good friend. I knew about his kids because I went myself to reap them out of respect for him. I was back on the Netherworld for the most part and made frequent trips to Earth to visit my friends.

I checked in with Loki, but I should have ignored him when he said he was fine. I should have barged into his life and crashed on his couch until he actually *was* fine. My friend was one of the most hardheaded and stubborn people I knew, but he wasn't violent except for Baldur. I wouldn't have been able to talk him out of any of his usual shenanigans, but I'd always felt like if I'd just shown up and refused to leave, I could have talked him out of what happened to Baldur.

Death was my domain. I taught Lilith necromancy so

she could teach her witches because even though every-thing died, sometimes it was helpful to temporarily bring them back. I didn't have to sacrifice and bleed like a witch would, but the rules were the same. The essence had to be *willing* to come back, and the vessel had to be undamaged.

I *tried* with Baldur, but his vessel was too damaged. I could have done what I did with Freya and kept putting him into mortal bodies, but his parents didn't want that. They wanted to wait until the fates decided it was time for him to come back and gave his vessel back. I didn't kill Baldur, and I did exactly what his family wanted and let the fates decide when he came back.

I still felt responsible for how he was now.

I wanted to delve in and fix it, but memory wasn't one of my powers. We had to wait for Muninn. And I had to deal with some stupid supernatural politics.

The college dodgeball league wasn't about to kick a god off one of their teams. Even if she was terrible, they could have used her for ratings. But she wasn't. I watched tryouts and practice. George was actually good and when Michael and George teamed up on something, they were showboats. I'd been watching dodgeball on two realms and I'd never seen *anyone* do what they did with the Air Ball. Dexter, Oscar, and Drake also made amazing plays with her that was going to make their team exciting to watch.

The league would have seen the footage and known what they were going to do for their ratings. But they had to make a show of investigating when they got the complaint and stress my girlfriend out. I wanted her to take the necklace off, but when *she* was ready. I was starting to realize why she left it on.

People were treating her differently and the only reason the board wasn't exploiting her for publicity was because

Church Senior did a hostile takeover and wouldn't let them. I'd dealt with the old board president when I was temporary headmaster. He would have had people hiding in bushes to take photos of her all over campus.

No one knew George, and I were together and the *real* reason I agreed to do what I did to keep her on the dodgeball team. The board of the Academy of the Profane and the board of the other school seemed to think that idiot warlock wasn't responsible for the injuries he gave himself shortly before he tried to get George banned from playing college dodgeball.

Personally, I thought he should lay there in bed while the healers mended his bones so he could really stew on the consequences of his actions. I hadn't hung out with a lot of pixies and the angels mostly kept to themselves, but even I knew what that warlock tried was going to end badly without an angel.

Between Dexter's video and Gabriel and Church Senior going to bat for George, the other school was starting to realize they were looking like poor sports in all of this. George *did* have advantages on the dodgeball field, but she wasn't using them. She could have portalled from one end of the field to the other and used her strength to throw the ball past the goalie, but she wasn't. She was running, flying with the aid of her brother, or passing the ball.

I'd gotten on video chat and informed all of them of this as well. There was one last thing they wanted and the other school would withdraw their complaint against George. It was stupid, and I didn't want to do it, but I couldn't risk being wrong about the league not wanting to lose the ratings that would come from George and Michael playing together.

Apparently, their Team Warlock was a local celebrity

because he was the best dodgeball player on their team. This stupid stunt was going to take him out the whole season. He also tore his rotator cuff in a few places when he tried to avoid breaking his face on the tree he hit. The healers weren't sure if they could heal it properly so that he would play dodgeball the same again.

The other school said that if perhaps one of the many gods who were now on our campus could come heal their star warlock, they'd withdraw their complaint and we could just settle all of this on the field. Problem was, all the gods here adored George and didn't want to do it. We weren't about to tell George they were asking this, even though she would have done it without complaint.

I agreed to do it for various reasons. Freya had known George longer than I had and thought of her like an adopted daughter. If we sent Freya, she'd heal that boy and leave something nasty behind. He'd probably play dodge-ball like he always did and his dick would never function right again. I wasn't mad at that idea, but I didn't want to give them any reason to make a big deal about George being a god again.

I wasn't going to pull Odin away from Baldur and Odin didn't really give a shit about a mortal dodgeball player. I wasn't about to ask Reyson or Loki because they were both hotheads and a little short sighted when it came to George.

So, I went to heal the warlock who tried to take some-thing from my girlfriend. I knew damned well when Loki found out about it, he was probably going to fuck up this kid's life and he wouldn't use a single drop of magic.

In fact, I was counting on it when I went to heal him.

GEORGE

College had gotten wild. I was ignoring everyone kissing my ass and my professors treating me differently. I'd gone from one of the best students in my witching classes because my family had been teaching me my entire life, to the literal worst student in class because I was taking classes for things I didn't even know I could do and I was now a semester behind everyone else.

It was pretty awesome. I was having a *normal* college experience, and I was having to work my ass off to keep up. I had friends in all my classes who were trying to help me catch up. I was in class with nearly every magical species. My dad and Azren had decided not to put me in class with the species with sex magic. I'd probably only be able to use it at moon orgies when there were incubi and succubae around, but I was seriously curious about their magic and how it would heighten sex for everyone.

I'd have to stay curious about that because my day was

full of a lot of classes I was now terrible at. I couldn't really work on honing my animal senses and controlling my inner beast like the rest of my class because I hadn't exactly figured out how to tap into that yet. I couldn't shift at all. Matilda, Mags, and West were trying to help me and Bram told me to come home and he could try, too.

My vampire classes weren't much better. They were teaching fang and feeding control. Vampires could also compel, but it wasn't totally reliable. The compulsion didn't last very long and anyone with strong mental walls could fight against it. While everyone else was being taught to put those walls up, the vampires were being taught to slip in the cracks. I hadn't even figured out how to drop fang yet.

My Fae classes were small, but I was faring worse in those classes. There were multiple different types of Fae and they all used magic. My class just had Seelie, Unseelie, pixies, and one lone Brownie. Dexter was helping me, but I was still terrible.

My classmates were generally *much* better about it than most of my professors at first. The majority of them got I was just an idiot eighteen-year-old trying to figure my shit out like they were. My professors needed a little more convincing that I didn't slide out my mom's vagina as an infant knowing how to do everything and I didn't go to college just for fun. I actually needed them to *teach* me.

It took a day, but I managed to get it through all my professor's heads. History and magical combat were my only classes where my teachers didn't treat me any differently. Zion paired me with West like usual and I was distracted because this was my last class and this had been a *long*-ass day trying to convince my professors to actually teach me.

So, West was kicking my ass.

"That's *embarrassing*," Paris scoffed, tossing her destroyed hair over her shoulder. "Imagine being a god and getting your ass kicked by a lion that didn't even go to college."

West gave her the biggest stink eye he could manage.

"You got some glitter on you when a pixie bested you."

I hadn't been paying attention to the rest of the class, but I would have *loved* seeing Dexter kick her ass. Paris wasn't just covered in glitter. It looked like Dexter gave her a black eye. Dexter's green hair was messed up like Paris resorted to hair pulling in a magic fight.

Zion never acknowledged I was a god in magical combat and he rarely gave out compliments. He taught like Beatrix Halliwell intended for teachers to do their lessons. Zion never played favorites, and he mostly gave us all the same learning experience. I was kind of limited to really hot body contact with my boyfriend instead of sparring with other supernaturals, but I got why he was doing that.

I didn't realize Zion was even paying attention until he strolled over.

"You've been trading barbs with George in my class all year. Which was pretty bold because we all knew she could whoop your butt when we thought she was a witch. I've been holding *her* back and you've just gotten bolder. You're going to settle this like supernaturals—with a magic fight. And I'm unleashing her on the rest of you. There are a lot of gods on this campus. You need to learn how to hold your own and she needs the full experience of my class. So, take your places. We've all watched you try to start something. We're going to see if you can finish it."

"I can't fight her! She's some butch dodgeball player and a god."

"Excuse me, but we are nearly identical and neither of us are butch," Matilda said. "Maybe you should have kept your stupid mouth shut after the first time a god fucked you up."

"I would have stopped after my hair got trashed because girl, not even an exclusive lion's only salon is going to fix that," West pursed.

"Enough!" Zion roared. "Your generation likes bickering and trash talking, but you need to learn how to finish it. Paris, you had the lady balls to start something with someone everyone thought was the strongest witch in the school and decided to keep it going when you found out she was a god. You can either settle it in my class in a fair fight or you can wait until she's good and pissed at you and you end up dead."

Honestly? Up until recently, I would have said my mom and most of my dads had instilled such a sense of patience in me that it wouldn't happen. I used to be a terror that caused all kinds of thunderstorms. That hadn't happened in a long time and then Kaylee hurt Oscar. I caused another thunderstorm and if I hadn't heard my dad and felt his hand on my shoulder, I actually might have killed Kaylee. She probably had it coming, but I'd never killed anyone before and I didn't know if I'd be as cavalier about that as my dad was.

I squared my shoulders and faced Paris.

"He's right. You can face me now when you're just a minor annoyance or I can be the last thing you see if you keep this up like Kaylee did and my dad isn't there to calm me down."

"Well, is everyone going to watch?" Paris demanded.

Zion just chuckled.

"Yeah, they are. You tried to humiliate her loudly

enough for the entire class to hear. It's only right everyone watches you get your ass kicked. I thought you witches believed in that kind of justice from the stars? Now, take your place. You're barely passing my class. If I kick you out because you're refusing this assignment, it's going to drop you an entire letter grade. Azren says you aren't doing great in their class either. Shifters can't *smell* academic probation, but that smells like academic probation. And you're starting something with the new headmaster's daughter. Choose wisely."

Damn. *The* Zion Skinner just defended me. I *knew* he was a softie who actually liked me. He solved this exactly like he should have. By letting us duke it out magically when the stronger of us wasn't pissed off and would hurt the other. It would be a simple magical sparring fight. We'd been in the same class with each other all year, so I knew what we'd been taught. I knew what *level* to fight her on and I wasn't mad enough to hurt her.

Paris decided she was going to fight me. This could either be really good or really bad. This could end things or escalate them. We faced each other and just stared. Paris looked like she was bracing herself and found some bravery.

"Fight!" Zion yelled.

I was intending on fighting fair, but Paris flung a particularly nasty hex at me that Zion didn't teach us in class. I guessed it was from her family grimoire because I wasn't intimately familiar with it, but I could *feel* how nasty it was. I didn't have to pretend to throw up a shield. I just had to be me.

Paris grinned because she could feel I didn't have my magical shield up. She didn't *get* it. She saw her hex barreling at me and she just assumed I was going to get blasted back with what was probably the nastiest thing in her family grimoire and spent weeks in the infirmary trying to get it healed.

I was counting on that. I *needed* her to know she could fling her absolute best at me, and nothing was going to happen. Paris clearly hadn't learned that after the Basilisk potion just dripped off me and did nothing.

I just stood there smiling as the hex hit me. It barely even blew my hair back. Paris's smug grin fell, and she started to look a little horrified. I think Paris was starting to realize who she was fucking with, which was all I really wanted.

I wanted her to leave me alone, and I didn't want her to pull a Kaylee and do something that was going to hurt my guys, but I also didn't want to destroy her. I flung a basic spell at her that we learned the first day of class. It was a *get the fuck away from me* spell that was more like a little love zap to warn someone you weren't messing around.

That was what I hit her with, but I put a little extra punch behind it to blast her back a bit. Paris would have known I just beat her with something we learned on day one and her best did nothing to me. She jumped to her feet and glared at me. I think she expected her friends to flock around her and come up with a plan to strike back, but they were all looking at her like I'd blasted her into a pile of shifter shit.

Maybe it was finally over with Paris, maybe it wasn't. It looked like she wasn't going to have help from any of her friends now and I could handle one spiteful legacy student.

OSCAR

It seemed like a lot of the minor drama was working itself out so we could focus on the giant, insanely hot, god-shaped drama who didn't remember who he was or if he'd been murdering witches. Kaylee and Lindsey were in jail, we *finally* had a decent headmaster, George put Paris in her place in magical combat, and Zion Skinner was pretty terrible at hiding his emotions, so I was pretty sure he was about to give the dodgeball team good news.

"We worked it out with the league and the team who made the complaint. They *will not* be banning George from college dodgeball and we'll be settling this on the field in two weeks with the school who made the complaint. George Bell isn't going anywhere."

I could literally hear West shriek all the way from the field. When I looked at the bleachers, he was shaking his ass with the cheerleaders in celebration. We did what dodgeball players did. Someone body tackled George, and we all piled on top of them. Drake and I showed her affection in the bedroom one way. On the dodgeball field, it was chest bumps, ass slaps, and dog piling on each other. It was just how things were done. When everyone got off of her, Drake and I smacked her ass.

"Now, I don't do the whole social media thing, but I was told Dexter already embarrassed the warlock that tried to get George kicked off the team. He's going to be on the field with his team when they play us. I'm going to need you all to do it the old-fashioned way, too. I want all of you to beat their team so badly, they regret what they did.

"Back in my day, a god on the other team would have been seen as a *challenge*. We would have busted our asses with extra practices and if they beat us, we wouldn't have made it easy. What we *wouldn't* have done was go bitching to the league and try to get someone kicked off the team. Your generation is a bunch of soft-ass baby whiners. Now, warm up so we can show them *you're* not a bunch of soft-ass baby whiners and if someone starts something with us, we're going to finish it like actual supernaturals instead of little bitches. Though, I might have to check out this social media thing just for Dexter's account because I've heard some things. Stretch and impress me."

Dexter was beaming with his chest puffed out. Honestly, Dexter had millions of followers and most of his posts went viral, but I don't think any of that compared to getting our grumpy dodgeball coach who hated the internet with a fiery passion on social media just to check him out. That was some *serious* cred right there.

Zion had already moved on with his life and was chatting with the cheerleading coach on the sidelines while we warmed up, but the rest of the team was losing their shit. We were used to Zion ranting about our generation being soft and social media being stupid, but we also knew he gave a shit. For a lot of us, he was our favorite professor, even if you weren't on the dodgeball team.

I had a feeling a lot went on behind the scenes in keeping George on the dodgeball team. And I had a feeling Zion, her dad, and Azren were involved. George hadn't put the pieces together that if the warlock was going to be playing against us, then a god had healed him. It was probably Azren because I couldn't think of anyone else who would. Azren probably didn't want to, but they adored George and if the condition for her playing dodgeball was a god healing him, Azren was going to do it rather than someone telling George she had to.

I was guessing they were some kind of dream team. Zion yelled at some people about the rules and regulations of dodgeball and that there was nothing that specifically said George couldn't play, Gabriel handled the politics and smoothed over any of the fallout if Zion offended anyone, and Azren used their magic for any demands only a god could handle.

Zion would probably punch me in the face and make me run endless laps if I ever brought that up in his presence. Gabriel Morningstar scared me at first. He *looked* like a guy who had descended from a fallen angel and knew a ton of dark magic. He also had a snake for a familiar and it was always draped around his neck whispering in his ear.

But then I got to eat dinner with him at home with his family and it just broke the entire mystique of Gabriel Morningstar. He was just a guy who adored his wife and kids. I needed to talk to her dad, anyway. I was in an insane amount of pain as my flesh was being eaten down to the bone, but the rest of my roommates said George was literally two seconds away from killing Kaylee until Gabriel showed up.

We all needed to figure out how to do that for her. One of her dads was a god, but the rest of them were regular supernaturals like us. George had Azren and maybe she'd have Baldur if that worked out, but the rest of us needed to figure out how to calm her like Gabriel did with just a touch and a word.

Azren would swear me to secrecy if I approached them about this. As they probably should. If George never figured it out, I didn't want her to know this bastard didn't have to suffer for trying to take this away from her.

George offered, but sometimes, my girlfriend was *much* too nice. I had no idea what it was like to be her, but I wouldn't have offered to heal that warlock.

And I would have done *much* worse to Paris when Zion paired us up.

GEORGE

I finally felt like I was getting the full college experience. Yeah, I nearly got kicked off the dodgeball team just for how I was born, but I was sucking in my classes and I was sitting in Halliwell Square with the dodgeball team and cheerleading celebrating the fact that I didn't get kicked off the team.

Michael finally realized Innis was *very* gay and not into me and stopped threatening to beat his ass any time he touched me. I think it helped that Innis already had his sleuth and most of them were on the dodgeball team. They were crowded around Drake, Oscar, and me fawning over us.

"So, like, you could conjure this beer I got with a fake ID in Ireland when I was fourteen and on vacation? I remember that beer fondly. My balls hadn't dropped yet, so just the one got me shit faced. The pub I was in refused to serve me another, so I stumbled into a different pub.

"I didn't know it was a gay bar, but every twink, daddy,

and bear knew I was drunk and underaged. They wouldn't let me drink, but they talked to me and fed me until I sobered up. I talked about some of the confused feelings I was sorting through. If I hadn't snuck out of the hotel while my parents were seeing a play and had that beer, it probably would have taken me *ages* to figure out I was gay," Innis said.

I'd already conjured a ton of food and booze for our little party. I didn't see the point in making anyone leave to get some or raid their stashes in their dorm rooms when I could do that. It was honestly kind of great. When I said I could wave my hand and make any type of food or beverage they wanted to appear, they started telling stories like Innis did.

It was little stories about food they tried on vacation or locally and the memories associated with them. Some of them weren't as big as Innis's beer, but they were happy little memories associated with something I could easily make happen. And I was getting to know them all a lot better.

"Give me something to go on and I'll make that beer happen for everyone."

We were all getting pretty drunk because I had been conjuring drinks for about two hours. Innis gave me what I needed and everyone got their beer. I didn't even get to taste mine when a shower of daisies appeared in Halliwell Square. My teammates and the cheerleaders hadn't met Freya yet, but they knew she was a god.

I didn't know if Zion did this on purpose, but everyone on the dodgeball team was *super* respectful in addition to being very talented at dodgeball. They would have stopped horsing around as soon as she appeared because Freya looked upset.

"I hate to break up the party, but I need to borrow George for god stuff."

"You'll have to do without the team forward and goalie, too," Drake said. "We aren't gods, but we help."

"I'm just here because I'm insanely pretty," West said.

I reached over and flicked West on the forehead. He gasped, but he knew *exactly* why I did it. The *only* reason West wouldn't have gotten into the Academy of the Profane or another college when he was eighteen was because he didn't like school.

"Everyone grab a god," I said.

All my guys grabbed me. Innis was probably the drunkest out of everyone in Halliwell Square. They hadn't really seen all the things I could do. I could hear him drunkenly scream how badass it was as we all disappeared in a cloud of purple smoke and daisies.

WEST

Icouldn't see the future and I wasn't well versed in god stuff except for my girlfriend, but I *was* excellent at reading women. I didn't know Freya that well, but I knew that look on her face. That was *not* the face of a woman who just got visited by a raven who gave her friend his memories back. Something bad had happened, and a god was scared. She was trying to hide it from the dodgeball team and George, but I didn't work at becoming the best boyfriend ever for George because that kind of thing slipped past me.

We arrived at a different cabin than Azren's. Azren was pacing and Odin was sitting with Baldur. I didn't even know what happened but Baldur looked like he felt terrible about it. If they caught him blacked out trying to kill witches, we were going to have to seriously reconsider letting him be a boyfriend-in-law if things didn't work out with his wife when he got his memories back.

My lioness was *much* too nice. She didn't know what he

did either, but she flew to Baldur and wrapped her arms around him. The big guy looked like a puppy who had been kicked, but he melted into her like she could fix it.

"What happened?" George demanded.

"I got another heart," Freya said. "It's not fresh. It's been preserved and was left on my pillow wrapped in a bow with a rose."

Ew.

"It *has* to be me," Baldur moaned.

"Well, did you black out today or over Yule break?" I asked.

Everyone just stared at me. What? It was a good question. Azren ran their fingers through their hair.

"Ah, fuck. The lion has figured it out. I've been agonizing over this since Yule and he figured it out," Azren said.

"I don't get it," Baldur said.

"Take it away, West," George beamed.

No pressure or anything.

"Okay, so the killer is taking trophies. *You* don't remember, but a blackout you would. If you didn't black out today or over Yule, then you couldn't have fetched the nasty hearts and brought them to Freya. Or you'd remember you did and could tell us."

"Or he's lying," Mags pointed out.

"Mags," George warned. "You can *feel* he's missing his magic. Baldur, did you black out on those dates?"

"No. I was alone over Yule break. I usually decorate my cottage and cook, but I'm never around anyone. I didn't black out. I've been working all day. I remember everything."

"Then it can't be you," George said.

"Good job," Odin said. "You've been pretty spot on so

far with a lot of things. You remind me a lot of my son, Thor."

"Oh, shit. He's totally like Thor!" Freya said.

George reached over and squeezed my hand.

"No. He's my West. He's *all* lion."

I puffed up my chest and started purring.

"If it's not me, then who is it?" Baldur asked.

That, I didn't know. I mean, I guessed why Baldur didn't have his magic and that if he didn't black out on certain dates, he couldn't be the killer, but who was actually killing witches was beyond my skill set.

"It's someone connected to Freya and I think my parents," Drake said. "My mom might have seen something, and that's why she was killed. Belladonna was probably right. If someone left the heart with a rose, it's probably some sick fascination with her."

Ew. Some of my distant feline ancestors liked to leave dead mice for their people, but that wasn't a sign of affection. It was because they thought they were shitty hunters and didn't want them to starve. Mostly because it would cut off their supply of wet food, but that was neither here nor there. Pretty sure this asshole wasn't a house cat.

"Drake is also probably right," Azren said. "Freya, can you think of someone who could do this?"

"No. No one in Asgard could do this. None of the Vanir could either. I met many of the other gods when my ex-husband went missing and plenty of them offered to replace him. Some of them were pretty aggressive about it and didn't like being turned down. A few reached out again when they heard I found him and he admitted he was too much of a coward to dissolve our marriage the way gods do and just disappeared, but I decided to enjoy the single life for a while.

"Some of them had the kind of egos that didn't like being turned down, but I don't remember *any* of them being deranged or having the kind of magic that would mess with mortal's minds without killing them. Also, I'm pretty sure whatever magic is being used on those witches is responsible for Baldur's blackouts. They probably know who he is if they know me. They don't want him dead, they just want him out of the way while they do this."

"Okay, so I may finally be convinced of Baldur's innocence," Mags said.

"Well, George and Baldur are clearly into each other. He might not be a killer, but before my twin gets hurt, someone needs to tell the big guy about his wife," Matilda said.

Matilda was savage. I was ride or die for George. I'd probably overthrow the government or start shit with the werewolf mafia if she casually mentioned she wanted me to but was actually joking and didn't mean it. George knew about Baldur's wife. We all did. We hadn't mentioned it to *him* because he'd kind of suffered enough and we didn't want to drop anything big on him until he got his memories back. We were loyal to George, but Baldur might be one of us someday, so we were looking out for him, too.

Matilda's loyalty was only to her twin sister. Yeah, I could see where that needed to be addressed, but the big guy literally *just* found out he wasn't a serial killer. He just looked so relieved. Baldur smiled at Matilda.

"Odin and Freya have been filling me in on my past, including my ex-wife. She didn't want to wait and found a light god from another family to replace me with. My parents dissolved the marriage. I might be upset about it when I can actually remember her, but right now, it doesn't mean much."

Well, that settled it for me. Bro wasn't a serial killer, and he wasn't married anymore. If he got his memories back and wanted to go further with George, I think we all approved. We didn't share a womb with her, though. This next bit was all on Matilda and she was currently having a stare down with Baldur.

"Fine. You can proceed with my sister and I won't bite your ass off while you have no magic and I technically can."

Baldur just bowed his head.

"Your approval means the world to me. I couldn't do this without it."

Smooth motherfucker. He didn't remember who he was or have a drop of magic flowing through him, but Baldur handled Matilda like a pro.

"It's time I open that box I found in my dorm room," Drake said. "I can *feel* it's my mom's. She might have left it because it wasn't safe to take it with her. It might have a clue who killed her and who might be killing witches."

Azren put their hand on Drake's shoulder.

"I'll take you to get it. Did you still want to risk it and try the lock with your blood?"

Baby Drake was keeping secrets from me. I didn't know about secret boxes in his dorm room, but it sounded like a blood lock. If he was wrong about the box being his mom's, the box could kill him.

At least there were enough gods here to fix it if Drake was wrong.

DRAKE

It was time. This box had felt like a live grenade in my dorm room. I pulled it out and ran my hands over it every night before bed. It had been under that floorboard for a while, but not so long it couldn't have been my mom's. George confessed it had been her in my closet and not a ghost trying to help me, but so far, the campus ghosts had been super unhelpful and kind of violent when it came to your nut sack.

I didn't really want to ask George or Oscar to summon Bethany again to ask about that box because I might say something nasty if she refused to help again. George and Azren could say things to ghosts the rest of us couldn't, but they couldn't really *do* anything to Bethany to make her stop assaulting my nuts if she wanted to without her body and that was impossible to get.

Azren portalled me to my dorm room. There could be a major clue in this box or it could be nothing. It could answer everything Azren had been looking for when they got their feeling. Whoever was doing this could do it again at any moment. They'd been quiet lately, but they might escalate now that Freya was here. But Azren was always going to be Azren, and I loved them for it.

"You don't *have* to do this because you think everyone wants you to. Don't open the box until *you're* ready. We know it's not Baldur now and Freya is probably right. Someone either recognized him, thought he was harmless because he didn't have magic, or they were causing his blackouts to set him up for the murders because he'd make a good suspect. Muninn will get here soon and Baldur will remember. We don't all know each other, but he might have an idea."

That was so Azren. Azren wanted to catch this god so badly, they could probably taste it. Only a god could hurt another god and killing them was next to impossible unless you knew their weakness. And god weaknesses were weird random shit. Baldur was the biggest man I'd ever seen across two realms and could literally die if he got scratched by a tiny plant like mistletoe.

Azren didn't play by those rules. They could pull someone's essence out of their body and put it in one of their little jars until they decided to let them out. Azren told me they'd done that to a ton of misbehaving gods who thought that was just an urban legend. I was guessing whoever was murdering witches while Azren was on campus thought it was just a rumor, too.

But I wasn't doing this because I thought it was expected of me. I'd been watching Baldur come through all of this a stronger person. He didn't know what would happen either, but he approached George and asked her to bring him to Azren just like I didn't know if I had all my hopes up that I'd find a clue in this box. Baldur found his dad and he would get his memories back soon. I had to hope it would work out for me, too.

I just smirked at Azren.

"You've known me most of my life. When have I *ever* done anything I didn't want to do because I thought other people expected it?"

Azren fell out laughing.

"Pretty much never, even when Ketura wanted to wring your little neck. You ruined that school play, by the way."

"I regret nothing. Basilisks aren't meant to play sheep. Take us back."

The room felt *much* different in the few minutes we were gone. The tension was gone. Baldur was looking more like a light god and less like a beaten-down man now that he knew he hadn't killed anyone. Matilda and Mags weren't giving him stink eye anymore because they knew that, too. Everyone knew Baldur wasn't married anymore and he and George felt something.

Everyone was trying to get to know each other. I'd give it to Odin. George was still a young god, and she told us she and Michael kind of wrecked Odin's house when they were kids, but he seemed to like the idea of George and Baldur together. Odin and Freya looked like co-conspirators on the loveseat watching them together with content smiles on their faces.

Yeah, never let it be said that Drake Nathara didn't know how to ruin a whole mood. George and Baldur could figure out where this was going and we could all get nasty at the next moon orgy *after* I figured out if my mom left a clue behind in this box. Of course, I could prick my finger on the lock and find out it *wasn't* my mom's box. It would ruin my day in more ways than one until a god healed me so whatever nasty curse in the blood lock didn't kill me or make my hand rot off.

I understood now that not all witches were evil, even after what Kaylee did with my hair, but if you were dealing with something made by a witch designed to keep people out, you should probably keep out if it wasn't meant for you.

"So, I found this box in my dorm room. It was under the floorboards and it's got carvings of Basilisks on it. All Azren and I have been able to find out is that a student was randomly attacked with an arrow shortly before my mom went home for break and never came back. No one knew she was thinking of dropping out, not even her roommate.

"Church, your grandfather was headmaster then. He told Azren my mom was at the top of her class and wasn't the type to get burnt out and drop out. She met my dad and had me shortly. They were murdered by someone they didn't see, but told the reaper was so powerful, they could feel them coming. I also know they were living in a small town in the middle of nowhere like they might be hiding from someone. I think the reason she dropped out is in this box."

George had been wrapped up with Baldur because it looked like he needed her. Azren could have healed me if anything bad happened, but George didn't treat us like we were minions here to worship her. She was amazingly supportive of all of us. If I was about to risk a possible deadly curse and find out this box didn't contain any answers, she was going to hold my hand and heal me herself.

I came to this realm hoping to find answers and only knowing Azren. I thought I was content to just get an education and answers, but I was so wrong. I loved my girlfriend. I loved my friends. It meant so much to open this box with these people.

I didn't know what would happen or if George was going to have to cure me before a curse took hold, but I shifted the ornate cover on the blood lock and pricked my finger.

AZREN

I always wanted more answers for Drake. When Ketura came home with a baby from another realm and told me why she wanted to raise him in mine, I was hesitant at first. Ketura didn't play fair. She told me something powerful and unknown killed his parents to get me interested and then shoved a fat little baby Basilisk in my arms because I'd always loved kids and she knew that.

Drake was going to stay, so I tried traveling back to his home to get some of his things and anything of his parents that he could remember them by. His parents had been renting a two-bedroom house in a very small town in the middle of nowhere. I had the extreme displeasure of meeting their landlord.

They had only been dead a day, but he had hired people to trash their stuff and put it on the curb. Normally, I wouldn't have been above going through it for a baby, but this shit-stain slumlord dumped their belongings before a really bad thunderstorm. Everything was ruined. I was only able to salvage one photo for Drake and nothing else.

The slumlord was more worried about getting blood off the walls and having to disclose the murder to renters and if he ever sold than what happened to the baby or that anyone would be coming for their things. I yelled at him until I felt better and then I snapped my fingers and collapsed the house. He was seriously slacking on upkeep and I found him rude.

Acts of God weren't covered by insurance. Fuck him. If he had waited, I might have had more to give a kid who wasn't going to remember his parents. I wanted more than anything for this box to have something for Drake. I didn't care if the box contained a big neon sign with the murderer's name on it as long as it had something to help Drake, too.

Blood locks were a complicated bit of spell work and machinery. I watched the gears whirr as Drake's blood activated it. Drake's hand wasn't turning black, and he wasn't crying out in pain, so this was a good sign.

Fuck me. The box sprung open. Drake's mom left a box under the floorboard at the Academy of the Profane. She protected the shit out of this box. When she was a student, Lindsay hadn't published the spell she stole from Minerva. The only person who could have opened that box would have been one of her descendants. Maybe she somehow knew Drake was going to end up here with help.

Drake pulled a very expensive camera and a golden arrow out of the box. I remembered Church Senior telling me a student got shot with an arrow. I had dismissed it because I thought it was a student playing a prank. The student was only injured, and no one died after that. A god wouldn't have missed. But that was definitely a divine arrow.

"The wounds in the witch's necks that we couldn't figure out could be arrows," Church said. "It doesn't fit with vampires or shifters, but it could be an arrow."

West gasped.

"Did fucking Cupid go feral?"

I grabbed West and planted a kiss on his lips because he figured a good bit of this out again. He was beating *me* on getting the right answer first and I was *much* older than he was.

"You're a genius, West!"

West touched his lips and looked stunned.

"Maybe it *is* weird to kiss your straight friends, even if you don't use tongue."

I had no idea what that meant, but West had just narrowed down the killer, so I just winked at him.

"I'm not straight. A lot of gods are associated with arrows, but their arrows are all distinctive to them. Cupid is part of a bigger group. Before the Romans adopted those gods and changed their names, he was part of Aphrodite's retinue and there were seven Erotes associated with different emotions. There were seven of them with the Romans, too, and they were *all* called Cupids.

"The group was called Cupids but there was also a god called Cupid. He was by far the most popular and went by Eros among the Greeks. It wasn't just his emotion that made him so popular. His origin story got a little muddy where everyone thought he was Aphrodite and Ares's kid, but he thought that was hilarious and never bothered clearing it up.

"Sex is a primordial force. It creates life and we couldn't have made the universe or anything that lives there without it. Our creations wouldn't have been able to populate and grow. And it's just fun. Eros is a primordial like me. He thinks it's amusing to play among gods and mortals."

"It's fucked-up sex is killing people like that. That could ruin a whole moon orgy," West moaned.

I smiled. West couldn't be smarter than me all the time.

"Eros isn't doing this. He loves mortals. Eros isn't in the Aether like some of the other primordials. There are always going to be people on every realm who worship sex above everything else, even other gods. Eros is *somewhere* soaking that up. He'd know more about the other Erotes and which one might have done this."

"Aphrodite introduced me to a ton of people when I was in Olympus looking for my husband. I remember Eros because he was the only one I actually decided to sleep with. I *barely* remember the other Erotes, just that they were half feral and *really* horny."

"One of them remembers you," Oscar said. "He's been leaving you his trophies."

"And I honestly couldn't tell you why. I spent most of my time in Olympus with Aphrodite. She doesn't have all the same domains as me, but we have some in common. When I was looking for my husband among other gods, I went straight to the love and fertility gods because we always connected better.

"She introduced me to her kids, and she had a lot of them. I had a lot of respect for Aphrodite and considered her a friend by the time I left. I wouldn't have slept with, or disrespected *any* of her kids when I was letting them down because I genuinely like Aphrodite. The only reason I messed around with Eros was because she said he wasn't hers and you've met him, Azren. Can you blame me?"

No, I absolutely did not. Eros was created to appeal to

everyone. He was *everyone's* type, and he smelled amazing. I don't think anyone who had met Eros would have blamed Freya. But clearly, one of the Erotes remembered this situation much differently and had a bone to pick with Freya.

That still didn't answer *why* they were killing witches or even how they were doing it. I didn't know much about the Erotes. The only one I'd met was Eros. I knew they all handled different emotions related to love and sex and some protected certain kinds of love.

"What does it mean that my mom had an Erotes's arrow?" Drake demanded. "Or that she left what looks like a very expensive camera behind?"

"I'm guessing there's film in that camera with a photo of the god who fired the arrow, but it's not like they could have arrested him or called Azren then, so I don't get why he went after your parents," George said.

I *should* have dug into them more. They weren't major gods in that whole arcana. I had a role in every god family, but sometimes, I could be completely *hands off* because of the death mythology in that culture. I thought Zeus was a crude man who needed to stop raping women and Hera needed to be beating his ass over that instead of his victims and their kids. I mostly avoided that entire family and let Hades handle all that.

Problem was, now I needed to *ask* those people why one of them was butchering witches and an entire Basilisk family, and Hades was the only one I liked. Hades didn't care much for them either and made his own realm just so he didn't have to share Olympus with them. I was guessing he didn't know much about Aphrodite's kids and I wanted this answer for Drake.

"Develop the film," Freya said. "I can't promise anything, but I might be able to recognize who it is in the photo. We might all be divine beings, but we have several things in common with mortals. For instance, if someone is misbehaving and you need to pinpoint who, you go talk to their momma to find out which of their kids is secretly a psycho and what's so important about those arrows that they'd murder a family over one. I'll probably miss Baldur getting his memories back, but this is important."

"Go," Baldur said. "If it's not me, I've been wanting to stop this for a long time."

I would have gone to Olympus and made nice for Drake and to stop witches from dying, but it was kind of public knowledge I punched Zeus in the face and threatened to put him in god time out if he didn't stop raping mortals. You would think Hera and some of the female gods would have had my back on this, but they called me a big, mean bully. They probably hadn't forgotten that.

Freya was *much* more diplomatic than I was, and she at least had friends in Olympus. Freya was the type of person who could get all the information we needed without damaging her friendship in the slightest.

GEORGE

I was glad Drake finally opened that box. The art program at the Academy of the Profane had a photography studio. Magical film couldn't be developed just anywhere or by anyone. There were special materials that reacted to the magic in the film and if you didn't know what you were doing, the whole thing caught fire and ruined the film.

We didn't need to hunt down an older art student to develop the film. Oscar was a versatile artist. He learned how to do it in high school. We just needed to find my dad to let us in. Gabriel had always had keys to the photography studio. He could have set up a dark room at home in his art studio, but he decided not to because he always wanted to be accessible to us if we needed him.

Oscar, Ren, Azren, and Drake were in the photography lab developing photos over the weekend. The rest of us were at my mom's library researching the Erotes. The library was technically closed on the weekends, but I knew the librarian. We'd been in a deep dive for hours until my mom made us stop.

"Take a break and come eat. Your dad made sandwiches and Felix made chips."

I moaned. My dad didn't *just* make sandwiches. And it was always a treat when Felix made chips. He cut them super thick with vinegar and salt. I set my book down and dragged everyone upstairs. Michael and Dexter were with us since we'd filled them in on what we were doing and they wanted to help.

"Those are the most beautiful fries I've ever seen," West said.

"Those are chips," Felix said. "If you're going to date our daughter, show some respect."

"I'll call them whatever you want as long as you gimme."

Felix smiled and slid them over. Felix liked my guys. All my dads did, but they were going to have to give them a hard time first.

"You'd better compliment my sandwiches, too, or I'm going to be butt hurt and you don't want a butt hurt God of Chaos."

"Is that pimento, bacon, and avocado?" Church asked.

"Yeah, it's amazing," Matilda said. "If you don't have that one, grab the BLT where the tomato is a fried green tomato. Reyson picked it up when we were in New Orleans."

"Yoink. That one is mine," Dexter said, snatching it. "I've *always* wanted to go there."

My dad just shrugged.

"We'll take you all when you graduate. I'm sorry I can't help with the research, but I couldn't stand Zeus any more than Azren could. Did you find anything before your mom did the 'mom' thing and made you all eat?"

"Oh, hush. You were all in here cooking because you knew they needed to eat, too."

"None of us are complaining about that," Belladonna moaned. "I like to pretend when a god made it, the calories don't count."

"Ooh, good call," Dexter said. "We won't have to run an extra mile in the morning."

Belladonna was jogging buddies with Dexter and Michael. Matilda and I both enjoyed running because it kept us in shape for dodgeball and cheerleading, but *not* at stupid o'thirty in the morning when the three of them did it. We'd probably never be morning people.

"There's not a lot written about them," I said. "Some seem to be more popular than others. There's a lot about Eros and Cupid. We found art and the basics of who most of them were, even if there weren't epic stories like there were with Eros. Some of them barely got an honorable mention. We know what their main power is, but it's like the people didn't care enough about them to record their stories, make statues, or put them on pottery."

"That's enough to make a god go on a killing spree if they are petty enough," Dad said. "But we have shitty attention spans since we live so long. They'd do all that while people were actively worshipping them and it wouldn't be limited to just one race. It would be *everyone* they thought was snubbing them and they would have been bored with it when their whole family was getting snubbed, too. It still doesn't make sense."

"What if it was another god?" Mina asked. "The killer has only been going after witches and he's leaving the hearts for Freya. Freya didn't create witches, but haven't they left offerings out for her, too?"

My dad just shrugged.

"It's possible, but not really our style. Like, I *knew* Ripley was going to be my wife as soon as I laid eyes on her. I can see possibilities and she was my wife in nearly every one. There were a few scenarios where something went wrong and she rejected me. I wanted this woman more than anything I'd ever wanted, but if she didn't want *me*, I would have accepted that and left her alone.

"Some of the other gods aren't like that when mortal women don't want them. They think they are beneath us and should be grateful, so they take what they want or hurt them. It's different when another god doesn't want you. Those gods can fight back. They live long enough to figure out your weakness and kill you if you really pissed them off. Besides, how would this Erotes even know Freya would eventually end up at the Academy of the Profane to give the hearts to if he was butchering witches and collecting their hearts to give them to her?"

My dad understood gods *much* better than I did, so I always deferred to him when there was something I didn't understand. I knew gods all had wildly different personalities just like mortals did. Some of them probably *did* react badly if another god rejected them.

But my dad was also right about a lot of other things. Most gods treated other gods differently than they did mortals because there were actual consequences with other gods. And unless there was some kind of connection we hadn't pieced together yet, *no one* knew Freya would be asked to guest lecture our history class because our headmaster got hexed by her own kid. I didn't even know I was going to have a god teaching history until orientation.

There was *no* way in fuck an Erotes could have predicted that. I was related to two seers who always tried to give me a heads-up, and *they* didn't see that. And if Freydis saw there were going to be two hot gods at the Academy of the Profane that I felt a connection to, she wouldn't have just told me. She'd be blowing up my phone wanting details. The fact that she hadn't, meant she hadn't seen a thing about Baldur and Azren and I was a shitty cousin for not telling her yet.

We were missing something.

"Hey, Balthazar? Can you peek at the Paranormal Investigation Bureau database without getting caught?" I asked.

Balthazar gasped.

"I've been your dad for eighteen years and you think someone is going to catch me when I don't want to be caught? Besides, the Paranormal Investigation Bureau knows I keep looking because I keep helping solve cases they don't consult me on, so about three months ago, they created an account for me to look the legal way. What do you need, sweetness?"

"Seriously? Congrats. Can you see if there have been groups of unsolved murders of witches in different areas of the country that involve hearts? We've been trying to figure out the significance of the Academy of the Profane but maybe it's just one of many places they hunt in when they want to kill."

"They didn't just give him access," Bram said. "Two years ago, they hired him to completely rewrite their database. The old one was archaic. It took forever to search and sometimes, it didn't connect all the dots. Balthazar can find this out in minutes. And don't let him fool any of you. They know he's been hacking them and they know he's stealing from rich criminals. Proving it would be insanely difficult but they aren't even trying because they all adore this motherfucker. He's lovable, cuddly, and *really* good at what he does for them."

"And I'm absolutely adorable. It was a good hunch, but the only case files related to a serial who was targeting witches and removing hearts were at the Academy of the Profane. It was always independent study witches and it would just stop with no one arrested.

"Some of the detectives put the pieces together that it happened before, but most of them assumed it was some coven who was ritually killing witches and using the hearts for dark magic. Some of them thought it was a guy in maintenance who made everyone uncomfortable. I'm guessing that's Baldur.

"Most of the detectives were good cops who were frustrated with the whole situation because they couldn't do their jobs and question students. I know you all said they were being dicks to Azren, but I'm pretty sure that's all for show. The God of Death isn't bound by the same rules they are and Azren is pretty important. The board wasn't going to fire them for breaking the rules.

"There's also a note from the most recent cases that they saw Azren over the body and waited to approach because they didn't know if it was safe. They did the same thing at the second crime scene. Now that I know more about what's going on, that's detective speak for malicious compliance. They used any rule they could to let the God of Death do their thing because they knew the protocol about murders on campus."

"Damn," Church swore. "That doesn't answer a damned thing. We know he tried when Drake's mom was a student and no one died because he disappeared after he lost his arrow. There is something important about the arrows. I don't think he killed Drake's parents because of what's on the camera. I think he wanted his arrow back."

"Probably," Dad said. "We are very possessive of our property, but there could be something special about it. There is a lot of mythology about getting hit by one of Cupid's arrows and there are technically seven Cupids."

"Which means back to the books," Michael said.

I pulled my mom aside to stay back. I told my mom *everything, but* I still hadn't told her Azren and I were together so I did that after everyone had left. She just fell out laughing.

"You're my child and you've never been able to keep a secret from me. I knew you had a crush just from our video chats at night. You might have been able to keep that he returned your feelings a secret a bit longer, but he's eaten at my dinner table. Azren *was not* fooling me when they pretended like they were inviting you to the Netherworld to celebrate Yule with Drake. A mother knows. Your aunt guessed, too."

I groaned.

"Do my dads know and is one of them planning some kind of celestial beat down?"

My mom was laughing at me again like that wasn't a possibility My dad could start a fist fight and I wasn't all that sure Balthazar couldn't hack Azren's bank in the Netherworld and make all his money disappear.

"Your dads love all your guys. Your dad would have been happy if you ended up with a mixed bag of supernaturals, but he's always wanted you with at least one god. The problem with that is that the ones he knows are either still happily married or he knows how they treated their ex-wives.

"Azren is an old friend and your dad is happy for *both* of

you that you ended up together. Your dad has wanted Azren to find their person for a long time, too. Everyone is reserving judgment on Baldur until he gets his memories back. We know he's not killing anyone and your dads have been grilling Loki on how he treated his wife when they were married. It's none of that and we trust you explicitly, but no one can predict what Baldur is going to feel when he gets his memories back."

I sighed and leaned into her. My mom wrapped her arms around me and kissed the top of my head.

"I really like him. He's like this giant teddy bear and he might not *remember* being a light god or have the magic that goes with it, but he's thoughtful and considerate like he still is one."

"I know, sweetie. Just remember what I taught you. Keep sex and feelings separate until you have a full picture and you know they *deserve* your affection. Get to know him and be supportive because he's obviously going through a lot, but don't fall too deep until he gets his memories back."

Baldur had basically told me the same thing in very different words. The problem was that we were constantly being drawn to each other whenever we were in the same room.

I could try to fight it until he got his memories back, but I really didn't want to.

GEORGE

We stayed at the library researching all day. The information we had on the Erotes was limited unless it was Eros. Felix convinced us that if all the Erotes used arrows and one of them murdered an entire family over one, we should deep dive into the one we had the most information on to see if we could find out more about the arrows.

A lot of stuff that had been passed down through history probably started out true, but then things got changed as the story was retold. Some of the inaccuracies were because the gods started the rumor in the first place. Like, everyone thought Freya hated Loki because he was always slut shaming her in front of everyone, but those two loved each other. Loki slept around just as much as Freya did. They set each other up and covered for each other all the time.

Cupid's arrows could be fact or fiction since everyone

we found who claimed to be hit by one didn't have a wound on their body and no one actually *saw* an arrow flying through the air. With gods, that could literally mean anything.

We stopped for the night to have dinner with my family. We invited Baldur and Odin. My mom usually would have tested Baldur and made him apply for a library card, but with his magic gone, none of us knew how the library was going to react, so she just took him upstairs to the living room.

We were all looking at the photos Oscar and the guys had developed. Most of them were of Drake's mom on campus, but it was the last few that had what we needed. Kind of. Gabriel told me about magical photography. He figured out once he met my dad and Loki that you needed to adjust the aperture for god aura. It was a different setting than other supernaturals.

Drake's mom was photographing a man in black standing by Shrieking Woods. He was holding a golden bow and had an arrow nocked. We couldn't see him at first because he was surrounded by a *very* strange aura for a god. Ours were usually gold, but his had bits of black and red in it.

She figured the settings out at the last picture and he didn't look like any god I'd seen. He wasn't as tall. We could only see his profile from a distance, but he seemed a little plain for a god. And none of the other gods at the table who were much older than me knew who he was.

Azren and my dad hadn't met any of the Erotes. If Baldur had, he didn't remember. Odin was pretty famous for his walkabouts in all the realms that weren't closed off to him. Odin squinted his one eye at the photo and sighed.

"I've never met that guy in my entire life. Olympus isn't

bad if you avoid Zeus. Aphrodite and Ares are impeccable hosts and Dionysus throws fantastic parties. Athena and Artemis are brilliant conversationalists. The Erotes were around when I was there. I couldn't pull up their faces from memory, but I'd remember if I saw them again. I remember the Erotes being a wild and feral bunch that I had a good time with, but I honestly don't remember there being seven of them.

"That was a very long time ago and I haven't been to Olympus in a while. I've never met him. He wouldn't be distinctive in a crowd full of humans, but he'd stick out like a sore thumb among gods. There's something wrong with his aura and his appearance isn't as shiny as the rest of us."

"That's what our auras look like when they get tainted," Azren said. "If we do something horrible, our auras do the same as mortals. Loki's nearly did the same after he killed Baldur, but he was so eaten up about it, he was pretty much never going to do anything like that again. It's when we do something terrible and we *like* it and intend on doing it again that our auras get tainted. His aura might not have looked like that when you met him."

"He must have learned to shapeshift his aura like you and Loki did," Gabriel said. "Most supernaturals can recognize a tainted aura, even if they don't know what they are feeling, but it's the first thing I start teaching as soon as they start taking Dark Arts. I hired one of my best students to replace me and they'll be doing the same. No one might have witnessed the murders, but they would have remembered those witches talking to him if he hadn't."

"The arrow has to be important," Baldur said. "If gods can shapeshift, I don't think he cares about the photos. He went after Drake's parents to get his arrow back."

"I agree," Azren said. "That's why it's stashed in the

Netherworld where he can't go until I can bring it out to examine it and find out what's so special about it."

Before anyone could say anything, a flash of flame appeared in our dining room, which meant Loki was here. He had my aunt, Uncle Bjorn, and cousin Freydis with him, which meant someone saw something, but I don't think he realized Baldur was going to be here. He had been trying to give him space.

"Ah, fuck," Loki sighed, disappearing again.

"Sorry," Ravyn said. "Bjorn and Freydis had a shared vision from the Fates and those are *always* important, so Loki brought us, but if we had known Baldur was here, we would have walked. Loki told me his version of what happened when we first met and now that I've been with him this long, he only tells stories like that when he feels insanely bad about what he did."

"Can you bring him back?" Baldur asked.

"Um, do I need to bring him back outside? This is a historical building with a lot of dangerous books in it and my sister is going to have big opinions about you dating her daughter if you break it," Ravyn said.

This was it. I knew Loki was beside himself wanting to make things right with Baldur but was keeping his distance out of respect. I think Loki would feel terrible, but not quite this bad, if Baldur had come back with his magic and memories and wanted to beat his ass. It was the fact that he came back like that, no one found him to help him, and the killer had probably been fucking with his head to make him think he was a murderer.

I think we all got that Loki was grieving and lashed out at the wrong person to make his point. Even Loki's wife would agree Baldur had the right to react to that how he wanted to. Baldur didn't have magic, but he was still the biggest god I'd ever met. He was bigger than my dad. If Baldur wanted to throw down, he could still do some damage.

"No need," Baldur said. "Maybe I'll feel differently when I have my memories back and can remember dying. Odin and Freya have been telling me what I was like back then and filling in the gaps surrounding my death that didn't make the history books. If I just went off the internet, Loki killed me because he's a terrible person and he thought it was funny. I don't remember him, but I've asked enough questions about the man responsible for my death to know he's a complicated person. I'm not going to hit him. I just want to talk to him."

Total God of Light move.

I wasn't the same kind of god as Baldur and I was much younger, but I can't say I would react the same. I'd make an attempt to understand why he did it and would probably forgive him once I found out his reasons, but I'd still want to hit him. And I said that as someone who deeply loved my uncle and understood him.

My aunt just gave Baldur a curt nod. She loved him and accepted everything that came with being married to a trickster. They were mostly maliciously helpful and not violent. If someone got hurt by a trickster, they usually didn't need to lay a finger on them. Ravyn wasn't just married to a trickster. Her daughter was one, too. She was used to talking them out of things and she knew Loki *and* Baldur needed this.

I knew they needed it, too. Also, if Bjorn and Freydis had gotten a shared vision *now* with everything that was going on, it was probably important. My aunt was a master at being married to a trickster and how to handle them. She whipped her phone out and hit a button.

"My love, get that perky butt back here. It's someone else's turn to spank it."

Oh, fuck. That was *so* my Aunt Ravyn. Baldur had only been around my mom for the duration of this dinner and he'd just met my aunt. Odin pounded on his back as Baldur choked on the lamb my dad cooked.

I was glad he wasn't married anymore because I wanted to keep him.

BALDUR

I was about to face the man who was responsible for my death. I knew I should probably be furious at him. It probably wasn't normal that I didn't even want to hit him. It wouldn't make me feel better and it wouldn't change anything I went through. It felt bad holding onto any kind of negativity being angry about it.

I had an amazing support system after centuries of isolation and loneliness when I didn't know who I was. My wife may have given up on me, but the rest of my family didn't. My father said he and my mother were still very much in love, but they set up shop on two different realms just in case I came back on one. They met once a week on either realm to catch up and be together. I had several siblings who missed me, too.

And then there was Freya. I was honestly feeling bad about the fact that I didn't remember a thing about her because she was helping me a lot. She had changed my diapers when I was a baby, but she rarely talked about that.

Freya was probably one of the few, if the *only* god who got what I was going through for the most part.

Freya had an arrangement with Azren to have her essence dropped in a stillborn baby. She lived without magic *or* memories of being Freya until she turned eighteen and her witch magic came in. She didn't always end up with a ton of magic or the greatest families. Freya thought she was going insane until Muninn showed up and made her earn her memories back.

Her mortal bodies had technically died more times than I had. She told me it sucked and a few times, she got murdered for no reason, too. Odin's admission of what he had done to Loki and Freya sharing some of the reasons someone killed her when she was living in a mortal body were why it was easier for me to just want to forgive Loki and move on.

Loki appeared in a flash of flame and shot his wife a look.

"Never mention the kind of spankings I like in the same sentence with what's about to go down. I've got this coming and I have to sit back and not even use my safe word."

I asked Odin and Freya a lot of questions about Loki since I couldn't remember. They said they could never predict what he was going to do, but he could usually fix any problem and had been a fiercely loyal friend until they hurt his kids. Odin said he was always like my fun uncle. When I saw him standing in front of me with tears in his eyes looking at me like that, I had this intense feeling and a flash of something.

"Did we ever do anything together involving butter-flies?" I asked.

Loki fell on his knees in front of me sobbing.

"When you were a kid, I'd take you to different realms after your lessons to watch the butterflies. You had to learn to fight and hunt. You hated both because you loathed the violence, so I took you to fields of flowers and let you play among the butterflies. I'm sorry. I'm not sorry for most of the shit I've done. I'm not sorry I tricked Thor into doing drag or all the times I stole Freya's fabulous falcon cloak. I'm not sorry about the time I helped Balthazar coat Felix in magical glitter that wouldn't come off. But I'm sorry about what I did to you and what happened after. I thought you'd come right back."

"Dick," Felix muttered.

"Are you starting to remember?" George asked.

"No. When I saw Loki, I didn't remember dying or feeling angry with him. I felt this extreme feeling of happiness and saw butterflies. I know you've been giving me space and I appreciate it. This might all change when I get my memories back, but I'd rather just move past this. Staying angry with you just feels bad. I don't want to do it."

"You might not remember the past, but the old you would have said that, too," Loki said, smiling at me.

The young seer tossed her white blonde hair over her shoulder and struck a pose.

"Yes, thank you for not beating the shit out of my dad. You both needed this, but you also need to hear our vision."

"Freydis," Ravyn warned.

"No, we really do," I said. "I needed this, but I also really want to catch this killer and I'm guessing the vision was about that."

I didn't know the first thing about real seers. Freya taught a few of us Seidr, but it wasn't the same. There were plenty of fakes around when I was still alive. George told me her Uncle Bjorn was a seer created by Loki and Freydis was her cousin who had her magic activated early from a horseback incident.

"First of all, this is a set vision," Bjorn said. "If you try to change anything beyond what we tell you, it's just going to happen to someone else. It's vital you do *everything* we tell you or this is going to end badly. Especially since it involves your dodgeball team."

West gasped. I really liked that guy. He wasn't just insanely enthusiastic for dodgeball. He really loved George.

"Tell us," George said.

"We don't know who is doing this. He's cloaked in darkness and he knows shapeshifting just as well as Loki does. He's moved his focus from witches to George now that he knows she's a god. He's been watching the dodgeball practices and I don't think he realizes any injuries she gets on the field are because she's letting herself get them to play fair."

"That doesn't make sense," Ren said. "He wasn't interested in her when everyone thought she was a witch. She would have been the strongest witch in the whole school. If his target has always been talented witches, why did he ignore her until he found out she was a god? As far as I know, her necklace would have hidden that from him, too."

"It would," Reyson said. "And the only reason I can recognize these fuckers when they've shapeshifted their aura is when they left their face the same. If we want to hide what we are, we can. The only people who would have known what George is are her family. You're right. We are missing something. He wasn't interested in her when he thought she was a witch, but he's willing to piss off a *lot* of gods now that he knows what she is."

"How do we stop him?" I asked.

I knew killing a god wasn't that easy because their

weakness could be anything. I also knew it fucking happened to me and I wasn't going to let it happen to her. I wanted my memories and magic back, but I was also scared as fuck to get them because being a god wasn't even on my bingo card when I was trying to figure out who and what I was.

I didn't remember my ex-wife, but Odin and Freya had filled me in. No one liked her or wanted me to marry her. I couldn't explain the pull I felt to George Bell or if I felt the same with my ex, but Odin and Freya had been actively encouraging me to pursue it.

I *needed* my memories and magic back now because this asshole was targeting her. I couldn't force Muninn to appear any faster, but I could hear the rest of this vision.

OSCAR

That awful feeling in the pit of my gut was back. It was there when we knew the killer was targeting witches and I didn't know George was a god. It had been blissfully gone now that her secret was out, and I knew she was pretty indestructible. It had stayed gone because his MO this whole time had been witches.

Why was he interested in her now when he wasn't before? From what I understood, killing a god was insanely difficult and if you got it wrong, they were going to come after you. George wasn't just some lone god the Fates created. Her dad was the God of Chaos. She was dating the God of Death. Her mom was just a witch, but she had one of the most dangerous libraries in the country at her disposal and I was guessing she could come up with something to fuck-up a god, too.

Chantico was wrapped around my neck. I could feel her vibrating and she chittered, and she booped my cheek with her nose. She sent me an image of me scoring the winning point and putting my team in the running for state dodgeball championships. I got hurt before the playoffs, but we would have won if that witch hadn't cheated.

I was under no grand notion my magic would do a damned thing against a god if it came down to me keeping her alive. I wouldn't even be able to hear them coming. But George's uncle said dodgeball was important, and I happened to be *very* good at that.

"Our visions aren't date stamped and we haven't had time to research everything we saw. Catching the killer is going to come down to a dodgeball match and a moon orgy that's going to happen after. We could tell you what team once we've had time to look at the uniforms we saw, but I don't follow college dodgeball and the sports Freydis likes involve horses because she's very much my child.

"Every single person on the team you're playing against has a bone to pick with someone on your team. One of them cheated on a bear shifter in high school and is bitter he got dumped and the bear shifter moved on. Some of them are mad at George over a video. There's an incubus who is really mad at Michael because he dated Dexter in high school before he transitioned and he hates that Dexter isn't hung up on him because of Michael."

Dexter just snorted.

"I was over him five minutes after he left for college."

"Wait, we're playing against *that* guy? Why is he mad at me that he's an incubus who is *really* bad at sex?"

That immediately set George off. She covered her ears and started singing. I usually adored that her family was loud and chaotic. I usually joined in, but I really needed them to focus. So did the massive seer with the man bun.

"Yes, anyway. Even their coach has a problem with your coach. They want to beat your team and they aren't going to play fair. I can't tell you *who* but one of your strongest players is going to get injured. It's not going to be enough to take them out of the game, but they aren't going to ask George to heal them because they don't want anyone to make a stink about it and get her kicked out of the league.

"The game is going to be close because of this injured player. It *has* to be close and I won't tell you who is injured because if you heal them or spend the whole game trying to stop them from getting hurt, someone else is going to get hurt because this is a set vision. Right now, this injury just affects one dodgeball game and can be easily healed. If something changes and the Fates hurt a different person, I don't know what will happen. So, don't change *anything* about that part of the vision.

"The killer thinks he's found George's weakness. He's going to test it at the dodgeball game. I don't know if it's magic, or he just used sports rivalry to convince someone to hurt George. I can't tell. He's going to have a knife dipped in something from the dodgeball field that he thinks can kill her.

"It's going to come down to the last few seconds of the game. George will have the Air ball. You'll think you can easily score and win the game, but that's when the player gets you with the knife. The killer will realize *that* is not your weakness and go back to the drawing board. If the player gets the knife in you, the killer *will* eventually figure out your weakness from watching you and testing it on the dodgeball field and on campus.

"Since I've known you your entire life, I know you're going to be trying to figure out how to avoid all this and still win the game. You're going to think you're the *only* person who can win the game, but you aren't. You have to *pass the ball.* All of this is hinging on you passing.

"The person you pass it to is going to score and win the game. The person who was meant to hurt you is going to call it off because the game is over and they'd get banned from the league. It's going to *piss* that killer off.

"The school you are playing is going to have players and students on campus and some of them are going to get invited to the moon orgy since they are away from home. Some of them will be given space in Halliwell Square if they are shifters and witches and they weren't invited.

"The killer is going to blame that player for their plan going wrong. They will try to punish them during the chaos of the moon orgy. Follow that player and he'll lead you to your killer. The arrow is also important. Also, this is where the Fates are being assholes with details, but when the killer starts talking, don't listen to him.

"Also, I can *see* the arrow. I used to live during a time when you wanted meat, you learned to set traps and use a bow. I've *made* bows and arrows. Freydis might have been born in this century and loves the internet and indoor plumbing, but she's also interested in the old ways. My kid could easily kill most of you with an arrow and she knows how to make them rather than buy them. I don't know why that arrow is important."

"It's not functional either," Freydis said. "It *looks* like an arrow I would make, but it's the wrong material. It's too heavy to shoot properly. He might be a god, but he answers to physics, too. The only way *that* arrow could go anywhere in the air is by magic, but then how would he lose it? It *should* hit its mark if it was aided by magic. I just shoot my bow with skill, but I *only* miss when I want to, and this guy is much older than me."

I didn't know about arrows or Norse seers, but one of them just told me I could keep my girlfriend safe by making sure she passed the fucking ball at the last minute at a dodgeball match. Based on *everything* Bjorn just told us, it was going to be our first game. The players *and* the coach wanting to beat us that badly and the game taking place on a full moon all added up. They didn't usually schedule major events on a full moon, but dodgeball was different. Everyone's adrenaline was pumping, and the sex was better. Dodgeball games were the exception.

I could help that vision come true by just positioning myself right at the end of the game so George could pass the ball to me. I'd take it from her and deal with the laps Zion would give me for not respecting a female teammate if I needed to.

GEORGE

had been raised with the knowledge a god might eventually want to hurt me just for being born, but now that it was happening, it didn't really make sense. If the killer was an Erotes, then he was like me. Aphrodite would have been his mother. And no one could figure out why he was changing his whole MO to come for me now instead of when he thought I was a witch.

When we got back to our dorm room, there were pieces of paper folded hotel style on our pillows. There were three of them, so there was one for Mags, too. The only way you could get into our dorm room was if you had a key or you were a god.

"I swear to shit, if there's a heart in my silk sheets, I'm going to be so mad," Matilda groaned.

"Stay back. I'll look," Mags said.

"No, *you* stay back. I'm mostly invincible and he's not going to try to kill me until the dodgeball game."

"Oh, fine."

I picked up the note and opened it. It was blank, but it felt spirit touched. Everyone's phone went off. I looked down. I had texts from Oscar and Drake. They had gotten them, too. Matilda announced that Mina and Belladonna had as well. The family group chat I had with Matilda and Michael went off that Michael and Dexter had gotten blank notes on their pillows.

I asked everyone to meet in the Sigmis common room. I had a feeling I knew *exactly* what this was, and it wasn't a bad thing. I looked at my siblings and Mags.

"I think we're finally getting help and we get the bonus of the thing Mom and Aunt Ravyn talked about."

"Spill," Oscar said. "This feels like ghosts."

Matilda just grinned.

"We're about to go on a treasure hunt and get access to the secret Academy of the Profane speakeasy."

"No way. That's an urban legend," Drake said.

"I asked my grandfather and he would neither confirm nor deny, but told me to work my ass off and maybe I'd find out."

"I got one, too," West said. "I'm not a student."

"You can't get in without an invite. You're still a part of this group and if these are from the ghosts, they think you deserve to be there with everyone," Michael said.

"Put the notes on the table," I said.

I waved my hand. I hoped the ghosts didn't think we were cheating. From what I understood, unlocking the text *and* the treasure hunt were how you got access to the speakeasy. But they'd also known I was a god this entire time, and the notes were coded to be unlocked with each supernatural's specific magic.

We leaned forward when the blue text appeared.

You're close to the answer. Find the forge, get your reward.

The blue text floated off the paper and dissolved into the air. The ghosts knew we were close to catching the killer and were finally trying to help us. I didn't know what the forge was or why it was important, but I was guessing it was connected to the killer.

"Any guesses?" Ren asked.

"The Erotes were Greek. Didn't Hephaestus have a pretty famous forge?" Belladonna asked.

"Yeah, but I think the forge they want us to find is on campus. I'm *really* bad at realm travel unless I've been there before. We could end up fuck knows where if I tried to get us to Olympus and I don't know any of those people. They could get really mad if I crashed their realm with a bunch of people. Azren and my dad don't really like Zeus, so they probably wouldn't be welcome with strangers. I can't say for *sure* my Uncle Loki didn't fuck anyone in that realm over, but he probably did. Freya is there now but we all wouldn't get a note about finding the force if it wasn't somewhere we could all easily go."

I'd actually never tried traveling to a realm I'd never been to before, but once when I was little, I wanted some of Lucifer's cookies and my dads wouldn't take me. I tried portalling there myself and ended up *very* lost. Hades and Persephone found me in their realm sobbing. They gave me cookies and got me home. I got *much* better at traveling to Hell, but I was still too chicken shit to try somewhere I'd never been before. Hades and Persephone were super sweet, but I didn't want to end up somewhere with nasty gods.

"It's probably on campus. They built the Academy of the Profane to be self-sufficient. There used to be stables for the horses. I'd imagine there was a forge and a blacksmith on staff for things they needed that might get expensive," Michael said.

"Azren?" Drake asked. "They'll be awake. They usually run on a few hours of sleep, coffee, and spite. I'm guessing they are poring over Bjorn's vision and that arrow."

"We also need to ask my dad," Michael said. "He's the headmaster now. If there's a forge on campus, he'll know."

"He's also sleeping right now," Matilda pointed out.

"Oh, he's not sleeping," Mags chuckled.

I put my hands over my ears and started singing. I knew my parents and my brother had sex but I really didn't want to think about it. I stuck my tongue out at Mags when I realized she didn't intend to continue.

"My grandfather might be awake," Church said. "He's been spending his retirement gambling with his friends and doing those diamond paintings. He would know."

I didn't know if Azren would know for sure, but if our current and past headmaster didn't know then there was one person I knew would. Freya was really Beatrix Halliwell. She knew all the Academy of the Profane's secrets.

If there was an important forge here, Freya could tell us when she got back.

AZREN

This arrow was *fascinating*. The little seer was right. It wasn't functional. I knew a little about archery. It wasn't just the metal. The arrow wasn't balanced right. The only way it would fly was through magic and if he used magic to shoot it, he wouldn't have lost it.

I kept turning it over in my hands trying to figure it out while chatting with Baldur and Odin. Odin was used to staying up late writing, but I think the big guy liked to go to bed early because he was yawning. It was honestly kind of adorable.

"This isn't any metal I've seen before. I thought it was gold when I first saw it, but it's not. It's not brass either. It's almost like a stone."

I thought it was just an old arrow that had been under the floorboards for a while, but when I polished it, it became clear it wasn't metal.

"Pyrite?" Odin asked. "It could be Fool's Gold. Most pyrite is harmless, but iron pyrite has a little arsenic in it."

"You know, I think you're right. It's metal, too, but it's not completely metal. This has someone's essence in it. I can literally feel it. It's just a tiny piece, but I've never known anyone to go that long without it. It's not enough for me to tell who it is, but I've never met them before."

Just then, George appeared surrounded by literally everyone. These cottages used to have families in them, but they weren't really meant for this many people, especially when a lot of them were god sized. Baldur alone took up half the couch. I conjured a few chairs. I thought she was worried about her uncle's vision and Drake wanted to know about the arrow, so I started talking. She was here for something else because she started talking, too.

"Sorry," I said, giving her a nod.

She couldn't show me the notes because ghost writing never lasted after it was read, but George told me what it said. I didn't know about the forge, but I *did* know about the speakeasy. That was all Freya. Then she came back as either a teacher or a student and drank there because that was the kind of badass my friend was.

"I wasn't headmaster long, so I don't know about forges."

"My dad is either sleeping or doing things that are going to upset George, so I haven't called," Michael said.

George shot him a look that could cut glass.

"I texted my grandfather, but he hasn't responded. He might be sleeping or he could just be enjoying his retirement."

"It can wait until morning," Odin said. "You all said you know which dodgeball match this is and you have time."

"Have you learned anything about the arrow?" Drake asked.

"I think it was created by magic. I know the ghosts said to look for a forge, but this wasn't made by a normal blacksmith. It seems to be a combination of stone mixed with metal. There are zero impurities like it was made on a forge but I don't know why it was conjured either if it was. There's definitely a bit of someone's essence in this arrow, which doesn't make *any* sense. Everyone's essence leaves them, but it always comes back."

"What?" Oscar said, paling.

Explaining this to mortals *and* gods always blew their minds because they didn't know. Honestly, I wasn't sure where they thought their magic came from.

"What makes gods and supernaturals different from humans is that our essence is supercharged. When either of us uses magic, we're essentially tapping into it. Gods eventually get tired, too, but for the most part, we use it and it comes right back to us unless we expend massive amounts of it. The reason supernaturals get tired after shifting or complicated magic is because your essence leaves you and goes to the Aether to recharge.

"You *always* get it back and the amount you are born with comes from your parents. It goes to the Aether every time, not a random object. When you hex someone, you are sending them your essence and your intention. It infects the other person's essence and goes to the Aether to recharge. Spelled and cursed objects are a little different, but the essence doesn't remain.

"The *only* bit of magic I know of where a supernatural leaves part of their essence in an object are sentient books and that why most of them are feral little assholes that bite.

I've never *once* met a sentient book that wasn't a complete dick but making them was all the rage for a little while."

"We used to ask to go in that room at the library all the time when we were kids. We thought it would be so cool. Even when my dad showed us the scar where one of them bit him, we still wanted to. The first thing I did when I got my library card was go to that room. Some bitch ass book screamed at me and tried to hit me in the face," Michael said.

"I *told* you not to go in there. The sentient book craze was big the first time I was alive. Everyone's books were assaulting them and keeping them awake all night screaming and they were pretending like it was the coolest thing ever. I didn't know it was because their essence was in there," Mags said.

"Mm, yes. Being separated from your essence isn't meant to happen. It only makes the person feel slightly off. They probably can't even put their finger on what's missing. The essence that has been cut off feels it the strongest. It's not very smart and can't tell you why it's angry and bitter, but it wants to go home.

"Whatever this arrow was forged for, it's protecting the essence. I can't hear it and it can't speak. I could probably pull it out, but it would destroy the arrow. If two seers tell me this arrow is important, I'm going to leave it until I know why."

"Couldn't he feel it? If he killed my parents to get his arrow back, wouldn't he know they didn't have it? He didn't murder them just because my mom took it, or he wouldn't have left it under the floorboards of my dorm room."

That was the part that was bugging me. This arrow was

important, and I was pretty sure Drake's parents died over it. His mother left an amazing opportunity at the Academy of the Profane because she saw the god who fired it and stole his arrow. She had no way of knowing what was lurking in this arrow, but she didn't want to take it with her when she left. Maybe she had plans for it when she thought she was safe and found someone who could do something with it, but she didn't get the chance.

"In theory, the two essences should be drawn to each other. When people were making magical books, the intention was to sell them for a lot of money, but they found they couldn't part with them when it came time to turn them over to a buyer. They became status symbols to show off when their rich friends came over.

"The material this arrow is made of is unusual. The essence inside should be reacting and it should either be trying to stab us or fly home. It's not, which makes me think something about this material is doing something that's blocking him from sensing his own essence. I can feel it because that's my domain. If it's important, I'm going to figure out why and make sure he can't get his hands on it," I said, waving my hand and disappearing it to my safe back on the Netherworld. "You should all get to bed or you're going to fall asleep in my class. Just because I like all of you doesn't mean I won't give you a little love zap to wake you up."

George slinked over and wrapped her arms around me. We hadn't been affectionate with each other around other gods, even though Freya had easily figured it out.

"I told my mom about us. They already knew and they are all happy for us."

"No shit? Even your dad?"

I could predict how the God of Chaos would react as easily as I could Loki. Which was not at all.

"He's happy about it because he thinks you're good for me and I'm good for you."

"That's because you are," I said, kissing her nose.

My girlfriend gave me this look, and I already knew it meant she was up to something. She never had it in my class because she was an excellent student, but when she had that face matched to her twin sister, it meant some shit was about to go down.

"So, the headmaster knows about us and he's not going to fire you. I know we can't be obvious in public, but you know I can get back to my dorm without being seen. Can I stay with you tonight?"

I groaned. How was I supposed to say no to that? Because she was right. If Gabriel was headmaster now and he was okay with this, there was nothing stopping us. The only person who had any reason to come to my cabin was Gabriel. The rest of the professors here valued their private time, and they weren't going to encroach on me when I was at home. The only reason Gabriel would was because he knew the true reason I was here.

"I'll bet it's hot as fuck when the two of you get together," West whined.

I cocked an eyebrow at West.

"Are you sure you're straight?"

"You can totally get turned on by your sexy as fuck god friends fucking your girl as long as the swords don't cross."

Ren rolled his eyes.

"He also says kissing men is totally straight as long as he doesn't use tongue."

"I'm a lion shifter. Don't be racist. We do that."

They actually didn't. I was there when they were made

and hung out with them for a long time. They didn't kiss anyone on the mouth unless they were family or into them that way. I wasn't going to say a damned thing because I really liked West just the way he was.

"Get the fuck out of here," I growled. "She's *mine* for the night."

GEORGE

I knew Odin and Loki had their problems and Loki still ranted about him sometimes. He scared me at first when I was little, but then he started telling us stories and I decided he was kind of cool. I knew he was here for Baldur, but it was nice having him around. Baldur was ready for bed. It wasn't really safe for everyone to walk back and he just *got* that I was trying to have filthy sex with the God of Death. Odin offered to portal everyone home while Azren and I went to their place.

I wasn't quite done. I may or may not have had a fantasy. So, when Drake went to touch Odin to leave, I snagged his sleeve.

"Oh, no you don't, sir. I have an idea unless you think it would be weird."

Drake just shrugged.

"I'm down. I don't think it would be weird, but I'm not bisexual so kinda like West. No sword crossing."

"It wouldn't be any weirder than that time in ancient Babylonia with the incubus and the bees," Azren said.

"Okay, you're going to have to tell me that story one day. Right this way, people," I said, snagging Drake's uniform tie and portalling him to Azren's cabin.

Azren wasn't that far behind me. I hadn't been in Azren's bedroom yet in their cabin. They had waved their hand and remodeled the entire interior because they could either just put it back when they left or leave it if anyone wanted to live here in the future because it was really nice.

Azren definitely had an aesthetic that completely fit the God of Death. They generally wore black suits or black dresses with black nail polish. Their hair was long, silky and inky black. They usually wore it down or pulled back. They'd decorated their cabin to fit those vibes, but it was also insanely comfortable.

The cabin didn't have the same ornately carved bed as their bedroom back home. They were mostly like my family and me. We preferred hiring artisans for the big stuff. It was mostly a big comfy bed. I took a running start and starfished on it. I'd been stressed to all shit with visions, gods wanting to kill me, and the possibility of us losing the dodgeball game. I just *really* needed to relax by getting tag teamed by the god everyone feared and a Basilisk who got a little dominant in the bedroom. I looked directly at Drake.

"You'd better not change a damned thing about how you did it at the moon orgy now that you know I'm a god."

Seriously. Because he'd been bossy and a little disrespectful, but he only did that right before he gave me the best orgasm ever. Drake had been rude to me before but that was just because he thought I was dangerous. Drake was polite and respectful to anyone who didn't give him a reason not to be and he learned not every witch was out to hurt him. Even when a witch *did* violate him, he saw how swiftly they paid for it and nearly everyone turned on them.

"Um, no offense, but we did a thing that Azren specifically raised me *not* to do to women. I'm completely *not* into getting spanked by the God of Death."

"Ooh, I am. Let's do that," I said.

Azren just let out that velvety chuckle that was always sexy as fuck.

"Drake, anything I taught you about treating women doesn't count if it's in the bedroom and she's *asking* for it. And I'm countless millennia older than both of you. It's nothing I haven't done or asked to be done to me. I can't believe you thought *I'm* the type to kink shame. I've only had one night with George and I'm still learning what she likes."

"I've just had the moon orgies, but she likes it when I top her."

"Ooh," Azren said, flopping on the bed next to me. "I'm into that, too, sometimes. Do both of us. We don't have to touch each other."

Drake just stood there with his mouth open.

"I *cannot* top two gods."

"Why not?" Azren asked.

"Please?" I begged. "You're really good at it."

The big scary God of Death got down on our level and started making puppy dog eyes at Drake.

"Please? I haven't been topped well in *ages* and she likes it. She just found out someone wants to kill her, and she might lose a dodgeball game. George *hates* losing, Drake. That might be worse than someone wanting to kill her. It's our *duty* to make our girlfriend feel better. Forget us being gods. Tonight, we are just two people pleasing our woman."

Drake's whole demeanor changed. I saw the minute he

went from not thinking he could do this to being totally on board with it. Drake had the whole 'glowering bad boy' thing going on. He knew he was deadly, an amazing musician, and a talented goalie. *That* Drake was back, and he was ready to proceed.

Drake had that dangerous smirk back on his face.

"Kiss our girlfriend," Drake ordered. "But pin her down first. She likes that."

Fuck. Azren rolled me over and did exactly what Drake told me to do. They pinned my arms above my head and stole my breath kissing me until Drake told them not to.

"Take her clothes off and show me that beautiful body."

"She has beautiful legs, doesn't she?" Azren purred, unbuttoning my shirt.

"She does. They go straight up to that perfect ass. I want to see those breasts."

Azren could have easily disappeared my clothes, but Drake didn't want that. And Azren didn't really like doing that. No, Drake wanted to watch Azren slowly undress me, so that's what they were doing. And they couldn't remove a piece of clothing without leaving a kiss or bite behind. Azren was old enough and had shapeshifted enough that they knew exactly how to undress a woman.

I made eye contact with Drake. He had removed his shirt and was stroking his cock through his trousers as he watched us. At this point, I was totally naked and exposed. Azren was lazily massaging my clit with their fingers and nibbling on my breasts while we waited for Drake's next command.

I was so into this and I knew why Azren was, too. It was fucking amazing to not be in charge for a bit and let someone else be the strongest person in the room. Especially when Drake was so fucking good at this. Drake unbuttoned his trousers, pulled them down, and then kicked them across the room like a boss.

"I think I want to watch Azren devour George's pussy while she sucks my cock," Drake announced.

I think Azren and I *both* groaned and broke into goosebumps. I had a feeling I knew how Drake wanted his cock sucked and I was here for it. Azren settled themselves between my legs as Drake crawled into bed with us.

"Gimme," I said, making grabby hands at his cock.

Drake just chuckled darkly and grabbed my hand.

"You aren't in charge here. You can have it when I say you can."

Oh, my fuck. I would have sent someone through the wall for saying that to me under any other circumstances, but when I was naked and it was Drake, it just went straight to my vagina.

"Yes, sir," I said, putting my hands down.

"Good girl," Drake growled, stroking my cheek.

I died right there and turned into a little pile of goo on the bed. It didn't help that Azren was flicking my clit with their tongue. Drake seemed content to just watch Azren devour me for a few minutes, but then he ran his thumb along my lower lip and pressed like he wanted me to open my mouth. I did *exactly* what he wanted me to do because Drake was running this show and Azren and I were just here for the orgasms.

Azren slid two fingers inside me right when Drake finally decided to give me his cock. And they both knew how to do that just right. Azren curled their fingers to massage my G spot and Drake was never going to be a passive guy. He was growling and fucking my mouth. I couldn't see his face, but I could see iridescent scales on the parts of his body that were visible to me. Drake *only* lost control of his Basilisk when he was angry or during sex.

When he was angry, it was just his eyes. I got the serpent when we were having sex and honestly, he was beautiful like this. He'd eventually learn to control it better, but for now, I'd just enjoy the snake while I had it. Maybe he'd get enough control over his Basilisk to bring him out to play in the bedroom sometimes.

Things were getting pretty intense. Azren had brought their black smoke to the party, and I was about to lose my shit. I actually lost it when Drake grabbed my ponytail and pulled. Drake thrust into my mouth three more times beforeI felt him cum. I swallowed him down as my entire body was shaking with my orgasm.

Drake pulled his cock out of my mouth and let me calm down. Azren had their head resting on my stomach as I played with their hair. My legs felt like jelly. Drake snuggled in next to me.

"Did you get what you needed?" he asked.

"Yeah. You're really fucking good at that."

"You are," Azren said.

Drake just started laughing.

"I hope you don't think we're done. I have the refractory period of an eighteen-year-old guy and Azren hasn't orgasmed at all yet."

I wasn't scared of Azren, but the laugh they let out was sheer evil.

"I hope you're prepared for what you asked for, George."

Duh, or I wouldn't have asked for it. I could *totally* handle getting railed all night by the God of Death and a really dominant Basilisk.

GEORGE

It felt amazing to wake up snuggled between Drake and Azren. It felt less amazing to wake up earlier than usual so I could portal Drake and me back to our dorm rooms so some nosy bastard didn't see us *proudly* doing a walk of shame back and made a stink with my dad. Gabriel could only do so much if we were careless.

It was Monday and no longer the weekend, so it was back to classes. I got back to my dorm room with just enough time to shower, throw my hair up in a bun, and slap a little eyeliner on. I was very much feeling like wearing the men's uniform today, so I did. I used magic to tailor it so it fit me like one of Mag's suits. She looked *much* better in a tailored suit than I did, but I wore what I wanted.

Everyone was already in the dining hall ready to work. Ren slid my latte over when I joined them with my plate.

"How is it you look hotter in that uniform than I do?" Ren moaned.

"She's hotter than all of us. It's not fair because she's also sexy in the girl's uniform," Oscar said.

"I'm glad I don't have to wear the uniform since I'm not a student. I like airflow to my balls," West said.

"Really?" Matilda said. "Right in front of my toast?"

"Sorry, little lesbian," West said, winking at my sister.

"If my sister wasn't attached to them, I'd rip your testicles off with my teeth."

"Then, you'd have to have my balls in your mouth."

"Touché, lion."

Church's phone rang, and he told us it was his grandfather. Freya wasn't back yet, and my dad never ate breakfast in the dining hall. We were going to talk to him later. Church's grandfather was the only other person who would know about any forges on campus. It wasn't a person, and I was guessing it wasn't magical. A locator spell was our next step just in case there was something magically significant about it. Church's grandfather could cut that step out.

"You said you needed help. Sorry I missed the text."

"I think we got invites to the campus speakeasy and the ghosts are finally trying to help us with the mystery. Do you know anything about a forge on campus?"

"There are two and the only reason I can even tell you about one of them is because Azren ran their big fat mouth when they shouldn't have. Both of them haven't been used in decades as far as I know. They converted the old stables to locker rooms when they built a sports field on that land. The old forge was preserved as a bit of history and it's off the side of the dodgeball stadium.

"The other is in Shrieking Woods. The caretaker of the garden that grows out there needed to live off the grid while they were building up the mythology. No one could be seen coming and going so there was a place for them to make and repair tools. They don't use it anymore. There's Wi-Fi out there. If they need tools, they have a credit card and email the headmaster the invoice.

"I know the God of Death spilled the beans about Shrieking Woods but it's still not safe to go in there unless Gabriel warns the groundskeeper you're coming. The groundskeeper is usually a hedge witch or some type of Fae because of their connection to nature, but they only hire powerful supernaturals for this job. I'm talking, the kind of supernatural that could make college students *think* there's the ghost of a banshee serial killer living there. They are also dangerous enough to knock someone out and make them forget they found someone living in Shrieking Woods instead of deranged ghosts.

"The caretakers are usually hedge witches who tend to hate people or high-profile Fae refugees who are hiding in Shrieking Woods because they don't want to get kidnapped back to their realm. It's a *big* job to take on and not everyone can do it. The Fae do it because they have to. Some of the hedge witches just like the idea of living in the woods surrounded by rare plants and terrorizing any teenagers that come close.

"Since this is a speakeasy quest and might have something to do with the killer, I'm guessing the ghosts don't want you looking for the forge that's right next to where you play dodgeball most nights. I'm serious about this. Don't go looking for the other forge until Gabriel can let the caretaker know you are coming. George is the only one who wouldn't get hurt. The caretaker might get spooked and plants could get damaged. The garden has some of the biggest crops of medicinal plants in the country. They've tried growing them in special greenhouses and they don't flourish the same."

"I'll talk to my dad," I said.

"I'd go with you, but I don't know this caretaker. They were hired after I left. The board isn't involved in secondary staff hiring. All I know is that they are an Unseelie refugee and really intense. I'm guessing they will show you the old forge and then want you gone."

We could do that. Between Oscar, Mags, Azren, and me, we could just touch the forge and see if there were anything fishy about it. West, Ren, and Matilda all had the killer's scent. They could tell if the killer had been out there and meddled with the caretaker's memories like he had the students.

We hung up with Church's grandfather and made a plan to meet in my dad's office. Some Fae had been in this realm for generations and the Fae Court didn't care. Some of the Fae that escaped that realm, they wanted back. They had to apply for asylum with the right supernaturals, but they were always worried soldiers from the Fae Court were going to swoop in and steal them back.

We could do this without traumatizing the caretaker.

WEST

At first, I thought it was weird the ghosts were including me in their little notes. After watching Bethany repeatedly assault Church's nuts, I wanted the ghosts to pretend like I didn't exist. Which was unusual because I was a very needy lion who needed everyone to notice me. I'd never admit that to a single soul, but I knew myself very well.

I didn't want my beautiful balls punched by an angry spirit, but I was glad they included me on this now that I knew what they were. I wouldn't have been able to join my people without getting that note. The ghosts would have known there were other people who were close to Oscar who could have signed for him while he was in the speakeasy. Church was not only picking up sign language superfast, he studied it over Yule break to get better.

I left the TV on in our dorm room before I shut the door when I left for breakfast and whispered a thanks to the ghosts for including me. I meant it. I would have felt left out if they all got to go and I couldn't. And I figured showing gratitude would keep my dick safe.

We'd already gotten Grandpa Church's story on the forges. Church was my boyfriend-in-law and he was in my pride, so Church's grandfather was practically *my* grandfather at this point. He wasn't as cute and cuddly as our Church and might bite my beautiful neck for calling him Grandpa, so I wasn't going to do that to his face just yet.

We were all in the headmaster's office to see what George's dad knew about the forges and see if he could get in contact with the caretaker. The *only* reason I knew George's daddy was cute and cuddly and not some dark warlock who could ban my ass from campus for the unspeakable things I'd done to his daughter under the full moon was because I'd seen him with his family and knew he approved of us.

"I can email the caretaker, but the other forge is being used. I'm not sure how to tell you by whom."

"Baldur," George said.

"It was one of the reasons he was hired and they overlooked the whole lack of magic thing. There were a lot of things previous maintenance had to contract out if it broke. He knows how to fix a *lot* of things. He can also make things on that old forge that plenty of people they interviewed can't do. When he was just Sol, he saved this college a ton of money and kept her bones strong by fixing what was broken."

"We cleared him though," Ren said. "West figured it out. He might know how to work a forge, but he still doesn't have magic."

I didn't get vibes from Baldur that he was a killer even before I asked if he had blackouts on certain dates. I might not have witchy-woo intuition with auras, but my vibes hadn't let me down yet. Baldur might not be a criminal, but for a hot minute, I was. I didn't *kill* anyone, I just vandalized or stole their shit, but we could smell our own. Baldur struck me as the kind of guy who had never just kind of slowed down at a stop sign at two in the morning because no one was coming. Nah, that big motherfucker always came to a complete stop.

"I haven't thought he did this from the moment you told me he was Baldur and having blackouts. He could have learned to blacksmith once he came back. He's been around for a while with no magic or memories and he'd have to learn skills to feed himself. It could be muscle memory. He might not *remember* learning to work a forge, but his body does."

"Why is that important?" Church asked.

"Okay, I'm not a god, but I have plenty in my family and my wife is a librarian. A lot of the gods have a weapon associated with them that they use to focus their magic. All of them could have just waved their hands and made one, but they didn't. All those magical god weapons were forged. Hephaestus made all of them for his family. Asgard has dwarves that make fantastic magical weapons. They made Thor's hammer. I'm sure the other realms have similar weapons and blacksmiths.

"Baldur was beloved by everyone, even the man who killed him. He could have befriended the dwarves on Asgard and learned to blacksmith. I've known him longer than all of you and that just seems like something he would do. Just so, we know the arrow is important and two gods can't figure out how it was made. Hephaestus was supposed to be one of the best. He could have taught an Erotes if they asked.

"Baldur might not be the only god using the campus

forges. Or another theory is that if this god can manipulate memories and pull people away from moon orgies, they are somehow having Baldur do something with the forges and arrows when he's blacked out. If someone reported they spotted a giant blond man without magic at the forge by the dodgeball field, I'd know who it was.

"I've only spoken to the caretaker a few times, but they are super paranoid and very in tune with the forest since they are Unseelie. If someone was messing with their memories, they couldn't erase all the little details they'd been in that forest using the forge. They would have gotten spooked and ran by now. And because of their respect for nature, they would have notified the headmaster so we could hire a replacement to care for the plants."

George and I both let out a little growl. I wasn't into Baldur like she was but come on. He was a giant teddy bear. I was sure he also had some big, scary god powers but fucking with him when he was like this was like kicking puppies. I might be a giant cat, but I happened to really like puppies. Assaulting puppies was worse than assaulting kittens. A kitten would remember and grow into a cat who kept a grudge and shat in your shoes, so they weren't completely harmless. Those little puppy brains had short memories and sometimes they didn't get big and get their revenge.

"I don't know," Gabriel said. "It's just a theory. Guys, the speakeasy wasn't just put in place to give some of the more restless ghosts something to do. It was meant to be a reward and an exclusive club for students. The ghosts could see things the rest of us might not. Even the professors get invitations. I got one shortly after I started teaching here. Your mom and I go there to drink sometimes when it's just the two of us. Some of the other professors were students here and are still waiting for their invites.

"The quests the ghosts give are meant to be personal and help the person doing them, but they also benefit the spirits. They are moving pieces as part of a bigger game the rest of us can't see because we aren't dead. I was content with just teaching, but my quest ended up giving me the idea that I might eventually want to be headmaster.

"You won't just get a clue when you find the forge. The Academy of the Profane doesn't have sororities or fraternities that would give some students connections when they graduate if their dorm didn't the points and get a letter from the headmaster.

"The ghosts are going to give all of you a token once you do what they ask. It's how you get the door to the speakeasy to appear and you'll have to show it to the bouncer to be let in. The bouncer is the ghost of a massive bear shifter and—"

"No one piss him off," Church said. "Bethany is just a frail witch, and it hurts like a bitch when she assaults my nuts."

"No, you really don't want to piss Theodore off," Gabriel said. "He takes his job very seriously. Anyway, that token isn't just how you get in and out of the speakeasy. You'll need to bring it with you on job interviews. There are a lot of Academy of the Profane graduates in the wild. If they don't have a token, one of their friends might have shown them theirs and explained what it meant. They'll ask if you did independent study, but some may ask to see your token. It's going to put you a notch above with the other candidates."

Everyone seemed excited about that but me. I was already doing my dream job. I didn't want to be a CEO and make more money in one hour than some people made in months. I didn't want responsibilities like that. All I wanted out of life was to sign for deaf people. I might not make millions of dollars, but I was happy, *and* it made me whole.

I was chosen by an amazing person to sign for him and try to help him learn to read lips and look what it brought me. I'd traveled all the way across the country to the Academy of the Profane, got to watch *the* Zion Skinner coach dodgeball, and I'd met my mate. I met my whole pride, and they were just as cool as Oscar and Ren.

Yeah, I'd take the token to get into the speakeasy with my friends, but I wasn't going to be flashing it at rich people to get a job I hated. I had *everything* I wanted. Well, except for a house for all of us with a giant bed where I could snuggle with George and make biscuits on her back when she wouldn't notice.

But that would happen when they graduated.

"Ah. I just got an email from the caretaker. They'll show you the forge, but they have conditions. His name is Hale and he would prefer it if only gods came out to look at the forge. Hale is aware of what's going on at the Academy of the Profane even if no one knows who he is. He says it's not really safe for anyone else to see his face if the Fae Court finds out where he is.

"Most of the Fae refugees who have direct knowledge of the Fae Court only give enough information to be given asylum because they are terrified of them. Hale is Unseelie and even though the Unseelie have been in this realm for a long time, they are super secretive of their actual abilities. I can ask Hale to give concessions for all of you, but he *lived* in the Fae realm until a few years ago. If he's saying it's probably only safe for gods to see his face, he's probably right."

"Dexter's family has been here for generations, but I don't want the Fae Court's attention on him and thinking they want to steal him back," Michael said.

Ah, yes. I wasn't dating Dexter like I wasn't dating Baldur. But Dexter was a cool little dude. He came out swinging when Kaylee messed with George after messing with him, too. He got his revenge and just kept fucking with her because she wouldn't leave either of them alone. Dexter was also a total beast on the dodgeball field.

Dexter needed to be protected at all costs.

"I agree with Michael," George said. "I don't know much about the Fae realm, but Hale would. We can all go check out the forge by the dodgeball field and Azren, Odin, and I can check out the one in Shrieking Woods."

Which was probably what we needed to do, but I was still butt hurt Azren asked me to sniff a dead body when they apparently could have shifted and done it themselves. I *traumatized* myself taking one for the team fulfilling that request, so I had the killer's scent. Matilda and Mags did, too.

I didn't have magical powers and I wouldn't know if the forge in the forest had been used to make some weird arrow. But I did have magical *senses* and I could smell if the killer had been out there. I *should* be out there with them.

I'd had a few good ideas so far, but I decided not to say anything about my sense of smell. God magic probably beat out a shifter's sense of smell. My girlfriend was *much* stronger than I was and I was okay with that. My boyfriend-in-law was a primordial.

They could handle the forest forge without me.

BALDUR

I wasn't expecting everyone to find me at the forge. Even with the Academy of the Profane having a dodgeball team now, no one ever went around back to the little closed-off nook with a blacksmith's forge. I was out here because Zion asked if I could spruce up the scoreboard on the dodgeball field. It was generic since the field had been rented out for so long.

The Academy of the Profane students voted to have a team, and they chose a Hydra as their mascot. If Hydras were ever created by a god, they decided they were too dangerous and killed them because they didn't exist today. Humans tried to wipe supernaturals out and sometimes, supernaturals got spooked about certain races and tried to exterminate them. Nature always found a way unless the gods were involved. There were two men in front of me that witches and vampires nearly hunted to extinction, but I was looking at them clear as day.

I knew there were newer methods to making a Hydra

for the sign, but some of it couldn't be done without the forge and I really liked working with my hands. I was just finishing up when George and everyone else appeared in my little nook. I'd only just started to get to know her. I couldn't tell you what her favorite book or food was, so I couldn't explain the pull I felt to her. I just went with it.

I couldn't help the smile that lit up my face as soon as I saw her. She walked over and tried to hug me. I stepped back. It wasn't that I didn't want her to. I did.

"Blacksmithing is dirty work. I'm filthy and I probably stink."

"And I care about that why? I need to do laundry anyway and I take a lot of showers," she said, pouncing on me and hugging me.

"Dude, she can't smell you like I can, but gods must stink differently than the rest of us because you smell amazing," West said.

"Bro, you can't say shit like that and insist you're straight," Ren said.

I just chuckled.

"I haven't known West very long, but he strikes me as the type of guy who is very secure with himself and doesn't have a toxic bone in his body. He gives compliments and does the things he does because he knows they are true, recognizes it might brighten someone's day when he does or says something, and he doesn't really care what people may think about it because *he* knows who he is," I said.

"I think you just totally summed up West," Oscar said.

West put his hand over his heart and pretended to swoon.

"My dude, only a few people have gotten me on that level before. If I *was* bisexual, I'd be totally into you because you may actually be hotter than me."

I threw back my head and laughed. I'd never done the group thing before. According to my father, I'd married really young to the girl I'd lost my virginity to. No one really liked her and thought she was bad for me. I'd also been pretty young when I died. I'd been back with no memories or magic longer than I was alive as a god. Supernaturals weren't exactly lining up to recruit me and humans hadn't really caught up on the whole polyamory thing. It was still illegal.

But if I was going to do a polyamorous thing with George for the first time in my life, I really liked these guys. Oscar and Ren had accepted me when I was just Sol in maintenance bringing them their luggage. West and Church were sure I wasn't a murderer long before I was.

"What are you all doing out here?" I asked.

George filled me in on their speakeasy mission. I had a token. The ghosts never spoke to me or told me the truth about who I was. They never visited me or tried to ease my burden about what happened during my blackouts, even though I knew they knew. They left me a note and a mission the very first time I got a job here and the token worked every time I got rehired. The ghosts might not have *helped* me, but they never ratted me out either.

I told everyone about my token and how hard it was to unlock the note without magic. The quest they gave me was completely unmagical, but getting texts written by ghosts to show itself required some finesse and me stealing some things from the potions lab.

"What was your mission?" Church asked.

"I had to find a certain library book and go talk to the campus blacksmith. That used to be a job here, and the stadium used to be where everyone kept their horses and carriages until cars were everywhere and they made a parking lot on the other side of campus. Fuck! The library book was on Norse gods and it had the story of Loki killing me in it. It didn't make sense at the time, so I thought they were fucking with me."

I really was pissed at the time because I was operating under the theory that a god was trying to make something, fucked up, and ended up with me. A lot of gods didn't want to be responsible for an entire magical race and didn't create any. Up until very recently, I didn't think any of the Norse gods tried their hand at creation, but I found out I was wrong and one did. I was still a little mad because they could have given me so much more than a library book with no context.

"The forge is also important," Oscar said. "We know the arrow is important, too, and Gabriel thinks all these weapons associated with gods were made by blacksmiths who knew how to infuse metal and magic. What happened when you went to talk to the blacksmith?"

Fuck. Talking to the blacksmith revealed *something,* but it also kicked open the door to about a million more questions.

"The blacksmith was a completely nonjudgmental werewolf. He didn't give a shit about my lack of magic because there were people that treated him like garbage for being a blacksmith instead of some fancier job. We just sat and talked while he worked. Honestly, it was nice not having someone talk down to me when I was among super-naturals.

"That was when I realized something. I didn't know *how* I knew and honestly, I still don't, but I knew nearly every step of what he was doing on the forge. This was back before I knew I couldn't age or die, so I thought it was just regular amnesia and told him. He let me help him out on the forge to see if it would help trigger some memories. It didn't, but I really like working with my hands, so I still do it. I can't always make fun things like Hydra signs for the dodgeball team, but it's still nice fixing things."

"Fuck, all those pieces are going to be a sign for the dodgeball team? Now I'm wishing I was bisexual. You might not *play* dodgeball, but making the mascot is still sexy."

"West," George laughed. "My dad was right then. He said you either learned it to survive after you came back or you befriended the dwarves on Asgard and they taught you. There's no magic coming off this forge, so I don't think the killer was forcing you to forge those arrows during your blackouts. That was another theory.

"The dwarves might have taught you to forge magical weapons, but you don't have magic. And I don't think *anyone* could forge a weapon with someone's essence in it except Azren and even they say that arrow doesn't make sense. The arrow is important, but I don't think it's like Thor's hammer or Poseidon's trident."

"Don't quote me on this because honestly, if I made a god weapon, I don't remember it. I'm going by me *now* and not me then. If I was making a weapon and I wanted it attuned to a certain person, I'd add their blood to my process. If I have to fix something or clean it when a class is in progress, I always pay attention to the lecture. *Every* supernatural race uses blood in some aspect. Even if the killer *had* figured out how to rip a piece of their essence out without Azren, why would they do that when they could just prick their finger?"

"That makes sense," Church said. "I'm an energy vampire, but I also get a boost if I drink blood. Most of my classes this semester have been about blood since I'm the only energy vampire here. Vampires aren't feeding off blood per se. It's the magic *in* the blood that sustains us.

"My dad tried to get me to use my energy vampire powers to convince a witch to sic a revenant on a rival he wanted gone, but not traced back to him. I got way more information on necromancy than a ten-year-old vampire probably needed. You can't raise the dead without blood. There are a lot of things that can go wrong and create a revenant, but if you don't have good magic in your blood, it's guaranteed. None of this makes sense."

"No, it doesn't," Oscar said. "Blood is important in my magic, too. It's not nearly as crucial in some of the other supernaturals, but they all have a few rituals that use it."

"Kitsunes aren't into the bloodletting and we get a lot of magic with each new tail, but even we have a blood spell. It's kind of an urban legend. Some people swear it works and some people say it's horse shit. There's supposed to be these potions we can drink with a drop of our blood that's supposed to give you a new tail and let you pick which power it gives you. My family said even if it actually worked, it was cheating. My cousin tried it anyway and ended up with diarrhea for a month so it's probably just a myth."

"I remember that!" Oscar laughed. "My Abuela was cooking for everyone and he ran out of her house and drove all the way home because he could never shit at anyone else's house. Your mom yelled to our whole neighborhood that he deserved to pee out his butt for being stupid."

"Thanks, Baldur," George said. "I can't wait to see your Hydra when you're done. I have to meet Azren to look at the other forge and see if that gives us any hint about why the arrow is important. Also, if we get our tokens to the speakeasy, we are kidnapping you and making you come party with us."

I grinned.

"Can't wait."

I watched her go with a smile. I felt like I wasn't helping because I couldn't remember anything and I didn't have my magic. But I'd actually done something today. And it was all thanks to what I thought was useless information from the campus ghosts over a hundred years ago.

GEORGE

It was a lot to take in. The forge Baldur had been working on was hot, but I didn't sense any magic coming from it. Azren had been teaching me to play with their magic in our private lessons. I might not be a master at it and couldn't really manipulate an essence like Azren could just yet, but I knew what it felt like. After Azren pointed out there was some in that arrow, I could feel it. There wasn't any coming from Baldur's forge.

There hadn't been any magic used on the forge at all. Mags, Matilda, and West had scented the arrow. We didn't know what it was made of, but they knew what it smelled like. I don't think we expected to find Baldur *using* it and all the scents out there were overwhelming because of it but they didn't smell anything similar out there.

That left Shrieking Woods. My dad met Azren and me to lead us to the cottage before dodgeball practice. The only reason I knew Zion and the coach from the other team we'd be playing had some kind of beef with each other was because my uncle had a vision. Zion would have called it bitching to even mention it to us, but he was being *brutal* at practice. I loved every minute of it.

"I know we're trying to be sensitive to Hale and his ties to the Fae Court, but the three people in our group who have the killer's scent aren't going to be out there with us. West is going to make you grovel for a very long time about using his nose like that, by the way."

Azren sighed.

"I really like West. If I'd known it was going to upset him, I wouldn't have asked. Is this one of those gift giving situations? Should I get him a card or something? Is there a certain apology flower you send when you ask a shifter to smell a dead body?"

My dad was just walking with us giggling like an unhinged psychopath. Azren was taking this very seriously and West might end up with a dorm full of flowers and gifts at this rate.

"Just be super nice to him. He was probably only upset about it for five minutes after it happened. He keeps bringing it up because you're nice to him after."

"Be honest, am I mean to the others? I don't know them as well as I know Drake and I'm trying. I'm just limited since I'm your teacher."

"Azren, you're nice to *all* of them and they really like you. West just likes getting compliments because he gives them out so freely, so he's kind of gaslighting you about this."

Gabriel fell out laughing.

"And you fell for it too. West is a shifter. He smells *every-thing.* He's probably smelled much worse. The kid was apparently a bit of a criminal before he got community service at a school for the deaf and decided that was what he wanted to do with his life. West has probably smelled some shit."

"Ah, fuck," Azren sighed. "I do like that lion."

"Just be aware, Ren will probably do it, too, and his weakness is Oscar. You bumped up a ton of notches with him when you realized Oscar was deaf and just started signing your lectures and never stopped. Most of our professors don't and some of them even stand in front of West when they are walking around doing their lectures and Oscar can't see. Church doesn't give a shit how you treat him. He likes you because you treat *me* well."

My dad seemed to find all this endlessly amusing, and I was so going to rat him out to my mom for giving my boyfriend a hard time.

"We all love you and George together but right now, I'm seriously enjoying the fact that the big bad God of Death also has to worry about the approval of some college students if they want to date my kid."

I was about to threaten to bring the wrath of my mom down on Gabriel, but Azren started laughing, too, so I guess I wouldn't threaten him with my mom just yet.

"It's kind of fucked up, isn't it? I never really thought I'd have anything with another god because of who I am, but when I find her, she comes with college students and one lion with a few misdemeanors. Except I really like all of them, even when one of them is trolling me to kiss his ass."

"The cabin is up this way. We can't see him, but Hale will already know we are here. He'll make himself known when he wants to."

"I'm right behind you."

The voice behind us was frankly creepy as fuck. I knew there weren't deranged ghosts out here and the spirit of a banshee serial killer but I still jumped straight into Azren's arms and let out a really stupid scream. I truly thought I was above that. I didn't scare easily. My brothers tried all the time and never managed.

I whirled around and got a look at Hale. He was pretty like all the Unseelie were but he was a little eerie. A lot of people said Unseelie were unsettling, but my old babysitter Beyla had a run-in with one who was the artistic director for the ballet company she was dancing with. She said she wanted to strangle him most days, but he had been a mostly decent guy underneath it all.

Something about Hale made me uncomfortable, and it had nothing to do with him being Unseelie. There weren't a lot of them on this realm, but I'd met them before. They never made me feel like this.

Hale was tall, like, nearly god tall. He was about my height and I was on the shorter side for a god. He was very pale and sickly looking for a gardener and I couldn't really read his aura. It was Unseelie, but complicated. There was some dark shit in his aura, but what did I know? Someone had hired him and my dad hadn't fired him yet. Hale could have been forced to do some shit in the Fae realm and this was his protection.

"Hi, Hale. This is Azren and my daughter, George."

"I'm aware. The forge is this way."

He was all business. Hale wanted to show us the forge and get us out of his forest. I got it.

"Have there been any signs someone was in this forest?" Azren asked.

"You mean aside from that unfortunate dead girl and

the agents who were stomping around my forest? No. The night of the murder I was out of the forest taking in a movie. No offense, but I'm not interested in moon orgies with anyone. I went to one staffed by humans. The Paranormal Investigation Bureau confirmed me there on their cameras and with my ticket. The only cameras here are on the rare plants. Usually, the trees tell me if someone is trespassing, but I was too far away to hear them that night. Other than the night of the moon orgy, it's been quiet."

"Holy shit, is that Fogbane?" I asked, seeing it growing on a boulder.

"A girl knows her lichen. I'm impressed."

I was kinda irritated this guy just called me a girl, but technically I *was* younger than him.

"My grandparents own a magic shop just off campus. They moved here after my brother was born to be close to the grandkids. They have charms, potions, potion ingredients, and a little greenhouse my grandfather built in the back where they try to grow plants like this. My grandmother has been trying to get Fogbane to grow on these rocks by the creek because of its healing properties and because it's so expensive. Any tips?"

"Mm. Have her pour orange juice on the rocks when the moon is full. Fresh squeezed is best with a lot of pulp. This is the forge."

Orange juice? We used to always love visiting the magic shop. We all had jobs there in high school. My grandma was going to lose her shit if the orange juice worked. I took in the caretaker's cottage. It was an old, charming place. It definitely gave off 'fairytale hermit who terrorized teenagers' vibes. I could tell someone had been updating the place as the centuries had passed as there were several modern amenities I could see. There was also an exit to the forest I didn't know about. There was a truck parked on a gravel drive leading somewhere.

We all crowded around the forge. This one hadn't been used recently. Baldur's forge wouldn't have burned me if I didn't want it to, but it was uncomfortable to be around and I didn't need to get close to get what I needed. Azren and I surrounded it and tried to figure it out.

There was no magic on this forge either but now that I was standing next to Azren, I had a stronger sense of essences. The killer's essence had been *near* this forge, but it wasn't *in* the forge. Before we left Baldur, he told us one last thing that was a major help. He said with a forge that old and what he knew about the arrow, if it had been made on campus, a little bit of the killer's essence would be left behind and trapped in the nooks and crannies of the forge.

The arrow wasn't *made* on this forge. I didn't even know if it had touched it. But I could sense the killer's essence near it.

"Hale, do you leave the forest often like when you went to the movies that night?" Azren asked.

"Yes. I'm a cinephile. I know some of the older movies are on streaming services and the newer ones will get there, but it's different when you see it in the theater. I see new movies I'm interested in and revivals of old ones all the time. The myths did their job. Everyone is too scared to come near Shrieking Woods at night. There are also motion sensors. If you trip one a recording of a banshee wailing plays. It wouldn't scare a god, but it would terrorize a college student into getting the fuck out of Shrieking Woods if I wanted to see a movie."

"Thanks, Hale. We'll be out of your hair now. Gabriel,

grab onto us. We'll get out of the forest the god way so we don't disturb anything."

My dad wrapped his arm around me. I hoped Azren had a theory because I certainly didn't. I also hoped this was enough for the ghosts and the hint with the forge played out a lot quicker than the help they gave Baldur over a hundred years ago.

REN

est was one of those guys who oozed confidence. He wore what he wanted and said what he wanted. One of our friends threw a costume party before we all went off to college and West showed up dressed like Marilyn Monroe for some reason not giving a single fuck what anyone thought.

Oscar and I knew he didn't have a single bisexual bone in his body. West was *very* into girls. I sounded like a broken record asking him if he was sure he was straight because I just kept hoping there was a tiny bit of bisexuality somewhere in that fabulous mane of hair that he'd find and decide he was also into guys. West would make an *amazing* boyfriend, alas, it wasn't meant to be. He was going to treat George like a queen, though.

Still, even with all that swagger and confidence, we needed to talk West up a little. He always joked he wasn't as smart as us, but I didn't think he actually believed that.

West was never going to write peer-reviewed papers on magical theory or cure diseases, but West was *clever*. And as a fox, I had a deep appreciation of that.

I wasn't shocked in the *slightest* it was West that figured out the right question to ask Baldur to figure out if he was the killer. He was also a big, sappy romantic. *Of course,* he saw that arrow and immediately jumped to Cupid and gave Azren a theory to work with.

But we needed to start talking West up because I was really starting to think he wasn't just saying he thought he wasn't as smart as us because he was fishing for compliments. I was pretty sure West actually thought that, or he thought we didn't value his opinions. Which was stupid because West was one of us. And even if his idea was fucking someone's shit up, that's what I was for. Hello? Kitsune.

"You should have said something because you're right," I moaned. "Azren and George don't have the killer's scent."

"I might threaten to bite your ass a lot, but I do actually like you. You're really good for my sister and you're right about this. My twin is powerful and so is Azren, but they don't have the same gifts we do as shifters. My uncle Loki said when gods shapeshift, their senses aren't as strong as ours, so even if Azren had, we'd still have a better read on the killer scent wise. George eventually *will* have the same senses we do as a hellhound and lion but she hasn't learned how to do that yet. We should be there."

I briefly had a brain fart thinking about George's superpowers. Because eventually, she'd figure out how to do the Kitsune thing too and could half shift like me. She would look hot *as fuck* wearing the men's or women's Academy of the Profane Uniform with fox ears and a few tails. Mm. That would be so sexy. I was pretty sure that was a new fantasy.

West just shrugged.

"I know you only threaten to bite my ass because you love me like a brother. Anyway, I *know* we've got super smell. Mine kicked in on my eighteenth birthday when I was in a shitty bar full of sweaty humans who had been playing a sport that *wasn't* dodgeball. I'm pretty sure some of them had religious objections to deodorant and washing their assholes. Sometimes, I want to turn it off. Azren will think of something. They are the smartest person I know."

Just then, George, Azren, and Gabriel appeared. Azren was probably the smartest person *anyone* knew. I had no doubt they figured out whatever they needed to figure out with the forge. I just had this *nagging* feeling in the pit of my gut there was *something* in Shrieking Woods that only the shifters were going to be able to help with.

Azren and George filled us in on what happened in Shrieking Woods and they both had very different theories about the forge, but Baldur had given her a tiny tip about blacksmithing that they both agreed the arrow hadn't been *made* in Shrieking Woods, but the forge was being used for something.

"You've met Hale," Gabriel said. "You've seen his aura. He's said he's not ready to talk about it yet, but the Fae Court had him doing some unspeakable things. Hale was an orphan and rather than giving him a chance to get adopted, they swooped him up and groomed him since he was a child for terrible things. Hale escaped, and he views the forest as his redemption. He doesn't much like people and from what I understand, the Fae Court would really like their asset back. How would a god get into Shrieking Woods and use the forge without spooking Hale? From what I understand, Hale was the kind of asset that had to sneak around in the shadows and would have known if someone was tailing him or been in his space."

This was getting weirder and weirder. Shrieking Woods wasn't being haunted by serial killer banshees, but there was a garden of super rare plants in there under the care of an Unseelie assassin or something. No one really knew. He seemed to suspiciously know a lot about gardening for a spy. I had questions.

"Hale said he was a cinephile. It wouldn't be that hard to watch Shrieking Woods for when he leaves for the movies, portal directly to the forge, do what he needs to do, and use magic to clean up the evidence. Especially if the killer was only using the forge and not actually stepping into the forest. Blacksmithing is a trade you have to learn. You said Hale sends invoices for his tools and I doubt the Fae Court taught him that while they were teaching him whatever they taught him, that made his aura like that. It's quite tainted. I'm shocked he was even hired," Azren said.

"Sorry, but gardening is a skill, too," Oscar said. "Some of us naturally have a better connection with nature than others, but there's only so much you can do with magic. Some of it you actually have to study and learn."

"Oscar is kind of right," George said. "My grandparents have been trying to grow Fogbane on the rocks outside their shop since they bought it. My grandmother has been all over the internet and deep in the bowels of the Library of the Profane and she's never heard the orange juice trick. Where did Hale learn it?"

"Aren't the plants in the Fae realm completely different from ours?" I asked. "I heard they bite."

Me and plants didn't get along. We had a very toxic relationship, and it all came down to me not knowing how to love them. It was a family tradition that everyone got a

Bonsai tree on their thirteenth birthday. We were supposed to care for it until we died and it would bring us Zen. I'm not sure what kind of chaos I introduced in my life, but mine up and died on me before I'd even turned fourteen and I *tried* to take care of it.

My parents gave me a whole-ass lecture when I got the Bonsai on how to care and nurture it and I even got on the internet when it started drooping. That was me growing up knowing about plants in this realm and still killing one. How would an Unseelie who didn't grow up here and wouldn't have even been taught plants back in his realm know a trick with Fogbane no one here knew?

The Shrieking Woods caretaker was super suss, and we needed to get some shifters to sniff him. I was more of a hybrid than a shifter, but my nose worked just fine. I'd smell this bitch, too.

"Like I said, I don't know much about Hale's background since he's not ready to talk about it, but I was in the room when Hale was interviewed since my specialty is Dark Magic. Hale has been here five years and I *do* know all the previous caretakers kept journals. There's a little library in the caretaker's cottage with all kinds of tricks and tips from the previous caretakers. What he didn't know about Earth plants, he could easily learn from those journals. Hale probably picked up the orange juice trick there. He's been here five years and the murders only started last semester."

Damn. That made sense. I didn't know why I was even hating on this guy. I'd never met him. Gabriel wasn't the type to vet someone for this school and give them a job if they were a bad person. I knew the final decision wouldn't have been his, but he would have given his input.

Azren and George had met him, too. They both said he was intense and his aura was seriously bad, but there was a reason for it and he had an alibi during one of the murders that was checked out by the Paranormal Investigation Bureau.

I needed to check myself. Was I just having bad vibes because the guy was Unseelie and used to be a tool of the Fae Court? Yeah, I'd hate myself if I was because I tried not to do that. I didn't even like it when someone hated me because I was Asian.

George's uncle said the arrow was important, and the ghosts said the forge was. No one with knowledge from the Fates or veil said to look at the caretaker. I was just being dramatic and probably racist. Oscar said he loved that I was a little extra most of the time but I usually wasn't racist.

I hoped the ghosts gave us a bit more to go on or a clue that would pay off faster than Baldur's did because we found the forge, but we still didn't know who the killer was and we didn't know why that damned arrow was so important that Drake's entire family got murdered.

DRAKE

I honestly got why Azren left us all behind. They were polite and respectful to everyone until someone gave them a reason not to be and even then, you had to push Azren really hard for them to get nasty. Azren liked to dress like the God of Death, but they only liked people to be scared of them when they gave them a reason to. Plus, Azren practically drilled boundaries and consent into my head when I was younger so I didn't grow up to be an idiot and no one stepped on mine.

Hale only wanted gods in his forest and he hadn't technically given anyone any reason not to respect that. Especially not me. Before Azren and George went out there with Gabriel, George's dad said Hale escaped the Fae realm six years ago and had been working in Shrieking Woods five years. The caretaker was on an entirely different realm when everything went down here with my mom.

Azren and George were right to respect Hale's boundaries. West was right, too. There were things Azren and

George were going to miss because they didn't have a shifter's sense of smell. There were things in Shrieking Woods we were missing out on without having *me* out there with snake senses.

The first semester of the Academy of the Profane had been dedicated to making sure we all knew how to shift. George should have been in *those* classes to figure out that part of her god magic, but it just wasn't possible and we couldn't change the past.

The second semester shifter classes were mostly about using our senses and not losing control. I hadn't grown up with my parents to learn everything about being a Basilisk and I was currently the only one at the Academy of the Profane. You couldn't be a teacher, much less a professor at a college like this, without learning how to teach *all* supernaturals and there had been Basilisks here before me.

I was currently learning all kinds of amazing tricks with just my tongue. I didn't know this and I couldn't really feel it, but I had an additional Jacobson's Organ—just like snakes—in my mouth. I could half shift and bring it out. I could sense all kinds of shit around me with just my tongue and the Jacobson's Organ.

It was cool as fuck. I wasn't at the first crime scene and I hadn't mastered shifting that part of my body at the second. I figured it out shortly before Yule break and Azren helped me figure out how to use it back on the Netherworld. I didn't have any information about the killer from the crime scenes, but I *would* be able to pick out what wasn't supposed to be in that forest.

We *all* had skills that could have been used in Shrieking Woods, but I understood why we weren't there. I didn't think it was remotely fair my mom had to leave the Academy of the Profane before she completed her education, nor the fact that both my parents were murdered later, but I *trusted* fate, even if I didn't trust a lot of witches.

We weren't going to catch the killer in Shrieking Woods. We were going to catch him by doing exactly what George's uncle and cousin said to do at the dodgeball game. I knew Ren felt differently.

We had to get to dodgeball practice now. I was in the locker room changing clothes. Someone had been in my locker, but they didn't break in. There was a golden token sitting on my cleats. If the ghosts were handing these out and people took them with them when they graduated, I was guessing someone was making them. I half wondered if Baldur was doing it because he was so nice and those bitches couldn't even settle his mind by telling him he wasn't a serial killer. I'd *never* say that out loud because I valued my nuts, but I could think it.

I turned the coin over. There was a loom and shears on one side symbolizing the fates. The fates showed up in many cultures and they were weavers in nearly all of them. Azren was sure they existed, but they said no god had ever met them, even though Azren was sure the Fates were the ones creating gods.

The other side of the coin had serpents wrapped around an athame. I *knew* my serpent lore. The other side of the coin was about the Furies. I got what this coin meant just by looking at it. This coin was an amazing opportunity. It wasn't just the speakeasy. This coin could get us all kinds of jobs. There was probably a little bit of fate involved that we were even chosen by the ghosts for a quest.

That could go to anyone's head. The other side of the coin was a warning not to turn into an arrogant fuck when the ghosts gave us an opportunity plenty of students weren't getting. I didn't think any of us would. Out of all of us, only West knew what he wanted to do with the rest of his life. After Azren finished teaching, they could decide to do literally anything.

I hid the coin in my jacket and shut my locker. Zion Skinner didn't give a shit I just got a magical coin from the campus ghosts to get into a secret speakeasy. If I showed up late and told him that, he'd tell me to leave my personal bullshit in the locker room and make me run laps. The entire team would also get a rant about how our generation was a bunch of lazy drunks if I was more concerned about drinking than dodgeball practice.

I had him pegged. Zion Skinner was a giant teddy bear who *loved* our generation. I met Oscar, Michael, and Dexter as we were leaving the locker room.

"You get your token?" I asked and signed for Oscar.

They all nodded.

"What's the protocol?" Oscar asked. "If we talk about this where other people can hear about it, is Bethany going to fly out of the floor to punch us in the dick?"

"She's welcome to try," Dexter laughed. "It's not secret if they ask for them in job interviews."

"No one is allowed to touch you there. That's mine," Michael growled.

"Yes, it is, cupcake," Dexter said, pinching Michael's butt.

I just smiled to myself. There wasn't much Michael could do about it. I was guessing if he did, the ghosts would make Angel Food Cake out of his nuts, too. They seemed to find nothing sacred.

"Just don't brag too loud on the field," I said. "That smells like extra drills."

"Ugh. Don't be distracted either. If Zion suspects we are

thinking about partying instead of dodgeball, he's going to kick our asses," Dexter moaned.

"I'll give you a rub down after."

We joined George on the field and started warming up. Honestly, Dexter and Michael were adorable. They were utterly devoted to each other. Michael would burn the world down for Dexter and Dexter would fuck-up anyone who came for his people. The two of them together might be more dangerous than Azren.

"You get a token?" Oscar asked George.

"Yeah. And we're kidnapping Baldur and going tonight. After everything, we just need to drink and get stupid for one night."

We definitely needed that. We'd been stressing about serial killers, arrows, forges, and I'd been wondering how I was going to feel when I finally saw the man who murdered my parents. We'd normally blow off steam at the moon orgy after the dodgeball game, but we were happily skipping it because that was when we finally caught our guy.

Checking out a top-secret speakeasy run by ghosts was *exactly* what we needed.

GEORGE

Dodgeball practice was brutal now that we were getting closer to our big game. Zion kicked our asses, then told us to go home and shower because our smell was offensive. I knew he really loved us. I had no idea what to expect from the speakeasy, but my dad told me enough that they served food. We were all skipping dinner to eat there.

I had to figure out what to wear first. The guys mostly saw me in my school uniform and dodgeball stuff. It needed to be impressive. Matilda was wearing her favorite pink dress. It had a corseted top and showed her legs off. She looked *amazing* in that dress. Mags had on a skin-tight tailored suit. She put a pink handkerchief in her pocket that matched Matilda's dress. Matilda straightened her hair and Mags had her short hair gelled back. They looked like this insane power couple that was ready to take over the world.

Me? I was standing there in my bra staring into my

closet trying to figure out what to wear. I could conjure something, but what should I make?

"You could wear a paper bag and pantaloons and those guys are still going to think you're hot," Matilda said.

"You're a god and everyone knows it now. If they saw you in a paper bag and pantaloons, everyone would start wearing them," Mags laughed.

"I don't want that kind of responsibility," I groaned. "I just want to look sexy tonight."

"You're going to look totally hot, and you know how I know that?"

"How?"

"Because *I* look totally hot and we are nearly identical."

"Oh, fuck you," I said, flipping my twin off.

"You know you love me," Matilda said, blowing me a kiss.

"I'd love you even more if you helped me pick out an outfit."

Just then, black smoke filled my dorm room. Azren and Baldur were here and fuck me, even *they* looked sexy. Azren was wearing a black button down and a black vest with red stripes over it. They paired it with this amazing long, black skirt and black combat boots. I was pretty sure Azren had dressed Baldur. Baldur was wearing a dark-grey Henley with the sleeves rolled up, which should be illegal because he had amazing forearms from doing all that maintenance work and dark jeans. He had scuffed work boots on his feet.

Fuck me. Was I the only one in my underwear who didn't know what to wear? Baldur might be a sweet, gentle giant, but he definitely wasn't dead anymore. He wasn't shy either, even though I'd made him before. Yeah, Baldur was checking me out. I was really glad my momma taught me to make sure all my underwear was comfortable, but sexy as fuck because this was Baldur's first time seeing me in it. I wasn't really expecting him, and I'd have to leave the entire realm if Azren brought him to my dorm and I was wearing granny panties with holes in them.

"Like what you see?" I asked, tossing my hair over my shoulder.

"Fuck yeah," Baldur growled. "Pity you have to cover it up to go to the speakeasy."

Ooh. I liked growly, horny Baldur.

"So, the ghosts didn't send me on a quest or leave me a note, but they decided to let me into the speakeasy. There was an enchanted coin on my espresso machine where I'd be sure to notice it. I'm guessing they knew I'd be a part of the quest, but it would have been nice to get a note like everyone else. Is it okay if I crash?"

"Dude, yes. This means all my people can be there! I was excited about the tokens but bummed you couldn't come. This is perfect!"

"I'll be pretending like I'm there to hang out with Baldur so no one accuses me of playing favorites. Plus, your dad is keeping our secret because he can. If we're being obvious in public, other students or professors can make a complaint to him and then he's going to have to do something."

"Gotcha. And it's not fair the two of you look *that* hot and I can't even figure out what to wear."

"I'd never presume to tell a woman what to wear, but do you want help, George?" Azren asked.

Azren was like, style goals. Even if they were just lounging around the house, they looked impeccable. They didn't even look messy when they slept in frumpy pajamas because they slept in the nude on silk sheets. Azren had their style completely figured out. I flung my arms out.

"Make me look half as good as you and I'll be happy."

"Hush. You have *much* better legs than me," Azren said, waving their hands.

I walked over to the mirror and gaped at my reflection. Azren captured everything I *wanted* to be in one outfit. It had girly sparkly accents, but it was also a lot of black leather and totally badass. They had me in a black corset with rainbow accents on the front and put this epic cloak over it. The black leather pants also had rainbow accents on the side and I was wearing some pretty tall 'fuck me' boots.

Like underwear, my mom also taught us how to do literally anything in a heel. She said her legs were one of the things our dads loved about her, and we got that from her. A good pair of heels would show them off, but we were supernatural and someone might try to fuck around and find out with us not caring what kind of shoes we were wearing. Matilda and I could ruin someone's day without breaking a heel, so these boots were fucking awesome.

Matilda walked over and hugged me.

"I told you that you were going to look awesome."

"You said it would be because we look alike."

"You're both beautiful, but in completely different ways," Baldur said. "It was weird overhearing people on campus mixing the two of you up and it's not just because you're different races and your eye colors are different."

"We should get going," Azren said. "Go get the guys. Baldur and I will meet you there."

This was one of those things my mom and aunt talked about, but wouldn't give us a huge amount of detail. We knew they got into the speakeasy and some of the stories that went down when they were inside, but those were the only details we got. My mom and my aunt told me about the time someone got drunk and threw up on their history professor, who was this ancient cranky vampire. He bit the shit out of them and then held a grudge until they graduated.

I knew about *that,* but I didn't know what the inside looked like or what kind of drinks ghosts served. I didn't know what kind of entertainment went on inside a secret speakeasy.

I was finally about to find out.

CHURCH

Ah, fuck. We all dressed up and tried to look properly groomed for our first big date with George. All of us had wildly different styles and I just now figured out I was the boring one of the group. I always thought I had decent style, but I looked like a generic, rich vampire compared to everyone else.

I had a dark-grey button down on with the sleeves rolled up and black jeans on. Five minutes ago, I would have said I looked stylish, but then I saw my roommates and Drake knocked on our door. Fuck. I needed to up my game.

Oscar was probably the most responsible out of all of us. He had a fairly good idea of what he wanted to do when he graduated and he had a backup plan if he changed his mind. I mostly only ever saw Oscar in his uniform, dodge-ball clothes, and comfortable clothes to hang out in.

Oscar going clubbing was an entirely different story. He went full punk. His hair was spiked, and he had eyeliner on.

227

Ren also had eyeliner on, but he looked like he literally just walked off a manga that Oscar drew with him as the main character. They both looked insanely hot.

Then there was fucking West. He spent way more time on his hair than he did on what he was wearing because he was West and a lion. West told all of us spending four hundred dollars on new jeans was stupid when he could buy a pair that were already broken in and just as nice at the thrift store. West still bought stylish clothes, he just didn't pay out the ass for them. West was just wearing a black t-shirt and jeans, but he had the whole hair thing going on that I didn't.

Drake looked like a fucking rock star. Did everyone own eyeliner except West and me? Drake looked dangerous and sexy. He looked like his whole body was venomous, played goalie, and he was a damned musical prodigy. I knew George loved me for me, but fuck, that wasn't fair.

We met everyone in the common room. Dexter and Michael were already waiting. Those two were adorable. Michael looked like Dexter's bodyguard and Dexter looked like a pixie about to go to a vampire rave.

Those weren't exactly the same thing as a ghost speakeasy, but the principle was the same. The location was top secret, you had to be invited, and if there wasn't a token, you had to know the password to get in. The vampires generally didn't care if you brought someone like the ghosts seemed to, but they expected you to bring someone cool. If you invited someone to the rave that brought the vibe down or attracted the attention of the cops, you'd never get invited to another one.

I'd been to vampire raves. I knew what to expect. I'd had my nuts punched enough to be terrified of pissing off a ghost at the speakeasy. It honestly hurt like a bitch and hurt my feelings every time Bethany flew out of the floor, shriek-ing, to assault my dick.

I finally had eyes on my girlfriend. Ah, fuck. She looked hot as shit and I felt underdressed and boring. George went around hugging all of us before we left.

"I feel like I dressed wrong for this," I whispered as I squeezed her.

"You can be neurotic with me. I couldn't figure out what to wear, so Azren dressed me. That shirt makes your eyes pop and your ass looks amazing in those pants," she said, pinching my butt.

Yeah, that was enough for me. I didn't need to be extravagant. She told me ages ago she loved my eyes and she once flicked my ass with her fingers after I'd fucked her at a moon orgy and told me I had the butt of a ballet dancer. I didn't know what that meant, but she said her old babysitter was a dancer and her coven was all ballet dancers. George assured me it was a very good thing.

George explained Azren got a token, too, and they'd be meeting us at the speakeasy with Baldur. We walked to Grimsbane Auditorium. It was one of the bigger buildings on campus. There was a door covered by ivy by the back garden. I only knew that because when we got close, the ivy parted to show us the door. You couldn't tell it was there unless the ivy moved.

Oscar and Mags conjured lights as we walked down this dimly lit, narrow staircase. We practically had to walk single file because there wasn't enough room. There was a solid brick wall at the bottom. There was blood magic on the wall. I couldn't sense what spell had been used, but I could smell the blood.

West had gone down first. He pulled his token out.

"Shit, mine didn't come with instruction. Is there a

magic word? I don't have to bleed for this, do I? I'm a very sensitive lion. Maybe someone else can bleed."

West wasn't sensitive. He just liked being dramatic. I literally watched him act like he was going to lose his whole arm over a paper cut.

"Try waving it in front of the door," Mags said. "There's blood magic on the door, but I don't think it wants yours."

"Yeah, but then I'll look like a dumbass and I'm sensitive about that, too."

"Fuck me," Mags growled. "You're lucky you treat George like a queen."

Mags pushed past West and waved the token in front of the wall. This super ornate wooden door magically appeared in the wood. Shit, did we just walk in? I was *not* trying to piss off any more ghosts. Mags took one for the team and knocked.

The door swung open and a massive ghost stuck his head out.

"No need to knock, friends. The token means you can just walk in. I'll be on the other side of the door and I'll know if you've brought someone we didn't invite. I've been told you're VIP. Pearl is going to be taking care of you tonight. She's a sweet girl, but she's special. She might get at least one order wrong. If you make her feel bad about it, I'll haunt you for the rest of the semester.

"When we set up the speakeasy, they taught us how to make the foods they were serving at them. We have no idea what they taste like. Back in our day, lobster was prison food. It's frankly fucking weird it's a delicacy now. We haven't updated the food menu, but we do change the drinks. Pearl will take care of you. And remember, be nice. We're all fond of Pearl. We'll *all* haunt you if you upset Pearl."

Officially consider me Pearl's new best friend. She could fuck-up my orders all night and bring me drinks and food I hated. I'd finish it and pretend I loved it. I'd kiss her spirit ass all fucking night because a ghost haunted my dick once and I had no intention of repeating that.

I finally got a good look at the speakeasy. The lighting was dim, and I was loving the vibes. There was a small stage up at the front and there was a band of ghosts playing instruments and singing. They were all dressed in Puritan garb because that's what they were wearing when they died, but ghosts weren't completely frozen in time if they were stuck here. They could watch and learn as time passed.

These ghosts happened to have a thing for jazz and they were really good. I didn't take the Puritan era for having a single ounce of soul, but the succubus up there at the microphone was killing it. My parents said classical was the only appropriate music for people of our station, but my grandfather really loved jazz and introduced me to it. It was *weird* seeing her up there doing Nina Simone proud dressed like that, but I was digging it.

The VIP section was pretty private. It was a booth off in the corner where we could see the stage and everyone else, but no one could really see us. Azren and Baldur were already there. Damn, they looked good, too.

Pearl came over to take our order. She used to be a werewolf, and she had an intellectual disability. I was a little mad the bouncer thought any of us were going to be mean to her. That shit wasn't cool, even if she was a ghost. Pearl looked embarrassed as fuck.

"We've had so many people in here before and some of them have gone on to become pretty famous. This is the first time we've had *gods* in our speakeasy before!" she squeaked.

Pearl looked absolutely terrified. I had a feeling she'd be scared of literally any god, not just Azren. I knew Azren and George could handle this. Azren just gave her that serene smile they always had.

"Please, treat us like you would anyone else. The only real difference between us and any of the ghosts here is that we aren't dead and we have different magic. Gods trip and fall, get their hearts broken, rip their pants, and make mistakes *all* the time."

"Okay, but sometimes, I get orders mixed up and people get mad about it."

And they got their dicks haunted by the ghost of a massive bear shifter. No thank you. Besides, my fucking parents were the type to berate the server when something was wrong, not me. Azren just shrugged.

"It happens. One time, I hosted an elaborate dinner party and completely forgot that three of the people I invited were allergic to shellfish. Which is actually way worse than you bringing us the wrong order. Someone could have died, and they were probably way less dramatic about it than some of your customers. We'll be fine. Do you have any specials tonight?"

"Yes, actually. The ghosts made something special since that one was coming and he knows who he is now," Pearl said, pointing at Baldur. "We've actually had it and it's been aging in the back. Someone snuck through the veil and found an old Viking recipe for mead to celebrate when Baldur *really* came home. There's enough for everyone at the table.

"Most of the food is new for us. We have lobster canapes, oyster toast, shrimp patties, and deviled eggs. We also have cheese balls if you want something to snack on. It used to be fruit cocktail for dessert, but one of the kitchen ghosts was feeling nostalgic and wanted to make something we'd actually tasted before. She made a cake that ended up more popular than the fruit, so we've been doing that since. I don't know why the lobster is so popular since that's what everyone ate in my time if they were poor or in jail, but the cake is delicious."

"Who is the singer?" I asked. "She's amazing."

"Oh, that's Morgana. She's always loved singing, but there were limited options for women when she was younger. Some rich human had his eyes on her and her parents were terrible people. They sold her off to the human, and he brought her to the New World with the rest of us. He didn't know she was a succubus, but he didn't like the attention she got from other people. He beat her a lot and forbade her from singing.

"If you don't like jazz, please don't say anything. She clicked with it the first time she heard it. Sometimes, people ask her to sing more modern music, but most of us prefer to listen to her sing what she feels."

We all agreed we loved jazz, and that Morgana was fantastic. We gave her our orders. Baldur said he didn't remember drinking mead, but his dad actually told him it was his favorite drink back in the day. I was guessing the ghosts knew that and couldn't be bothered to tell him that when they were giving him hints.

And I wasn't going to say a damned thing because I didn't want my dick haunted again.

BALDUR

I didn't go to the speakeasy much, even though I had a longstanding token. The ghosts were always kind to me, even if they hadn't really given me *any* information. It was some of the students and professors that weren't. This was some secret exclusive club, and they always wanted to know how the maintenance guy with no magic got a token once they realized I wasn't there to fix something.

I got tired of it and honestly, I never really even got much of a buzz from any of the drinks. I could taste that they were strong and not watered down, but they didn't do much to me. This secret barrel of mead was another story. I was pretty sure I was fucked up. George and Azren were, too.

Pearl was terrified of messing up our order and how we would react, but she kept the drinks and food flowing all night. She also was a trove of information about the history of the speakeasy and the ghosts that worked there. Pearl was an amazing waitress, and she took care of us.

Ghosts didn't really want money. They couldn't use it. They charged for the drinks and food only to keep the speakeasy running because it cost money. They didn't work in this speakeasy for free either. Yeah, it was set up because they were getting rowdy, but it was also considered an honor to be picked to work here as a spirit.

The ghosts didn't need to eat or have any need for money, but if they were unable to move to the Aether, they *did* have wants. They took their payments in favors from the living. We couldn't do the rites and get them to the Aether. The people who murdered them were long dead, so we couldn't get revenge for them. Sometimes, they wanted us to stop a student from doing something they were incapable of doing. Other times, they just wanted a message sent to a descendent. Most of the time, they would just alert me if something structurally needed fixing that wasn't visible to the naked eye but would become a problem later.

That mead was delicious and fairly strong. I was pretty sure I was drunk for the first time I could remember. I'd probably been drunk before I died but I didn't exactly know what kind of drunk I was now. Everything was funny. George was the most beautiful thing I'd ever seen and her boyfriends were pretty sexy, too.

Fuck, I was horny.

We all promised Pearl whatever she wanted. She mostly wanted us to stop the bad man and come back to talk to her again. Before we could stumble out, my phone went off. It was Odin telling me he didn't want to cut into my date, but Huginn and Muninn were back at our cabin to give my memories back.

"Ah, fuck," I mumbled. "Muninn is here with my

memories. I'm too drunk for this. I was having such a good time, too."

"I think we're all drunk, but we can heal it out," Azren said.

"No, I think I want to be fucked-up for this."

I really did. I wanted my memories for a very long time, but now that I was about to get them, I just wanted five more minutes not remembering a damned thing about who I was before. I didn't particularly like being powerless and shat on, but I liked who I was. I didn't want to change because I got my memories back.

But I knew I needed to. I needed to face my past. The killer would know my weakness. It was plastered in every history book in this realm and a few fiction books, too. He hadn't killed me yet, but I needed my magic and the knowledge to use it to be able to fight back. Getting mistletoe in me wouldn't be as easy as last time if I had my magic. George could handle herself, but I was fond of her boys, too. I could help protect them.

I also knew I could have *seen* the killer during my blackouts and we needed that information. So, I asked Azren to portal me to the cabin and George would take the others.

I didn't know what I was expecting, but as soon as my feet were settled, a very tiny goth woman dressed in black shrieked and practically tackled me. She was rubbing her face in my shirt and sniffing me. Was this weird or was I just drunk? She pressed something in my hand. When I looked down, it was a random jeweled bobby pin.

"I stole that off Ma'at's nightstand when I heard you were back. We were doing a walkabout in Duat when we got Odin's message."

"Why did you steal a bobby pin?"

"Because I'm a raven, silly. You don't remember, but I

stole trinkets for you all the time when you were a baby. Odin turned them into a mobile and hung it over your bed. It helped you sleep."

"There are some perfectly good reasons for stealing bobby pins," Ren said.

We were in my cabin trying to figure out serial killer stuff and Ren presented me with a woman's necklace. I couldn't see myself wearing it and I didn't know why he gave it to me until George told me Ren only gave stolen goods to people he cared about. I guess Ren had a lot in common with magical ravens.

"I know I need to remember our relationship in addition to a lot of other things. How can I remember?"

"I've known Freya for a while and how she got her memories back. I'm really fond of Baldur and I'm only eighteen, so I don't know if I'm the jealous kind of god. Is there a way to give his memories back *without* kissing him?"

Muninn looked horrified.

"Okay, first of all, Baldur was like an adoptive son to me. That's gross. Secondly, I kissed Freya because I wanted to show her what she was missing when she turned me down back in the day. Lean in, Baldur."

I had to lean down because Muninn was tiny. I didn't really know what was going to happen, but I couldn't predict what Muninn actually did. She tapped my nose like a puppy.

"Boop!" she gleefully yelled.

I was drunk enough to start laughing *that* was how Muninn chose to give my memories back because it was utterly ridiculous. But then my whole body tensed and rose off the floor as all my memories started slamming into my head at once. It hurt like a mother fuck. I was starting to *remember* the stories Odin and Freya told me. I remembered the people they hadn't told me about. Odin told me about my mom, but now I could remember her face and how much she loved me.

It wasn't just the headache either. I could feel my body filling with magic. I used to wonder what it would feel like to have magic. Now, I actually knew. And I could remember how to use it.

I was only twenty-four years old when I died, so I wasn't getting back hundreds of years of memories, but it was still a lot. It seemed to go on forever but in reality, it was over in less than a minute. I collapsed on the floor, dry heaving. Maybe I shouldn't have done this drunk. I *really* hated puking and definitely didn't want to do it in front of all these people I had feelings for.

Because that didn't change. I remembered my wife. I married the first woman I slept with. I wasn't an idiot kid anymore. Looking back now, I could see now that she tried really hard to isolate me from my family and friends. She was one of those people who would love bomb you so you didn't notice they were manipulating you.

My wife never liked it that most of the people in Asgard liked me better than her. If I was having a pleasant conversation with friends and family, she'd insert herself and ruin the moment. When we got home, it was never because she was being unpleasant.

Yeah, even some gods were young and stupid at one point.

But getting my memories and magic didn't change much about who I was today like I feared. I was still older, wiser, and a product of my experiences being reborn without memories and magic.

George wrapped her arms around me and helped me to

the couch. She snuggled into my chest. I *loved* it when she snuggled me.

"How are you feeling?"

Muninn squealed and jumped up and down, clapping.

"I'm *so* glad you have better taste in women this time. I actually like this one. Your ex would *not* be worried about how you are feeling right now. I'm just telling you this because I love you just in case you're thinking about finding her and getting her back."

I could actually remember Muninn now. She was weird, awkward, spoke in riddles if she wasn't being blunt as fuck, and I loved her to death. She had always been like a second mother to me. I lifted my other arm.

"Come here, you. I remember you now."

Muninn squealed and dove into my other side. I wrapped my arm around her. My father had told me how hard he and my mother had taken it when I died, but I knew Muninn would have been devastated. My father created Huginn and Muninn differently than most gods made their creations. They were both more magic and animal than they were person.

"Your magic is back," Odin said, smiling at me.

"So are my memories, Dad. After this, I *need* to see my family again."

"And I'll take you. First things first, whoever is killing witches was manipulating you. It had to have been mental torture wondering if you were doing this. I raised you and I know how you think. This god needs to be punished."

I could *remember* my blackouts now but I didn't know who the god was. I died young, and I hadn't met a lot of gods outside my family.

"I don't know who he is. He's very plain for a god. When I'd see him on campus, it would just be him and a witch. He didn't just make me blackout. He could make me leave and forget I saw him with just his words. And I saw him with his bow. Sometimes, it fires magic. Other times, it fires actual arrows like the one Drake found under the floorboard. I only ever saw it fire real arrows before a murder. When he'd see me and that I was going to try to stop him, he would hit me with one of his magical arrows. He'd tell me to turn around, go home, and go to sleep. I'd wake up in random places by my cabin remembering nothing."

We all looked to Odin and Azren. Those two were the smartest people in the room. Azren might even be smarter than my dad since they were much older.

"That's not possible," Odin said.

"It shouldn't be. A lot of gods have tried to take away free will like that. Some of them tried to program it in when they were making creations and the rest of them tried to do it when they were falling out of fashion with mortals. As far as I know, it's never been done before. They couldn't do it with magic. They had to gaslight the fuck out of people and even then, not everyone fell for it. The fact that we have a very drunk angel and his boyfriend in the room with us is a prime example."

Michael grabbed Dexter and kissed him.

"Lucifer will tell you he regrets nothing."

"The arrow is important," George said. "My Uncle Bjorn stressed that, but I think it's important in more ways than we think. This Erotes can shoot two types of arrows. He shot one that didn't harm Baldur at all and just redirected him. It sent him away. Why does he need the one Drake's mom had and made that wound in the witch's necks if he can control people with magic? Why did he hunt Drake's parents down and murder them to get the arrow back?"

"I actually have nothing. None of this should be possible. I don't think the Fates *wanted* gods to mess with free will. This Erotes is breaking the rules somehow," Azren said.

It actually felt amazing to have my memories and magic because I could *help* now.

"I remember Freya now," I said. "I remember her teaching me Seidr and trying to help me with girls. I have a feeling when she gets back, she's going to be able to tell us *exactly* why that arrow is so important and give us a hint which Erotes it is."

I had a *massive* crush on Freya when I was thirteen, but she let me down easy. The crush turned into a huge amount of respect, even if the romantic feelings left me. She was crafty, brilliant, and powerful.

She could get this information from Aphrodite without losing her as a friend.

GEORGE

Wow. Baldur was hot without his magic. I kept being drawn to him despite his magic missing. But all that Light God magic was sexy as fuck. We all went home to sleep it off since we had to go to class the next day, even if I really wanted to grab Baldur somewhere and have my wicked way with him.

All those people who shat on him or just pretended he hadn't existed before had been talking about him all day now that it was pretty fucking clear he was a god. Baldur decided to just go back to work like usual because he enjoyed working with his hands. *All* of my classes. The only students who weren't trying to hop on his dick were the lesbians.

Belladonna and Church were walking me from one of my vampire classes to my shifter classes. I was crabby as fuck. They all treated him like shit and now they were plotting the best way to throw themselves at him. First of all, even if he wasn't *mine,* history books said he was married. The only people who knew he was divorced were the people who gave a shit about him before he got his magic back.

Paris had mostly left me alone since our duel in magical combat. I think it had finally got through her head that I was a *lot* stronger than her and if I hadn't held back in magical combat, I could have obliterated her. Either that, or she finally realized my dad was the headmaster now and if I didn't fuck her up, he wasn't going to look the other way with her strikes.

A lot of Kaylee's old crowd had distanced themselves from Paris after she carried on that old feud because it had literally destroyed Kaylee and Lindsey. I was guessing they didn't want to get caught in the crossfire of gods and didn't want to go down with them.

But legacy students tended to congregate together and some of them had flocked back to her side. Belladonna stopped to tie her shoe near Paris and her posse. I wasn't *trying* to eavesdrop, but they were kind of loud. Paris had her hair pulled back and I could tell she had been trying potions to fix what Loki did to it. She haughtily tossed her ponytail over her shoulder.

"I *always* thought he was sexy and there was a reason he felt like that. It was probably a test. He was pretending to be like that because he's looking for a wife. I'm going to be that wife. I *need* my own god on my side. Which one do you think he is?"

I snarled and lunged at Paris. She didn't even know his name or what he went through. Paris just wanted him because he was a god and what he could do for her. I had this overwhelming urge to rip her throat out with my teeth. Belladonna and Church caught me and dragged me back.

"Yeah, she's terrible. I want to bite her, too, but you just dropped fang and figured out how to tap into the vampire stuff for the first time. You need to figure that shit out or you're going to take her head clean off by accident and I don't think you want that," Belladonna said.

"You look hot as fuck with fangs," Church grinned.

I touched my teeth. Yup, I definitely had fangs. And I still really wanted to bite Paris and drink her blood. Even though the idea of drinking blood kinda half grossed me out, I really wanted it right now. I could smell it and hear her heart beating.

"Ah, fuck. How do you deal with this shit? I have to get out of here," I said, grabbing them and portalling them outside.

Fangs were fucking weird. I'd just unlocked a new level to the video game that was my magic. This is what I'd been trying to do, but I'd like to turn it off now. Belladonna grabbed me and looked me in the eye.

"Hey, breathe. It's intense when it kicks in the first time. A lot of times, it happens because of an emotion. We don't just turn eighteen and drop fang. We're different from shifters. We don't have some animal screaming inside us to get out. Vampires have blood lust, and something has to trigger it for the first time."

"It's different for energy vampires, but kind of the same. It's an emotion. You have to breathe, calm down, and it will go away."

Yeah, I was trying, but I was just so *mad.* I knew Baldur wouldn't look twice at her; it was just that she thought she deserved him when she didn't even know his name.

"Hey, Paris is an idiot," Belladonna said. "My parents were vampire supremacists, but they thought some of the other famous families were acceptable for what they could do for us. They wanted me to be friends with her. She's a spoiled princess who thinks the world owes her everything, and she doesn't have to work for it. Paris is delusional enough to think she can bat her eyes at a god whose name she doesn't even know and he's going to fall in love with her. Baldur gives off giant teddy bear vibes, and he's totally into you, but something tells me now that he remembers who he is and has his magic back, the big guy might bite a little when entitled shits who treated him like shit before comes sniffing around his cock now that he's got his magic back."

"He's a giant, even for a god," I moaned. "I want him to throw me around the bedroom for a few hours, then snuggle me after. I also want to see him throw Paris through a wall."

Church started rubbing my shoulders. I'd say this for all the guys I'd caught feelings for at the Academy of the Profane. They all knew how to give massages.

"Blood lust makes you want to bite and fuck. Until you learn how to bite, think about fucking."

I immediately pictured Baldur naked hovering over me and ready to ravage me. Yeah, I usually had a fairly decent attention span and could multitask. Blood lust me was a little different. As soon as I pictured Baldur fucking me, I pictured them *all* naked ready to fuck me. And damned if I forgot all about biting Paris and drinking her blood.

As the kinky scene played through my head, the new senses that were bombarding me finally let up and I felt my fangs go away.

"Thanks," I sighed. "How do you deal with that every day?"

"Because it's not always like that, silly," Belladonna said. "That was blood lust. When you aren't in blood lust, it's fucking awesome. You've got amazing senses and super speed. It's totally awesome when you're fucking."

"Noted. The only person allowed to tell me about my twin's sex life is my sister, though."

"Please, I'm not that crass."

"Thank you. That was honestly a lot."

"It gets so much better."

"Now that you did it, can you do it again?" Church asked.

"Well, it was kind of an accident, but maybe?"

"Good. Belladonna and I can teach you from there and catch you up on what you missed last semester in our vampire classes. You'll figure out shifting and eventually get to bang Baldur. When you do, I want to watch because it's probably going to be hot. We'll catch the killer after the dodgeball game and Paris is probably going to flunk out of the Academy of the Profane. This was a good thing."

I grabbed Church and kissed him.

"Seriously, how did you get to be so perfect?"

I'd never had vampire blood lust before, but I had lost control of my god powers before. There were only a handful of people who could talk me down and I was related to all of them. The fact that Church and Belladonna could meant they were my people because this could have gone seriously wrong.

"My girlfriend is pretty special, so I've got goals."

"Excuse me, but I helped," Belladonna said.

I started laughing because I knew *exactly* what Belladonna wanted.

"I'll put in a good word with my sister and Mags, but they're already super into you. I'm pretty sure they are desperately in love with you at this point. My sister doesn't argue with someone she has *that* much in common with cheerleading wise unless she's interested."

I was happy for *both* of my siblings and I liked their people. Mina and Belladonna were really good for Matilda and Mags and I adored Michael and Dexter together. I loved my people, too.

The dodgeball game was in two days. I could fix *everything* by ignoring every instinct and passing the fucking ball.

AZREN

I trusted the Fates, even if they sometimes fucked with me, but I didn't like a damned thing about the vision they sent Bjorn. All this hinged on my competitive, driven girlfriend passing the ball when she *could* have scored and won the game for her team. She'd do what she needed to do because that was George, but she might hesitate.

I still didn't know *how* the killer was doing any of this. I did know George and I were immune to mortal magic, but not the magic of other gods. We didn't just need to catch him. We needed to get his bow away and stop him from talking because he was dangerous to all of us. I *needed* to know what was so important about the arrows.

Thankfully, Freya finally came through the day before the big game. Baldur's cottage was much roomier than mine, so I texted everyone and we met there so Freya could fill us in.

"Okay, so I tried to find out *which* Erotes it was first.

Aphrodite said most of them are still on Earth doing their jobs, even if no one worships them anymore. She said most people didn't pay much attention to them back in their day. Aphrodite added most of them are sensitive kids that just want to spread love. Some of the types of love they represent eventually became illegal and humans started killing people over it.

"They banded their efforts together and started using their arrows on people making the laws to give them a bit more empathy and stop legislating love. She said most of them come back every once in a while because they are all momma's boys.

"There's only two she hasn't seen in a while. Hymenaeus is busy with weddings. Hedylogus always felt underappreciated and hasn't talked to any of his family in a very long time. She has no idea where either of them is, but sometimes, one of the Erotes bumps into their brother at a wedding. No one has seen Hedylogus since he left."

I'd been researching all the Erotes, but I barely even remembered reading about Hedylogus. Was he even mentioned more than as a painting on a vase?

"What is Hedylogus's power?"

I couldn't even remember that, there was so little written about that particular Erotes.

"Sweet talk and flattery. Aphrodite said his brothers never gave him a hard time, but some of the other gods thought it was kind of a lame power. Mortals did, too. They never wrote any legends or stories about him, and he only ended up in a few pieces of art with his siblings. Any time his family tried to assure him that his magic was just as special as anyone else's, Hedylogus would get upset and think they were patronizing him. No one has seen him for a very long time. She didn't *say* he might be a psycho serial killer now, but she seemed uncomfortable talking about him."

I needed to *think, but* I also needed a lot more information to put together all the pieces.

"You're the only one of us who has been to Olympus and met him. He's hunting at a building that has significance to you and as soon as you came back, he's been leaving you his trophies. What happened when you met him in Olympus?" Baldur asked.

Yes. Good question. He was taking the hearts because he was an Erotes. It was all part of the lore. We'd been trying to figure out *why* the Academy of the Profane. Balthazar checked, and he wasn't killing anywhere else. He was sporadically showing up to this college, butchering a few witches, stealing their hearts, and then disappearing.

A *smart* god would have run when they realized I was here looking into the murders. I was pretty sure he had been waiting for Freya. Whether the murders had been to draw her out this entire time, I had a feeling all of this was connected to what happened in Olympus when Freya was looking for her ex.

"Honestly? I don't remember him. When Aphrodite was talking about her kids, I remembered little interactions with all of them except him. Which is strange. We're *all* just vain little monkeys with a lot of power. I remember everyone who gave me pleasure or made me feel good about myself. If I met a god whose power was sweet talk and flattery, I'd *remember* how they made me feel, even if they were just lying to me."

I was starting to get a pretty good idea of what went down in Olympus thousands of years ago and it all boiled down to some really lousy sex I had back when the universe was maybe two weeks old.

"You're forgetting when you were just a baby god and had to figure your shit out. Back when we made the universe and went there with our new vessels, we had to figure out what our magic was. We were also experimenting with sex and trying to figure out who and what we were into until most of them got scared of me.

"Eros is literally the God of Sex. He'd probably show up and threaten to beat my ass if he heard me saying this, but Eros was *terrible* at sex with men and women until he bothered learning to get better at it. We're immune to our own magic. I can't do a damned thing with my own essence. Hedylogus can gift other people the ability to be good at sweet talk and flattery, but he might have been terrible at it when you met him. Like, so bad you completely forgot about him."

"That's surprising because I fucked Eros, too, and that man knows a *lot* of tricks," Freya said. "Aren't our powers just kind of inherent to our personalities? Everyone I've met so far has been like that."

"Hello, I'm not," George said. "I'm stupid awkward. I couldn't even figure out what to wear to the speakeasy and when the vampire part of my mimic powers kicked in, I nearly killed someone."

"George, you know I love you, but you're basically a fetus. You're *supposed* to be awkward and not have your shit figured out yet," Freya said.

Freya wasn't wrong there.

"He could be a late bloomer, especially if some of the other gods tried to make him ashamed of his magic. I can't figure out why you not falling for it thousands of years ago started this attachment. If there had been a scene between you and him, you would have remembered. I *do* know after he left Olympus, he'd managed to figure out how to use his magic in a way that spits in the face of the Fates," I said.

"Explain," Odin said. "Because I don't see how any of this is possible, especially from a god that doesn't have a single story written about him and a lot of his own family didn't think he was that strong."

Odin knew. If he thought really hard about it, he'd figure it out.

"His power is pretty words. You know the saying the pen is mightier than the sword? Words have a *lot* of power. Everything dies unless you write it down. Every dictator who ever came to power feared words and ideas over people because you can't kill an idea. Pretty words have convinced people to die in someone else's war or vote criminals into office. Hedylogus is actually dangerous as fuck if he left Olympus to come to Earth and prove to everyone his powers weren't useless. Because they very much aren't.

"That's why the Fates didn't create more of him in other god families. I think some of us are just to see what will happen. They just fuck around and find out with creating gods and it ends up being this massive mistake. A lot of people end up dying and the rest of us end up having to fix it. If it's Hedylogus and we aren't completely off base about the entire thing, he was given this awesome power he could have done great things with. He chose this."

"Fuck," Odin said, mopping his face with his hands. "He might be even more dangerous than you are. I still don't get what that has to do with Freya. Everyone has always been in love with her. She always lets them down gently unless they are troglodytes who don't ask her directly and come to me instead. I could be a bit of an idiot back then, too, and went the long way around telling them no so the men wouldn't feel bad. Looking back, I should have just let her do it. She was better at it than me and we wouldn't have needed Loki to bail our asses out so many times."

George just shrugged.

"One of those times produced my Uncle Sleipnir, so it wasn't all bad."

Odin fell out laughing.

"If you think that boy wouldn't have shapeshifted and fucked a stallion anyway, you just need to spend more time around him."

I started laughing. It was so fucked up with everything going on, but I'd known Loki as long as Odin had and he wasn't wrong.

"That's actually fair, but I need to concentrate. Freya, did Aphrodite say anything about the arrow?"

"Yes, and all of you *owe* me because she didn't want to talk about it. Usually, I would use a little love magic to soften her up a bit, but since that's *also* her magic, it cancels mine out. I had to do it the long way."

"Freya," I warned. "Don't bullshit us. You lived countless lifetimes as a mortal witch without that kind of magic and you still *always* managed to get what you wanted."

"Bullshit doesn't work on Aphrodite!" she yelled, throwing up her hands. "It doesn't work on me either. You get a really astute bullshit filter when some of your magic is love and beauty and everyone is trying to get into your pants. I got what we needed, but I'm going to need everyone to kiss my ass and tell me I'm pretty for at least two weeks for getting that information without completely imploding my friendship with Aphrodite."

I rolled my eyes. Freya knew damned well she was gorgeous. When Loki and I chose to shapeshift into women, at least parts of us were stolen from Freya. The woman knew this, too. But we all swore to kiss her ass for a bit.

"The Erotes were all born gods. Eros and Aphrodite were companions. He was there for her birth and helped with her children. Eros was the one who helped her kids figure out their magic. Eros and Aphrodite realized all the brothers had domain over feelings.

"Eros was a bit of a trickster. Aphrodite said he liked to crash Dionysus's parties and shoot magical arrows at people and turn it into an orgy. Dionysus wasn't complaining, and neither was anyone at the party. Their magic works by speaking at people, but sometimes Eros wanted to get someone randy in a way they couldn't blame it on another person manipulating them, so he came up with the bow and arrow thing.

"He taught the Erotes this. They were created to do *good* things, but sometimes, they needed to give feelings a little nudge without someone saying another person had been manipulated. The bows are *supposed* to shoot invisible manifestations of their magic with a little bit of their essence at a person. It's not supposed to *harm* them. They won't even notice. It usually just amplifies any feelings they might have."

Except for Hedylogus. He could give someone the ability to find the words they needed to get what they wanted, but he had perverted that into some kind of abomination.

"The arrows take an immense amount of concentration. When Eros was first teaching them, they kept manifesting actual arrows that could hurt someone instead of magical arrows. They can't sense essences like you can, but it became clear the little Erotes kids were missing a part of them trying to figure out the arrows. They brought them to Hephaestus to destroy them and make them whole again. Hephaestus taught them all how to do it when they were old enough just in case they got distracted and accidentally created one away from Olympus. There used to be black-smith forges in every village, so destroying it wouldn't have been hard."

If Hedylogus had been trained to destroy those arrows by Eros, that would explain why he hunted Drake's parents down and murdered them. He hadn't tried that hard to find it outside of murdering them. Hedylogus hadn't gone after her roommate or searched her dorm.

"My parents died over the arrow we have and George's uncle and cousin say it's important. He's not creating them by accident anymore. He's using the magical ones to get *something* from those witches. Hedylogus is getting them alone and their covens are noticing. He's given them poorly planned-out lies the coven sees right through. He wants something from those witches and when he can't get it or *thinks* he's got it, he's manifesting real arrows and murdering them," Drake said.

Drake had a damned good point I hadn't considered. He wasn't just picking independent study witches. Hedylogus was looking for something. He was talking to the witches first because he was trying to find something out. I was fairly certain he'd approached several witches and narrowed it down to a few. He probably spoke to some and only decided to focus on certain witches.

I also knew one other thing for sure. Hedylogus hadn't just figured out how to expand his powers into taking away free will. I was pretty sure he'd mastered shapeshifting, too.

He could literally be anyone on campus.

DRAKE

I was a mess of emotions. I was pretty sure we had the name of the god who killed my parents. How it went down was pissing me off even more. He didn't *have* to manifest an arrow my mom would have found and tried to keep safe. He could have just shot a harmless, invisible arrow and they didn't have to die.

Unless he was intending to shoot something magical, got distracted, and manifested a real arrow. Even then, I didn't give a shit. If he hadn't been on campus in the first place, *none* of this would have happened. I didn't care.

I didn't give a shit if the other gods were mean to him or told him that his magic was shitty. From what it sounded like, his mom and his siblings had his back and tried to support him. He hadn't even gone home to talk to his mom in ages. Ketura was the only mother I knew thanks to this fucker. I called her every day from the Academy of the Profane. She knew about my love life and dodgeball practice. It seemed like Aphrodite loved her kids. He couldn't even be bothered to go visit her because he was too busy killing witches.

But it was time now. It was the night of our first dodgeball game and we were going to catch this fucker. We were going to have to turn the other cheek about a lot of shit to catch this guy and that wasn't the supernatural way. We knew the other team was going to be cheating. They were going to hurt one of our best players. Thing was, we didn't know *who*. We had a lot of people on our team who could be playing pro right now instead of going to college.

Oscar would be playing pro, but he had that accident. I found out Michael had offers, too, but he wanted to go to college. Innis turned down pro offers because he initially planned to go to the school we were playing against to be with his boyfriend, but his boyfriend cheated on him, so he said fuck that and came to the Academy of the Profane. We'd be playing against Innis's ex and he had an axe to grind because he thought Innis should have forgiven him.

Dexter was like the fucking Spanish Inquisition. No one expected him. He looked like a small pixie boy with a green mohawk and pretty wings. The only explanation I had for him moving that fast was pixie magic because it was insane. He was that fast whether he was in the air or using his legs. It was a little unfair to the rest of us.

George was a powerhouse just using witch magic and plain old skills she had practiced in her front yard instead of god magic. I was no slouch on the goal. The rest of our team was pretty amazing, too. We'd been trying to drum up support for our team by posting videos of practice that didn't give away any of our plays. The other teams would have good reason to be afraid of us, but which one of us they would try to take out was anyone's guess. We didn't really have a star player. We were a cohesive unit, and we were *all* vital.

We were dressed and on the field. The stadium was packed. I could see my people in the stands. Ren, Church, and West were sitting with George's massive family. Azren had joined them with Odin, Baldur, and Freya. Ketura knew about the game and she wasn't going to miss it, even if it wasn't on the Netherworld. She'd been to every single one of my dodgeball games and that wasn't going to change now that I was on a different realm. She was here, too.

They were all decked out in shirts with various names on them and holding signs. Except West. West had his naked thing with dodgeball games. He was in his trench coat again with some strategically placed girls sitting around him hoping something was going to happen on the field that blew the trench coat up and gave them a show.

I don't think anyone else on the team knew Zion and the other coach had some kind of feud going on. I don't think any of us that knew about it gave a shit what it was about. Zion Skinner constantly told us we stunk and various other insults, but we knew he gave a shit probably a lot more than some of our other professors. The people who *didn't* know what was at stake with this game wanted to win for Zion.

Zion was about to give us a pep talk before the game and honestly, he could say anything.

"Listen, you little shits smell horrendous and you're going to be even more offensive after the game, but you're all talented as hell at dodgeball and you can win this. And I mean all of you, not just our god and angel. You're all badasses and if you get the slightest bit of ego on my field because I told you that, I'm going to make you run laps until your buttholes fall off.

"They tried to cheat and get George kicked off the team, but it didn't work. That means they are going to bring it onto the field. I know their coach. If they can't win on their own skills, they are going to try to get someone out of the game through injury or they are going to make it seem like one of *you* is doing that, so the referee kicks you out. It's fucking dodgeball, so you have to be doing something pretty extreme to get kicked out of a game. It wouldn't shock me if they attack each other to blame it on us.

"You *will not* stoop to their level. We aren't them. I didn't just pick you for my team because you're good at dodgeball. You all have good heads on your shoulders, even though you are idiot kids who smell terrible. Now, go out there and win this fucking game."

Zion Skinner told us we were morons with offensive body odor because he cared about us. It was how he showed affection. We had him pegged because we were also taking his magical combat class. My group also knew all the things he *didn't* advertise. Like, he fought like hell to keep George on the team because he knew she needed the outlet and not because she was our team witch. He befriended Sol when he was just that guy in maintenance that made everyone uncomfortable.

"Let's win this shit!" Michael roared.

We were dodgeball players, and this was a game. So, even if a lot of us were dating each other, we punched each other on the arm or swatted them on the ass. Except for Michael and Dexter and Innis and his boyfriend. They had a pretty graphic make-out session.

But there was a point to that, too. That was to assert dominance and psych out the other team. Dexter and Innis both had exes on the other team. I didn't know who they were, but I could guess looking at the other team after I'd properly spanked my girlfriend's ass and punched Oscar for good luck. It was two guys who looked like they were going to be gunning for Michael and Cosmo the whole game.

I pulled George and Oscar into a huddle.

"I'm going to be at the goal all game, but keep an eye out for that incubus and the eagle shifter who look pissed off Dexter and Innis are blissfully happy without them."

"They'd better not. No one is allowed to assault my idiot brother but me and Cosmo is like the golden retriever himbo in romance books. He's an amazing dodgeball player and I really like him with Innis."

Everyone loved Cosmo. He was a lion shifter like West. I hadn't really met lion shifters until I came to this realm, but they all seemed to be really easygoing, lovable people. I'm sure they had their assholes like every other group, but the ones I hung out with the most were great. I couldn't do a damned thing to protect Cosmo or anyone else on the field from the goal. I knew no matter what George and Oscar did, someone was going to get hurt.

And I fucking hated it.

I took my place at the home team goal as the rest of the team took their positions. George faced off with the team warlock from the other team who'd tried to recreate her signature move and nearly killed himself because he's an idiot. I didn't like how he was smirking at my girlfriend. Especially since she was about to tame the Air Ball when he got flung halfway across the dodgeball field and his mediocre ass was probably going to go straight for the Earth Ball because it was easiest.

The referee released the balls, and they went zipping onto the field. George immediately tried to do her thing with the Air Ball. Instead of doing his damned job and taming a ball for his team, the warlock tried to send the Fire

Ball flying at her face. Which wasn't technically against the rules, but frowned upon.

And my girlfriend was a complete and utter badass who was much stronger than he was, so she just waved her hair and sent it flying back at him. I laughed like a maniac when he dove out of the way so his eyebrows didn't get burned off and the Earth Ball flew to my side of the field.

He lost a *lot* of time fighting dirty. George and Michael did their thing with the Air Ball and had it tamed while he was still chasing the Earth Ball down. And I totally had him pegged for going for the Earth Ball.

George passed the ball to Innis, who passed it to Cosmo because those two worked really well together. The Fire Ball was a little pissy about getting handled like that so early, so it was trying to take people out on our team *and* theirs. It nearly got Cosmo, so he sent the Air Ball to Dexter. Dexter scored before the other team even had a ball to work with.

It all went downhill from there. It was pretty clear who on our team was hurt. And it was our fault. We put a target on Michael's back when we were trying to keep George on the team. They knew they couldn't take out George, but we practically advertised George and Michael were siblings and George had several moves she couldn't do without him.

Michael was a fucking beast. He was our team captain because he was a good leader with an excellent understanding of dodgeball and teamwork. Michael didn't just have moves with George. He'd perfected several with Dexter in the air and he worked well with the rest of our team.

We could all tell they'd done something to his wings because he'd put them away and was moving like his shoulder hurt a bit. Michael's wings were *always* out unless he was off the Profane grounds where humans might see him. George *could* heal him because I could tell she knew. She kept looking to him to make sure he was okay. I could tell it was killing her knowing her brother was hurt and not being able to do anything about it. George would have snuck in a healing where no one could say she did it, but we had the vision. We had to let Michael's wings stay hurt for the duration of the game or someone might get hurt worse.

Taking our angel's wings away hadn't completely crippled us, but it had taken away a lot of our strongest plays. Michael had to pull out different ones to call where he was grounded. We didn't have a lot of those and he was still in a lot of pain.

We should have been *destroying* this team. They really weren't that good, and that school had a dodgeball team longer than we had. It wasn't just Michael. The rest of my team was trying *really* hard not to get taken out of the game because of an injury because they were playing dirty and the ref wasn't even calling them on it. Dodgeball was a dangerous game and injuries were expected, but this was extreme. I could see it from the goal.

It was the last two minutes of the game. We were behind by two points. We'd have to make a goal from behind a certain line on the field for a three-point shot to win the game. It was possible since George tamed the Air Ball, but we'd either need someone with magic or wings to make the shot since it was too far to throw it.

Fuck! Bjorn's vision was playing out before my eyes. Everyone who knew about it was supposed to stay close to her toward the end of the game, but we weren't counting on how dirty the other team was going to play. The other team's warlock who tried to get her kicked off the team was running at her. I could see where he had a knife tucked in his hand.

I couldn't leave the goal or any point we made wouldn't count. Oscar and Michael couldn't make it to her because the other team had blocked them and Michael couldn't fly right now. Shit! Bjorn said she had to pass the ball, or we'd lose *everything*. He said we could still win the game, but there was literally no one she could pass it to.

Fucking Dexter. No one expected the Spanish Inquisition. I was going to buy that boy whatever the fuck he wanted when we won this game. He went zipping across the field in a shower of glitter.

"Bitch, pass it!" he yelled.

Dexter had the magic to make the shot and win the game. George grinned and passed the ball and then turned to the warlock running at her with the knife. Shit. The look she gave him was scary as fuck. He stopped dead in his tracks and didn't do a damned thing. He *could* have kept going and blamed the momentum, but she was looking at him like she knew about the knife and was going to fuck his shit up if he continued. Their school didn't have gods teaching, so he wouldn't *know* they weren't precognizant and knew everything before we did it. She knew about the knife because her uncle saw the future, but he didn't know that.

Dexter threw the ball. The only thing stopping us from winning at this point was their goalie, but Dexter was a pixie. He had chaos magic *and* control over the elements. He sent the Air Ball at the goalie with a gust of wind and just enough fuckery attached to it that he tripped over his feet when he tried to catch it and the ball sailed into the net.

The stadium was packed with people rooting for us *and* the other team. I *should not* be able to hear West shriek from the field when we won, but here we were. George ran at Dexter and tackled him. I was finally able to leave my goal and joined the puppy pile on top of the pixie who won the game for us.

Zion Skinner was losing his shit. He was usually kind of reserved and grumpy. He was a showboat on the dodgeball field, but he never gloated. Oh, he was gloating now. I watched this man rip his shirt in half and let out a huge bear roar.

"Fuck you, Conrad!" he yelled at the other team's coach, who flipped him off.

Someone was going to have to tell us that story one day. Zion was about to give us this big speech and send us to the locker room.

"Nope," George said. "They played dirty and I know a lot of you are hurt. I know a lot of you didn't ask me to do anything about it because you were worried the other team was going to complain about us having an advantage and try to kick me off the team again. But the game is over now, so I'm healing all of you. Especially you, asshole. How are you supposed to get your stupid feathers everywhere if they mangled them?"

George healed Michael, but wow. More of our team was hurt than I realized. It took George a while to heal everyone. They'd, apparently, broken Michael's wing and a few people had some strains and sprains.

This was it. George passed the ball, we won the game, and that warlock hadn't come at her with the knife. Catching the god that murdered my parents was within my reach. We did what the Fates asked of us.

Something told me none of us were going to be prepared for what happened next.

OSCAR

This wasn't how I liked celebrating dodgeball wins. Ren and I would always go home and have furious sex. Maybe it was fucking weird, but I really liked to bottom when my team won. It certainly wasn't how I wanted to celebrate my first win at the college level when there was going to be a full moon that night and I had my coven now.

But I was part of a coven with responsibilities. Even if there weren't three gods in it, I'd still want to do something about whoever was murdering witches. So, we were all creeping in the bushes at the moon orgy watching the warlock that tried to stab George. No one minded if you snuck a peek when you were there fucking, but if you were fully clothed, hiding in the bushes, and watching? Yeah, that was weird.

I liked yanking Ren's tails because *he* liked it, feeling George between us, and I wondered what it would be like for Baldur to toss me around when he was just Sol in maintenance. Azren was older than the universe, so he could probably do things to me and teach me to do things to George and Ren that might have been outlawed in the Dark Ages. Some of the shit I wanted to do to George after a dodgeball game was probably perverse, but not as perverted as what we were doing right now.

Man, I didn't know what was up with their warlock. He didn't seem bisexual, which didn't have to be a problem at a moon orgy. You just focused on the woman or many women you joined. He was a warlock, so he didn't need an invitation to the moon orgy. His dodgeball team was here with their cheerleaders and a good bit of their students. The Academy of the Profane offered Halliwell Square to them for the moon orgy for comradery.

I had no idea why this dude was going for *our* cheerleaders and students and kept it up when they kept telling him no. He was persona non grata with our cheerleaders after going after George. He probably would have been even if Matilda and Belladonna weren't co-captains. The girls that weren't into dodgeball either wanted to be friends with a god or were into Michael. They kept hoping he'd see someone other than Dexter. *They* knew George was his sister and even if they were jealous of Dexter, they followed him on social media.

Basically, no one was letting that guy anywhere near their vagina after what he did to George.

I didn't know why he kept trying to jump in on our girls when his school was here. You had to be *really* bad at sex to not get laid at the moon orgy. Sometimes, if you had strong magic or good connections, they would just ignore that you couldn't find the clit for what you could do for them. No one in our group was like that, but some people were.

The warlock was furious no one from our school

wanted him to join them, but I wasn't sure why he didn't just join someone from his school. We all started moving when he stomped out of Halliwell Square like a child. There weren't many places he could go. The dining hall wasn't serving food and he couldn't get into the speakeasy. I was guessing he'd run into the same issue if he found anyone at the dorms who hadn't been invited to the moon orgy, but most people were. I think our whole school was out on Halliwell Square fucking.

We all snuck out to follow him. It was dark, so Azren was cloaking us in their smoke. I expected the warlock to go back to their bus. He started heading toward Shrieking Woods. That wasn't right. Even if he didn't go here, these grounds were famous. The Academy of the Profane was one of three magical buildings built on the site of the biggest supernatural massacre in this country. Beatrix Halliwell wanted to reclaim the land because of the ley lines by giving the ghosts a purpose.

Everyone knew that. I grew up in California, but I learned about the massacre, the buildings here, and Beatrix Halliwell in my history classes in high school. I learned about Shrieking Woods then. Some of us at my high school never intended to go to college, but we told ghost stories about the banshee who lived in Shrieking Woods and killed anyone who set foot in there to scare the shit out of each other at sleepovers.

I didn't know where this guy went to high school, but he would have learned about the history of Profane. He probably had one fucked-up teacher who told his class about the banshee to get them to behave. Supernaturals didn't like dealing with ghosts. They started out mostly annoying with the haunting but eventually, they figured their shit out. They learned how to move stuff and punch vampires in the dick. The adults used to *love* terrorizing us with ghosts.

This guy *shouldn't* be headed toward Shrieking Woods. We were all signing so shifter ears didn't pick us up. I was a little surprised that everyone close to me thus far knew sign language except Church and he had picked it up pretty quickly. Odin and Freya knew it and they gave that knowledge to Baldur. Azren signed to grab onto them. They took us to the edge of Shrieking Woods where the warlock was heading.

A tall, thin Unseelie stepped out. I felt George's hand tighten on mine. She knew him. I was guessing it was Hale, the caretaker, since I'd never seen him before. He could have been from their school, but he wouldn't have known about Shrieking Woods. It was an Unseelie and not a god this whole time?

I saw him conjure an ornate golden bow. Baldur had his magic back and remembered how to use it now. He waved his hand and stole Hale's bow from him. His eyes turned to where we were. West didn't sign for me when he spoke. West *never* did that. He signed everything.

I had no idea what Hale said, but everyone came stumbling out of the bushes. Azren shoved me behind them. I had no idea what was going on. I could see a flash of light. I peered around Azren's shoulder and could see where Hale had turned into the god in the photo Drake's mom took. I could see he was talking, but no one was signing for me.

I couldn't read lips yet. I might never be good at that. I didn't know what he was saying, but my party had several powerful supernaturals and multiple gods and they were all powerless around him. He couldn't do a damned thing to me because I couldn't hear him but my magic also wasn't going to stop a fucking god.

Azren was supposed to be our ace. They were the god everyone feared. But they were right. You couldn't kill words or ideas. If this was Hedylogus, that was their magic. Before Azren was too far gone, I saw them summon the arrow we found behind their back. They shoved it at me and then grabbed me.

The next thing I knew, I was standing behind Hedylogus. What the fuck was I supposed to do now? I might be immune to him because I was deaf, but he was a god and I was a Brujo. I was a powerful supernatural, but I wasn't a god. My magic would bounce off of him. Church couldn't bite George unless she let him.

I was so coming back and haunting Azren when this was over. They sent me right behind this fucking evil god with just an arrow he'd already murdered Drake's parents over. I was *definitely* figuring out the dick punching thing. Maybe Bethany would teach me.

Hedylogus was so focused on the others, he didn't notice me until I felt myself step on a stick. He whirled around. I didn't think, I just reacted. All I had was an arrow and a giant will to live. I just stabbed with the arrow. I had no idea if it was going to do a damned thing, but it sank into his chest straight into his heart.

His aura started flickering and his skin started turning a pale color. Fuck, did I just kill a god? Did Azren know that arrow was his weakness when they gave it to me and shot me over here like a human sacrifice? I was still thinking about dick punching Azren.

But *fuck*. I was pretty sure I just killed a god.

GEORGE

Mother fuck. That was intense. My family came out for the dodgeball game. Like, my entire family. My mom and aunt got my siblings and cousins home but some of my dads and uncles were here. We had a *lot* of gods and some pretty powerful supernaturals and we were all powerless against Hedylogus when he started talking.

I heard the warlock who was supposed to try to stab me demand money from Hale, who was just Hedylogus shapeshifted this entire time. He conjured his bow to kill the warlock probably and then Baldur took his bow. As soon as he ordered us out of the bushes, I lost complete control over my body. It was so fucked-up.

No one had ever been able to control me before unless I let them. It was the same for all of us because free will was a thing. It was like Hedylogus sapped all of it away from us. As soon as we heard his voice, we couldn't do anything except what he told us to. We couldn't even sign for Oscar, so he had no idea what was going on.

I was furious when I realized Hale had been Hedylogus the entire time. My dad had vetted him and the Paranormal Investigation Bureau checked out his alibi and cleared him. Hedylogus had been doing this longer than my dad had been alive. He learned about the caretaker job, figured out shapeshifting, and then applied for the job with a story about the Unseelie that would explain his aura.

He probably killed as he pleased and no one ever suspected him. I already knew how he beat his alibi. He drove to the movie theatre, bought his ticket, made sure he got picked up on all the CCTV cameras and then probably went into the bathroom and portalled back to the Academy of the Profane to commit his murder. Hedylogus could clean up and portal himself back to the theatre before the movie was over, and let himself be seen on camera leaving.

Fuck. How had none of us realized that when we were in Shrieking Woods talking to him? The ghosts literally told us find the forge. We did. The killer had been staying near it the entire time.

And he was a total fuckhead that seemed obsessed with Freya. He ordered us to come toward him and then stop. We all had no choice but to obey him. I was fighting with everything I had. I could mimic his magic, but I didn't have the skill to wield it like he did. And he basically told us all to shut the fuck up because that idiot warlock who tried to get me kicked off the dodgeball team was bitching about money, so even if I wanted to use his magic against him, I couldn't talk.

"Do you know how long I've been waiting for you, Freya? You disrespected me once, but you've been hiding in mortals for a very long time. I kept trying to figure out which one was you so I could have the satisfaction of cutting your heart out. I always thought I had the timing right when I got here and a powerless god without his memories would show up. I always figured you two knew each other, and he was looking for you. I killed every potential witch I thought you were hiding in. Tell me, did I ever get it right?"

What the fuck? *No one* knew about that. The only people that knew were Azren and Freya for the longest time. My Uncle Loki and Sleipnir kind of outed her as Minerva Krauss because she'd make the same perfume she made back then and they knew it. The perfume was literally the only reason my uncles even guessed. Hedylogus couldn't have known that.

And Freya was used to men throwing themselves at her. All the drama in Asgard where my Uncle Loki had to swoop in and save the day happened because Freya wasn't allowed to speak for herself. Even Odin acknowledged that recently. When Freya was Minerva, she sat Matilda and I *both* down and said sometimes, men were big babies who didn't handle rejection well. Even if we were stronger than they were, to always let them down so that we *both* came out looking good so he didn't hold a grudge. Someone didn't need to be able to overpower you to hurt you.

Freya could have hated this man and everything he stood for. He never would have known it. Hedylogus would have gone on his merry way neither upset, nor angry that Freya didn't want to be with him. He would accept that was just how it was. Matilda and I didn't exactly take her lessons to heart. We were both insanely bad at it if someone got gross when they propositioned us.

None of us could talk because he told us to shut up. Freya didn't even remember this dude and no one us could ask what went down that he started butchering witches hoping one of them was her. I think a lot of us would like to know how he even knew Freya was going to be walking this earth in a mortal body he could easily kill.

And then Azren sent my sweet baby Oscar right behind Hedylogus. Oscar was immune to his magic because he was deaf, but there were countless other ways he could be killed. Oscar was my rock. He was the guy who had a new page of a manga he was writing—where I was this badass superhero—for me every morning at breakfast. Oscar was probably the *only* guy I was in love with who might try to talk me out of it if I had this super crazy idea. Church would probably think it was insane, but he was the kind of guy who wasn't going to tell me what to do because I knew my mind best. Ren was a Kitsune, so if I wanted to fuck shit up, he at least wanted to watch. West was my ride or die. If I wanted to burn the world down, he was going to hold my hair back while I did it. Baldur had the whole God of Light thing going on, so maybe he might be a good influence. Azren was friends with my dad. They would just tell me to have fun and try not to get caught.

Azren had better have a *very* good reason to send my very breakable Brujo behind the god that had us all rooted to the spot and unable to speak with just his words. Because I didn't know what I'd do if Oscar got hurt. I might very well raze this realm to the ground.

Oscar stepped on a stick. I could hear it and there wasn't a fucking thing I could do about it when Hedylogus whirled around. He was obsessed with Freya. He wasn't interested in me before because he knew who my dad was and I wasn't her. I guess he had been trying to kill me to hurt her since he still didn't know her weakness but he thought he had mine. He'd been watching the dodgeball practices as Hale, but I guess he hadn't figured out it was Oscar we were all signing for. He probably just didn't care to find out.

"Stay still and shut up!" Hedylogus roared at Oscar.

I still hadn't figured out how his magic worked or how to use it, but he figured out it wasn't working on Oscar. I tried to scream when he went to grab Oscar and I couldn't even do that. I *couldn't* watch him die. Oscar was a powerful Brujo, but he wasn't a god. And this was the kind of god who went on a killing spree because Freya didn't want to fuck him. He was probably going to go fucking insane that he spent all this time perfecting his magic to defy the Fates and it didn't work on one deaf Brujo.

But then I figured out what Azren did. I was still mad about it because I was sure this was another one of their theories like when they handed me their scythe and hoped I didn't explode. Oscar whipped Hedylogus's lost arrow from behind his back and stabbed him in the chest with it.

Fuck me. Drake got the *real* answer why Hedylogus murdered his parents over that arrow. Aphrodite wasn't completely honest with Freya, but I got why. Freya wasn't honest with her either and those were her kids. God weaknesses seemed to be pretty fucked-up. Baldur's was a harmless plant that actually had a lot of medicinal properties. It could be used to heal a lot of shifter ailments, but it was fatal to Baldur.

Eros taught the Erotes to spread their magic like he did, but if they did it wrong, it also created their weakness. Hedylogus was kind of a dumbass. He was creating his own weakness because he thought he was hurting Freya more. Hedylogus could have done it with his words because he was doing it to us now. He created a physical arrow and shot them in the neck to get them to lie there while he cut out their hearts because it would hurt more.

I was guessing the arrow Drake's mom found happened by accident. Someone saw him and distracted him. I'm sure he thought if he butchered Drake's parents, the location of the arrow would die with them and even if anyone found it, they wouldn't connect it with him.

Big mistake. I kind of loved the look on his face when he grabbed the arrow and sank to his knees as his aura flickered while he died. It was the look of some guy who thought he was more powerful than death, but just got his ass beat by a mortal, deaf Brujo. I actually loved that for him.

Oscar was losing his shit and Hedylogus's hold on us was gone.

"Holy fuck, did I just kill a god?" Oscar shrieked. "Is his god family going to get mad about it and come seek vengeance?"

Ren and I ran as fast as we could and sandwiched Oscar between us. I *never* wanted to see my boyfriend in that kind of danger again. West found us and wrapped all three of us in a bear hug before stepping away. He grinned at Oscar.

"I *told* you the first day we met being deaf wasn't a weakness. You literally just kicked the God of Gaslighting's ass because he couldn't use his mojo on you."

Azren fell out laughing.

"He's not the God of Gaslighting, but that fits. And you aren't wrong. Oscar was the only one of us who could have beaten him. Bethany? If the ghosts want their revenge, now is the time to do it because I have questions."

Oh, fuck. Azren had been teaching me their power, but I'd never seen them go full God of Death before. I'd seen their scythe before. It was pretty massive and ornate and for some reason, I didn't look nearly as sexy and badass as they did when they held it. One thing about Azren is that they literally knew how to dress for every occasion.

They could have conjured a hooded cloak for this and we all would have got it, but that was a little boring for Azren. Azren looked like they were about to walk a runway in Milan just to teach history. Azren was *not* going to reap Hedylogus in just a cloak. No, Azren conjured this black leather ensemble and topped it off with a long, black-leather trench coat.

I had a feeling Hedylogus was about to spend a lot of time in one of Azren's jars in their safe back on their realm, but not until he answered some questions. And Azren brought out all the academy ghosts to hold him down. The ghosts were *pissed*. They weren't just supposed to help run the academy and the speakeasy. They threw tantrums and did things like repeatedly punch my boyfriend in the dick, but they were also here to protect us and make sure we graduated as functioning adults.

Magic didn't work when you were dead and that applied to ghosts, too. Ghosts didn't learn to do the fun stuff like work in the speakeasy and punch harmless vampires in the nuts until they'd been dead a while and could practice. So, yeah, Hedylogus might have been one of the most dangerous creatures when he was alive because of how he abused his powers, but he wasn't shit as a ghost.

The ghosts had him pinned down while they beat the ever-living fuck out of him. Yeah, Bethany had a weird kink about punching people in the dick, but I wasn't mad about it if it wasn't a dick I planned on using. Hedylogus had it coming.

Ooh, and he had an ego about it. He was doing the whole 'unhand me, you cretins' thing while the campus ghosts just wailed on him.

"That's enough. I have questions and then I'll get rid of him," Azren said.

Bethany straightened up and smoothed out her dress. Usually, she was the picture of a perfectly groomed Puritan, but she got a little messed up this time.

"Do you see now why we couldn't help you so until the Fates got involved?" Bethany asked. "His power is an abomination, and he's petty. We tried to get involved the first time he showed up, and he threatened to hunt down all of our descendants and wipe our lines off this realm. He'd do it. He can make gods his puppets. We left hints until the stars were aligned just right for his downfall. I know we frustrated you, but if you had acted before tonight, it would have been a disaster."

"You didn't *have* to haunt my dick when I got frustrated about it," Church sulked.

Bethany huffed and kicked Hedylogus for good measure. At least she wasn't kicking Church again.

"Yes, I did. We might not be your professors, but we aren't sending you out into the world as spoiled children who think you can be rude because you didn't get your way."

Church looked like he was going to argue, but Azren had this God of Death thing going on that was both sexy and scary, so when they held up their hand, we all shut the fuck up. Azren leaned down and got right up in Hedylogus's face.

"I know Freya better than you ever will. She only would

have disrespected you if *you* were an ass to her. We figured out an Erotes was doing this, and she remembered meeting you all when she was looking for her husband. She would have remembered having a bad experience with a god in Olympus. Especially one she'd just met and wasn't *expecting* to have a shitty experience with. So, you're going to tell the class why you *think* you were disrespected and that set you off on this whole nonsense of butchering inno-cent witches," Azren purred.

"Seriously," Freya said. "I met a lot of gods when I was looking for my husband. There were several I knew to avoid when I went to certain realms because I knew they weren't going to take no for an answer and shit was going to go down. I didn't have that experience in Olympus. It was pleasant. Aphrodite showed me around, I met several gods, realized my husband wasn't there, and left. And you *shouldn't* have known anything about me being on this realm as a mortal. No one knew about that."

"I have nothing to say to you," Hedylogus sneered.

West bounded over.

"Come on, dude. Your power is words. You worked *really* hard at that. Like, *we* all hate you, but props to the superpowers, even if you found the worst ways to abuse them. You *know* you wanna villain monologue. Every bad guy wants to do the villain monologue. Give us that tragic backstory. I doubt it's going to turn into *that* kind of romance book, but you pissed off the God of Death and you might want a little sympathy from them."

Hedylogus just scowled at West, but West wasn't my only chaotic boyfriend. Ren decided to jump into the fray. The *only* time I wanted to get double teamed by West and Ren was sexually. They might not be gods or been immune to him when he was alive like Oscar was, but I had no doubt they could get his ghost villain monologuing in no time.

"I *knew* there was a reason we should have gone into Shrieking Woods with Azren and George. You could shapeshift into an Unseelie and explain away your aura with a tragic backstory about the Fae Court, but you can't hide your scent from shifters. All that time making yourself that powerful and butchering all those witches and you got killed by *my* boyfriend. Suck on that, little bitch. Thousands of years old and all that fucking power and you handled rejection like some twenty-year-old human incel."

"Fuck you!" Hedylogus roared. "It's not that simple!"

"Girl, tell us how it is because this is all kinds of fucked-up," Ren said.

"I met Freya when she was in Olympus. She was one of the few gods outside of the family who met me, found out my power, and *didn't* make fun of me. Freya was sweet to me. We had a connection. My brothers left Olympus to spread love, but I left to prove those assholes wrong. Some of them were bullies. If you haven't met them, then you've probably read about them.

"I figured out shapeshifting and mostly traveled around trying to figure my magic out. I didn't want to go home until I was strong enough to make them *all* pay. I was shapeshifted in Europe hundreds of years ago. I was trying to drink at a pub and mind my own business. The gods had mostly left this realm at that point. I hadn't run into one in a very long time.

"I saw a flash of golden aura in the alley and peeked my head out. I saw Freya and another god I hadn't met yet shapeshift and come into the pub. I walked over to say hi. I told you who I was, and *you didn't remember me*. I tried to remind you and tell you about the connection we had and the fucking God of Death said I was making you uncomfortable and I should leave. I wasn't rude. You *both* disrespected me.

"So, I went into the alley and shapeshifted again. Everyone in that pub was so unimportant to the two of you that you didn't even notice me take the table right next to you. I overheard *everything* about your little plot to be mortal because of the massacre in the New World.

"Of course, I didn't think there was much I could do about it if I wanted revenge for how you both dismissed me like that. We can't sniff each other out when we're shapeshifted, so there was no way in Tartarus I could figure out who you were going to be as a witch.

"And then you made it *so* easy. News of a gifted spirit witch who tamed *that* many ghosts and set up a legacy that big reached me where I was living. The *only* way a mortal could have come up with that idea was if they had been inspired by a god. I *knew* it was you and that you'd be back. I just had no way of knowing when.

"I snuck around and eventually learned about the caretaker in Shrieking Woods. I'd hang around trying to figure out if you were there right under my nose while pretending to be the caretaker. Then, the broken god would show up. I figured you two knew each other, and he was seeking you out, even if he can't remember shit.

"That was when I started hunting. I wasn't indiscriminate about it. I gathered information on the witches and compared it to what I knew about Beatrix Halliwell and when we met. If I didn't *think* they were you, I left them alone. I only killed them if I was ninety percent sure. It was a fuck you to *both* of you for how you treated me."

I didn't say anything because there wasn't much for *me* to say. I wasn't alive then, but Hedylogus was probably one of the most toxic gods I'd ever heard about. Yeah, there were others with egos that big and some of them had stories and legends attached to them about punishing mortals. *Most* of them hadn't. They had their creations spread all these stories they did for fear and adoration. The rare few that started getting shitty with mortals were probably all in little jars somewhere in the Netherworld.

None of us spoke. We all just looked to Azren and Freya. Most of my dads were here and so were Odin and Baldur. They weren't commenting either. I knew Freya and Azren had their own version of what went down in that pub and it was probably quite reasonable. Even if it wasn't, it was no excuse for what he did. Matilda and I told guys they were being creepy and to go away all the time. We weren't disrespecting them. We were telling them the truth, and they needed to hear it.

"You fucking idiot," Freya snarled. "You never *once* killed me. The only reason Baldur showed up when you did was because he was being drawn to the closest god to seek help. He didn't even know that's what he was doing. You butchered a bunch of innocent witches because you approached me over two thousand years after we met, wearing an entirely different face and aura and expected me to recognize you."

Azren was absolutely dripping with disdain, which was saying something because I'd watched them handle Kaylee, Lindsey, and Paris with an utterly serene resting bitch face.

"No one was disrespecting you, you turnip. You were getting agitated and causing a scene in a pub full of humans when it was popular to burn witches *and* heretics. Those humans think there is only one god. They weren't going to have a come to Jesus moment if some random guy in a pub was ranting about how he and two other people were gods.

"They would try to arrest all three of us as heretics. If we used *any* kind of magic around them or showed our strength, they were going to get hysterical with the Satanic Panic again and there probably would have been just as big of a massacre as there was on these grounds. I don't have that much experience with gods when they are infants and if their little skulls are the same as mortal babies, but I'm half wondering if you got dropped on your head as a kid."

"Fuck you," Hedylogus spat. "I know what happens when gods die. It's not like the one who came back defective and cleaned toilets. I'll be back with my memories and magic in no time. The chances of you getting your hands on one of my arrows again are pretty slim and I overpowered you once. I could do whatever I want to *all* of you when I'm back."

Azren let out this low, dangerous chuckle.

"I usually hate it when people form opinions about me without getting to know me first, but in this case, I'm a little offended my reputation doesn't proceed me. Have you heard about my secret room in the Netherworld, Hedylogus? See, your superpower is words, but my domain is death. That means I have control over essences.

"If you hadn't immobilized me, I would have ripped yours from your vessel. I had a theory about your arrow and the real reason it was so important they be destroyed. It paid off and you're dead. See, if you want to go to the Aether and be reborn, I'm the only one who can take you there. Or, I can put your essence in this little jar that I'm going to hide away in my realm with the other gods I've put in time out. It's up to me when you get let out and allowed to play with the living again. I really like a jar for you."

Hedylogus was finally starting to realize what his giant *fuck you* to Freya and Death was about to cost him. I was pretty sure he figured he could overpower both of them and they'd never figure out his weakness. I'm pretty sure Hedylogus thought Azren and their god timeout were stories gods told their kids to get them to behave like my mom did with ghosts. He was starting to look a little panicked that if he wanted to get reborn and get a vessel again, that was all up to the fabulous god in the trench coat and scythe he just pissed off.

"No, wait—"

"You bore me," Azren said, pointing their scythe at Hedylogus's ghost.

"Remind me not to piss you off," Ren said as Hedylogus's shrieking ghost got sucked into their jar.

Azren popped a cork in the bottle and tossed their hair over their shoulder. I should probably not find them sexy as fuck right now, but Oscar and Azren were both sexy as fuck right now.

My dads surrounded me and crushed me into a group hug.

"Maybe for the rest of college, you stick to classes, moon orgies, and winning dodgeball games instead of catching serial killers," Dad said.

"Ah, fuck, can we *please* go back to dodgeball and moon orgies?" West moaned. "I nearly shit myself when Azren sent Oscar at the killer."

"I should hit you in the face again because you didn't know for sure that was his weakness," I growled at Azren.

Freya started giggling.

"I think Azren likes it when you do that. Seriously, did he go on this whole elaborate killing spree because I didn't remember his name, he was shapeshifted when he approached me again, and Azren tried to stop him from making a scene that probably would have started another witch hunt?"

"A man who thinks he's the most powerful person in the universe going on a killing spree because a woman and her nonbinary friend tells him to calm down?" Matilda snorted.

"Ah, fuck," Freya sighed.

"He only met you twice," Baldur said. "I grew up around you. If you had wanted to disrespect him, you would have enunciated it like a fucking lady and would have done it in such a way that even if *you* didn't remember it, Azren certainly would have."

"It's true," Azren said. "I barely remembered there was another god at the pub because it was such a small interaction. I came back from getting us drinks and thought it was a werewolf talking to you. I didn't even get his name, just that he was a god and kept insisting you knew him, and you had a connection. I told him to calm down, stop making a scene, and leave because the pub was crawling with humans. He left, and I thought that was it. Clearly not."

"Um, I am not okay," Oscar said. "Everyone stopped signing when he froze everyone and then I got portalled behind a god with literally *no* instructions. My whole-ass life flashed before me when he came at me and it was just instinct I stabbed with the only pointy thing I had since my magic wouldn't work. I'm only eighteen. I'd like to win the college dodgeball championships, see what it's like to get fucked by Death and my girlfriend at the same time, and I've wanted Baldur to throw me around since I thought he was Sol in maintenance. I could have *not* gotten to experience any of that because I got unalived by a fucking stupid powerful Cupid. Ren is usually balls deep in my ass after I win a dodgeball game. I can't handle this shit. Am I being dramatic?"

Ren waggled his eyebrows at Oscar.

"I could still be balls deep in your ass while you're balls deep in our girlfriend. It's still a moon orgy. Ah, fuck. Please don't smite, curse, bite, or eat me," Ren said when he realized my dads were *right there.*

My dad just laughed.

"She's a god. It's what we do. I'm not going to kink shame my own kid. The killer is dead, and we have our own moon orgy to attend. You all played a brilliant dodgeball game. Props to the pixie for making the winning shot. Have fun at the moon orgy, kids."

My dad portalled everyone back to the library. Yeah, it was still pretty early. It was barely midnight. We could all go have fun at the moon orgy. I could *finally* have my wicked way with Baldur and Ren and Oscar could make their kinky fantasies with him come true.

But not all of us. If Azren was going to stay and teach history now that the killer was caught, they couldn't participate with us. Azren loved teaching, and we had a thing. They could very well want to stay. I *wanted* them to stay instead of going back to the Netherworld.

"I know you aren't *supposed* to fuck inside during a moon orgy, but I'm not doing a moon orgy without Azren," I said.

I was pretty firm on this. I was a *big* fan of moon orgies now that I was eighteen and could go to one, but I loved Azren. I didn't like that I had to pretend I didn't have feelings for them in class, but I wasn't excluding them from orgies when there were workarounds.

Azren looked a little surprised, like they expected me to go off with the others and sneak back to them like I cared about them less. I grabbed Azren and pulled them down for a kiss.

"Don't look so shocked. You're just as much a part of this as the people my age. You, too, Baldur. I'm pretty sure Oscar and Ren want to play with you, too, but Church, West, and Drake are very straight. When we're *all* playing together, that means you, too, even if it means we have to use your cabin."

Azren chuckled.

"You want three gods playing with mortals in a wooden cabin? Especially when two of those mortals have been quite clear they'd like to be thrown around by a god of Baldur's size? The cabin wouldn't be left standing."

"Promise?" Ren whined.

"I don't want to fuck either of you. I only want George," Church said. "That said, I think it would be sexy to *watch* the two of you pleasure her. You're part of our group and should be a part of this. No one gets excluded."

"Stop being a dickhead," Drake said. "The Netherworld is on the same lunar cycle, so all the reapers are fucking under the full moon, too. You aren't alone anymore. You've got George and you've got us. Some of us don't want to fuck you, but others do. Take us to the Netherworld. You're supposed to be smarter than all of us."

Drake was grinning, and that was just Drake. I knew he was actually happy for Azren and trying to give them a solution.

"You're actually right, even if you were rude as always," Azren said, flicking Drake's forehead with his finger. "The gardens around my house are pretty vast, so if *everyone* would like to come to the Netherworld, you could have some privacy. My gardens are pretty romantic, too."

"They really are," I said. "You'd love them."

Matilda and Michael both wanted to see the Nether-world. They probably would have jumped at the chance even if Azren wasn't offering their private gardens for a moon orgy. I think everyone wanted to go. It wasn't often any god let you see their realm. Everyone knew what an honor this was.

And I was finally getting *all* of my men at a moon orgy. Two of them were gods. I might not be able to walk straight tomorrow and I was so looking forward to that.

BALDUR

We were seriously all going to need to decompress and process everything later. For some of us, Hedylogus was just a guy killing witches. For others, it was much deeper than that. I'd known Freya a long time, and I knew enough about Azren that I knew they'd be stressing about how they could have handled things differently in that pub so things would turn out differently. Even though they hadn't done a damned thing wrong. Anyone I knew who wasn't insane would have handled it like that.

Then, there was Drake and me. Hedylogus hurt me for much longer, but what he did to Drake was worse. I found out why I kept getting drawn to the Academy of the Profane. I was being drawn to the closest god to help me figure out how to get my memories and magic back. Hedylogus not only didn't help me, but he made it such a bad experience that when I was feeling the pull because there were gods in Profane that *could* actually help me and one that would recognize me, I ignored it for years.

He made me think it was me killing those witches for a very long time and I was the one that always had to clean the blood so the students didn't see it. So, that was an extra mind fuck. I hadn't even figured out what I was feeling when I finally saw his true face, much less how I was feeling now.

Still, I could process that later. I remembered everything about being a god. We had orgies, but not full moon orgies. I died young, so I'd never been to an orgy before. I also remembered everything about being reborn with no memories and powers. I'd had sex with humans, but never supernaturals. When I was around supernaturals, they never invited me to their moon orgies.

So, here I was, at my first orgy ever with someone I felt this insane connection to. Not only that, I was getting to do it in this beautiful garden in the Netherworld. I wasn't stupid. Most of the god families had their realms. A few individual gods made one for just them and their creations. It was considered poor taste to go to another realm without an invitation or you didn't know someone there. Realms like Hell and the Netherworld were locked unless someone let you in.

I didn't know how to get into Hell, but the Netherworld was smack in the middle of the Veil. You couldn't get there unless you were with a Reaper or Azren who could traverse it. Getting to the Netherworld was wild, but now that we were here, it was gorgeous. It was different than Asgard, but similar in a lot of ways.

Matilda wandered off with her girlfriends. I really liked Michael and Dexter together. They were adorable. Michael just picked Dexter up like a caveman, threw him over his shoulder, and went marching off into the gardens to find a place to be together. I smiled to myself as I watched them go. I didn't know a lot about angels or their magic, but I'd seen Michael in his classes and on the dodgeball field. He was insanely powerful and that tiny pixie with the green mohawk could bring him to his knees.

But now we were alone and George Bell very much looked like she wanted to eat me alive. I knew how to please a woman. My family took various aspects of my education differently. My brother Thor decided to take over my sex education because he said he didn't want me to embarrass myself.

Loki liked fucking with Thor, so when he came across Thor explaining orgasms to me, he lied to him that Freya was thinking about doing another orgy with the dwarves for trinkets because my brother lost his mind about that the first time. I was fourteen at the time and fairly mortified when Loki sat me down and told me to take sex advice from someone who could shapeshift and had actually had sex as a woman rather than my idiot brother.

Yeah, even though I remembered everything now, my feelings on forgiving Loki hadn't changed. I remembered all kinds of conversations like that when I was younger where Loki helped me.

I knew *how* to please George, but I was a little nervous about this because I'd never actually done this with an audience before. I always wondered what it would be like to attend a moon orgy when I didn't know who I was. Now I did, and it was happening. I barely knew what to do with that now.

And my new girlfriend was very different from my wife in *many* ways. She was much nicer and less manipulative. And rather feral when she was horny. She conjured a pile of blankets and pillows and just body tackled me like we were on the dodgeball field. I laughed and fell back with her so I'd cushion our fall. We weren't even naked yet, and she was already the most aggressive woman I'd ever been with.

And I loved that about her. There were things inherent about me because I was a God of Light and grew up surrounded by a loving, supportive family that didn't try to make me something I wasn't. Still, I could be aggressive, too, sometimes. I held back a lot when I was reborn because of my size. Fuck. It had been a very long time since I'd had sex at all and even longer since I'd had it how I liked it.

I grabbed her, flipped her on her back, and pinned her down with my body.

"Did you seriously just tackle me like we're playing dodgeball?"

Ah, this one definitely wasn't like my wife or anyone else I was with after. George wasn't afraid of me because I was so big and she wasn't going to lie there like it was a chore. No, this one just bit me and then snapped her fingers, so we were both naked.

"I regret nothing," she said. "Also, you look much better naked and on top of me."

I chuckled and kissed her. George was going to be a handful. So were some of her other boyfriends. Especially the two who propositioned me the very first time we met. They'd joined us on the blanket and were furiously making out and watching us at the same time. Fuck. Okay, that was hot and not weird at all. I didn't mind any of them watching. Maybe I was a bit of an exhibitionist after all.

I spent a while exploring George's body. She was a god, but all that dodgeball practice made her body even more divine. I desperately wanted to see what it tasted like when she came on my tongue. I kissed lower until I had exactly what I wanted and then I devoured her. She was so responsive. George was grinding against my tongue and crying out. And they were all watching us. I *loved* that they were watching us. I was watching George, but sometimes, I'd look over to Oscar and Ren.

"Touch her," I said to them.

This was my first moon orgy. I wanted the full experience. Oscar and Ren scrambled over to please her, too. They were touching and kissing her, but Ren moved like he wanted to touch me also.

"Uh, is that okay? You aren't going to smite me or anything?"

I chuckled. I didn't experiment with men back in Asgard, but I did when I didn't know who I was. I enjoyed men, but my preference was women. I could see myself enjoying their touch when we were all pleasing her and being good friends with them, but George would always be the center of my world.

"It's completely fine," I said, going back to licking George's pussy.

Oscar was kissing her and nibbling on her breasts. Ren decided he was going to take me in his mouth. He gasped when he saw me.

"Holy shit. Is that legal?"

"Is it big?" George whimpered.

"Girl, you are going to have a *good* time with that."

"Is it bigger than mine?" West asked. "You're blocking the view, asshole."

"Yeah, that's not straight, West," Ren called out.

"Comparing dicks is totally straight as long as you don't put it in your mouth after."

I'm sorry. I knew I was supposed to be concentrating on George, but I fell out laughing. I had Ren and West pegged long before we got to this moon orgy. West was a *very* secure straight lion. Ren knew that and kept poking at him because I think Ren kept hoping West would change his mind.

"Excuse me, mister, but I think you were in the middle of something before my other boyfriends distracted you."

I chuckled and went back to work. I groaned when I felt Ren's mouth around my cock. I fully concentrated on George because I didn't want to cum in Ren's mouth. I wanted that to happen in George. So, I devoured her until she came on my tongue while Ren sucked my cock. Her cries were muffled by Oscar's kisses.

I sat back on my heels. I wasn't going to presume to guess how she wanted us and this was my first moon orgy, so I asked. She actually blushed and looked a little shy after everything that just happened which was adorable.

"So, I have this idea, but it's only going to work if Baldur doesn't mind doing a little bottom action."

Ren snorted.

"Girl, sit up and *look* at his cock. The only guys who are going to let Baldur top them are size queens who are going to want to take pictures of his dick for bragging rights."

Ah, fuck. Now everyone was looking at my cock. And Ren wasn't wrong. The few times I was with men, I was either the bottom or I was with the guy Ren described perfectly because I *wasn't* a small man.

"Ah, shit. That's huge. And I can be a size queen," George said.

"Girl, me, too," Oscar said. "I don't want photos, but I'd try it at least once."

Now I was the one blushing, so I just told George to tell me what she wanted.

"So, like, I want Oscar in my ass, Baldur in my pussy, and Ren in Baldur's ass."

Ah, fuck. That was hot as hell and I'd never done that before. I was *totally* on board with this. We were a tangle of bodies as Oscar and Ren prepped us. I hadn't had magic in so long. I'd gotten used to not having it, but I needed to *remember* I could do certain things now, so I conjured lube. And I'd been powerless and without memories longer than I'd been fully a god, so I kind of got tickled when I did it.

George was absolutely *stunning* as she slid down Oscar's cock. When she was situated, I leaned over to guide myself in her. Oh, I intended to take her hard, but she needed to get used to me first. George moaned as I eased in and out of her.

"Fuck. Ren is right. Is your dick legal? That feels amazing."

"I'm just feeling it from back here, but damn," Oscar growled.

"Uh, thanks?" I grumbled.

My ex-wife usually just laid there. The humans I'd been with seemed to like how I fucked them, but not before I was fully seated inside them. I'd honestly never gotten this many compliments at once. It was nice. It felt even better when I was fully inside George. She was tight as fuck with Oscar in her ass. I stayed totally still until Ren was fully in mine.

It was intense as fuck and felt amazing. I finally realized what I was missing marrying young and never getting invited to one of these before because I forgot who I was. And then it just got even more intense when we all started moving. George was tight and wet. I loved how she felt around my cock. But I could also feel Oscar fucking her ass through the thin wall that separated us.

Ren knew *exactly* what he was doing behind me. I was trying to hold back because this wasn't just me and her. She could have it rough with all her boyfriends except Azren and me. We could actually hurt her.

But I should have known my girlfriend wasn't a delicate flower. She was the daughter of Chaos and she loved playing probably the most dangerous and violent sport in the universe. George also had *no* problem telling me what she wanted.

"It's the full moon, and we just won our first dodgeball game. Don't you *dare* hold back on me!"

"If she gets mad enough, she'll punch her god boyfriends," Azren chuckled. "Don't let the fact that she's on the smaller side for a god fool you. George has been playing dodgeball since she could walk and it fucking hurts. You should fuck her how she wants to be fucked. You'll enjoy it."

Yeah, I would. And she knew more about what she wanted than I did. So, I gave it to her. So did Oscar. And Ren was feeding off our energy and fucking my ass just how I liked it. And frankly, we were all feeding off the full moon. There were two moons in the Netherworld, so we were extra feral.

I was nearly losing my mind and trying to hold back waiting for George. It was hard because Ren was hitting that spot just right. When I made a little noise and he realized he found it, he just kept going. I had zero complaints.

When George came, she clamped down on my dick hard just as that cheeky Kitsune spanked my ass. He'd clearly gotten bold after worrying I was going to smite him. The *only* person I'd ever met who was bigger than me was my brother, Thor, so no one had ever spanked me before. I was pretty sure I was into it because when his hand connected with my ass as George came all over my cock, I had an explosive orgasm.

Fuck. I think we all went off, and it was pretty intense. If I was going to go again, I needed time to recover. I *knew* George intended to, so we all just snuggled while we calmed down.

I *liked* this. I had my family back in Asgard but I was always meant to go off and make my own. I'd found it now. We were *all* going to have to deal with the aftermath of Hedylogus and we could do that when the moon went back to sleep.

Most of the hard stuff was over. There would still be shit thrown our way, but hopefully not like this. Hedylogus couldn't hurt anyone anymore. We could all just focus on each other and healing.

GEORGE

I might be a god with all the blessings that came with that, but sometimes, I got sore muscles if I played a hard dodgeball game. I was *definitely* going to be walking funny tomorrow because all my guys were good at sex but I guess when I looked at Baldur and saw the biggest man I'd ever met, I didn't quite think his cock was going to be *that* big. That man was blessed.

I knew this was his first moon orgy, and I didn't know if he wanted our first time together to be just us, so that's what I was planning on doing. But then Baldur invited Oscar and Ren and it was just perfect. Baldur was spooning me and since he was a fucking giant, I felt cocooned and safe. Oscar had his head resting on my other shoulder and Ren had draped himself across all of us. His three tails kept flicking. I'd been slowly picking up on reading his tail body language. That meant he was content. Especially since Oscar was stroking his tails.

"You were all amazing," I purred.

"Wow," Baldur chuckled. "I've been missing out."

Baldur told me about his past after he got his memories back and we had five minutes to just hang out. He was sixteen when he met his ex-wife and she was older than he was. Even though that kind of thing wasn't frowned upon then and teenage marriage was common. Odin and Frigg desperately tried to talk Baldur out of getting married at eighteen. Everyone did, but he thought he was in love. Baldur said now that he was older, he could see how she manipulated him because she thought sharing his light would make her equally loved. The man had never had an orgy before this.

"Oh, we're going to do this again. And I'm going to kidnap you and ravage you alone, too. I'll probably steal you and invite Azren, too so I can see what it's like to be in the middle of a god sandwich. I can't explain why I keep getting drawn to you, but you're one of us now and you're *mine*. If your ex comes sniffing around here wanting your light back, we're going to have some god-on-god violence. My whole family taught me how to fight and my idiot big brother is an angel. I will fuck her shit up. That goes for *anyone* sniffing around any of you."

I meant it. I guess I *was* a jealous and possessive god. I was still kind of figuring that shit out and I meant it. I wasn't going to tell West not to watch our dodgeball games wearing nothing but a trench coat because my momma was a witch and I was raised with a certain level of superstition. I knew if he said teams lost if he wasn't free balling it, he was probably right. That didn't mean I wanted people peeking.

"You're cute when you're jealous," Church said, winking at me.

"It'd be kind of hot if my girlfriend fucked someone up for looking at me," West said.

"It really is," Drake said.

"You don't have to worry about that with me," Azren said. "Most people are terrified of me."

Church started giggling.

"The bisexual vampires in my classes have been discussing their student teacher God of Death fantasies in a room full of other vampires with good hearing."

"Shifters, too," Drake laughed. "The only reason George didn't beat the shit out of Innis and Cosmo when they were talking about their kinky God of Death fantasies is that she really likes them. They both have big opinions on cheating, so anything they do is going to be with the other's knowledge and if George told them you were hers, they'd immediately back off."

"After high fiving her and asking for all the details because that's the kind of guys Innis and Cosmo are," Oscar said.

I was pretty sure Innis and Cosmo knew. I kind of let out a feral growl when I heard them fantasizing about Azren. They apologized and never did it again. But yeah, Azren seemed a little shocked all these students found them sexy and were fantasizing about them.

Azren was the *only* one who was shocked. Azren was gorgeous, androgynous, and looked like a fucking model. They were constantly perfectly groomed and well-dressed. Azren was brilliant as fuck and they had that whole danger thing going on. I knew some of the other gods and mortals shit on Azren, but that wasn't us.

Ren snorted.

"You'd have to be completely dead from the waist down

to *not* fantasize about Azren. Like, West keeps saying he's totally straight, but I'll bet even West thinks about it."

West flipped Ren off.

"I fantasize about Azren ravaging our girlfriend, but even I will admit they are insanely pretty. We could all watch if you'd get off of her."

"We just had a foursome with *two* gods, West," Oscar pointed out.

"I think I'm ready to proceed," I said, kissing Baldur, Oscar, and Ren.

The rest of my guys grinned at me. I crooked a finger at Azren.

"You heard West. He has a fantasy we need to bring to life."

Azren just cocked a perfectly groomed eyebrow at West.

"I'm down for a little performance. Do you have any requests?"

West looked like a giant child who had just gotten a pony for Yule. Did Azren know what they were doing unleashing West on my vagina?

"So, like, I've been thinking about George sucking you off while Church is behind her fucking her with vampire speed, but you use that black smoke for sexual shit. Can you pinch her nipples and play with her clit with it?"

I moaned because Azren most definitely could. I just didn't talk about them behind their back. I knew we'd eventually get to this place, and we'd all learn about our strengths and weaknesses together. That was how relationships worked.

"I actually can. And I'd be honored to share our girlfriend with Church if he agrees. I know George is already naked because she wanted to play with Baldur, Oscar, and Ren first, but I do love unwrapping our girlfriend when she's dressed. It's sexual as fuck. I'm not going to make her get dressed so I can do that, though."

"I'm down for that," Church grinned.

"Then you'd both better get over here," I said.

Church and Azren pounced. They were *both* dangerous. A lot of my guys were. The other gods feared Azren and supernaturals feared energy vampires and Basilisks so much, that they were nearly extinct. Some of them felt that way about Brujos, too. Azren, Church, Drake, and Oscar could do a lot of damage *if they wanted*. They didn't.

Then, I had Ren, Baldur and West as their opposites. Baldur was literally a God of Light and West was the most easy-going person I'd ever met. Honestly, I wasn't *super* shocked I ended up with a Kitsune. My dad was the God of Chaos and my uncle was a trickster. Of course, I was going to be drawn to Ren.

I was happy Hedylogus was chilling in a jar in Azren's safe and couldn't hurt anyone anymore. I could focus on college, my guys, and actually figuring out how my mimic powers worked. I had been doing witchcraft for as long as I could remember, but I didn't *know* that. The vampire thing happened by accident around two vampires because I was pissed. I needed to figure my shit out.

But it was the full moon, and we'd just won our first college dodgeball game. I was going to *thoroughly* fuck my guys. Church and Azren were an interesting pairing. Church was my intense stalker, and he very much fucked that way. Azren was older than the universe. I had no idea why Baldur stayed dead for so long, but I imagine if anyone found out Azren's weakness, the Fates would boot their ass out of the Aether five minutes later because of what their job was. I was pretty sure Azren knew that too, so Azren fucked like they had all the time in the world.

West had never seen Azren in action, but West noticed everything. He wouldn't have known for sure what Azren's smoke could do, but I was guessing West had a pretty good idea how Azren was in bed and that they would have learned that. West was the boyfriend who noticed my drink was getting low before I did and if I got the slightest bit cranky when the situation didn't call for it, he would ask when was the last time I ate. He usually noticed I was hungry before I did.

I'm sure I would have eventually done this with Church and Azren because I planned to have a *lot* of sex with these men. I knew West had some spectacularly *bad* ideas before he ended up doing community service at a deaf school and found his calling. He'd been brilliant since then in helping us catch Hedylogus and West was hyper attuned to my needs and the needs of his friends. It's why he was so amazing as a sign language interpreter and as a boyfriend.

West didn't just suggest this because he thought it would be kinky to watch. I mean, he *did,* but West probably thought the two of them together was going to be pleasurable for me, but Church and Azren were going to get something extra out of it, too. My lion was plotting, and I loved him for it.

I also wasn't complaining *at all* about what Azren and Church were doing. Azren might enjoy undressing *me,* but I was already naked, so they disappeared everyone's clothes. We were all kissing and touching. Church was still super intense and kept teasing me with his fangs, but since Azren was acting like we had all the time in the world, so did Church.

And I needed that right now because my last foursome was a little intense. Church had been super into me before I even knew who he was. He was utterly devoted to me and always treated me like a god before he even knew I was one. We had a blip when he found out the truth, but it was only because he thought he was going to lose me. I assured him that wasn't the case and things were back to how they were when we first met.

Church loved to worship my body, but Azren did, too. Since Church was an energy vampire and I had absolutely no problem with him feeding off me, he'd sometimes get excited and frenzied because he was feeding off how I felt. I loved it when he did that, but he was feeding off Azren now, too. I didn't think he could help it since we were both gods.

Azren might be the God of Death, but I didn't get why so many gods were afraid of them. Azren's aura was insanely pleasant to be around. I'd watched people poke Azren in class because they were idiots and Azren never rose to it. I'd watched Azren get frustrated and angry, but they never once felt bad to be around because of those emotions. Azren was steady, like a rock. They weren't just teaching me magic. They kept me grounded.

So, Church was getting my chaotic energy because this felt fucking good and Azren's calming aura. I kind of had this thought it might overload his circuits, but I'd also never met an energy vampire before Church. I could feel the magic radiating off Church as we powered him up with just our emotions from touching each other.

Church was returning the favor by treating me like I was his queen. So was Azren. I had a lot of opinions about people kissing my ass just because I was a god. My guys treated me this way because they loved me. Azren and Church were nipping and kissing all over my body while telling me how totally perfect I was. Yeah, I needed that right now.

I was touching them and telling them the *exact* same

thing because I knew they needed to hear it, too. Azren had been walking this universe since they were created, thinking another god would never love them. If Church had *any* doubts I loved him and I considered myself part of his hive, I fully expressed my love for him through words and touch.

Church sat back on his heels and groaned.

"Sorry, I'm trying to only catch George's emotions and I've had longer than everyone else here to figure out my magic, but you're both insanely potent. I'm going to ruin this threesome and the blanket like it's my first time having sex if we keep doing this. Which is going to be stupid embarrassing because you're *both* gods and I might have to talk Bethany into dick punching West a bit for thinking I could do this. I think that's some weird Puritan kink she carried over with her when she died."

West gasped.

"You leave my dick alone, you monster! The first time I had sex with George, you were there. Aside from a kinky shower when I thought her dodgeball sweat was blessed, you've been there *every time* I've had sex with George. I believe in you, Sparky," West said, throwing Church two thumbs up.

Church just flipped him off, so I grabbed him and kissed him. Azren chuckled.

"Church, don't be embarrassed. George loves what you do to her. Every single god, whether we were created or born or a big, bad primordial, has some horrifying stories about figuring sex out. None of us had the internet and for a long time no one knew how to make parchment. There weren't exactly manuals we could read. Not everyone had parents either. Sometimes, the Aether just shot out a bunch of fully grown gods that knew what they needed to, but not everything.

"George loves what you do to her and you got the seal of approval from West, who doesn't have a single bisexual bone in his body, but watched you long enough to hatch this fantasy in his head. I've never seen you fuck before but I *have* had sex with vampires and I know what you *could* do to her. Let's bring West's kinky fantasy to life."

West blew a raspberry at Ren.

"I'll be watching them spit roast our girlfriend as straightly as possible."

Ren flipped him off, but Church got the pep talk he needed to proceed. I got Church because I got Belladonna, too. Their parents were awful and just wanted to use them. If Church hadn't run away, he'd probably be in the same situation Belladonna was where his hive wasn't people he really connected with, but were handpicked by his father. Church had time with his grandfather, but he needed certain reassurances that this was real and no one was going to take it from him.

Which I would always be happy to do.

Church was one of those guys who heard what they needed and immediately snapped out of whatever funk they were in. Church was totally back in the game. They all knew I was a fickle creature by now. Sometimes, I wanted to be kissed, petted, and cherished. Other times, I really didn't want to be the most powerful person in the room and wanted them to *respectfully* manhandle me a bit.

Church and West were the first guys I'd slept with here and Church stalked me long before that. Church knew damned well what I wanted now that he and Azren treated me like a total queen. He just picked me up, placed me on all fours, and then spanked my ass. I let out a moan because

I *loved* it when they did that and wanted to explore it a bit more when we had the room and privacy the Academy of the Profane didn't really afford us.

Azren was practically purring as they looked down at me on all fours with Church behind me. I might have heard them growl once, but Azren was probably just as feline as West was.

"Fuck, you're beautiful like that," Azren said in a low voice.

"I'd look much prettier with your cock in my mouth."

"Such a smart little mouth on a young god. I love that you have no problem using it on me."

I let out a little growl because Church was already inside me. I was just waiting for Azren to join the party.

"Gimme. I get cranky when I'm mad."

"And slightly violent toward your boyfriends who can handle a face punch from a god." Azren chuckled.

But Azren gave me exactly what I wanted and slid their cock between my lips. Church started thrusting, and this was *just* what I wanted. Church let me get used to him and slowly sped up until he was using his vampire speed. When he did that, it was like the Fates or the gods finally gave women what they really wanted—men with vibrating cocks. Because seriously, someone should have got on that by now. Nosferatu created vampires way before batteries existed, but I was going to thank him for that if I ever met him.

Azren was fucking my mouth, but they finally let their smoke come out to play when Church reached maximum velocity. Azren had a lot more control over their black smoke than I did with my purple smoke. I'd mostly only managed to keep it small so I could portal without raising suspicions.

This motherfucker was massaging my clit and pinching my nipples with it. I knew what blood lust felt like now. I knew it was slightly different for Church because he was an energy vampire but I could tell he was keyed up and right in the middle of it. I could hear his growls and snarls.

Dating an energy vampire had *huge* perks. I understood Church could abuse his powers and his dad tried to make him into that person, but Church was his own man. He used his. Magic to soothe people for the most part, but there was one trick that was reserved just for me.

Church could tell when I was closed from my emotions. He'd get himself right there with me and that's when he'd bite. Azren had apparently been with enough vampires before they met me that they knew this, too. Azren was fucking my mouth and playing with my clit and nipples with their smoke.

When Church flung himself over my back to bite my shoulder, Azren pinched both with their smoke and I utterly fucking lost it. Church might be a different kind of vampire, but his fangs still had venom he could use to cause pain or pleasure. And holy fuck, between Azren and Church, it was a lot. We *all* needed to be thanking West for this.

Azren grunted and spilled down my throat as I felt Church go off. My whole body was quaking. Moon orgies were about connecting and celebrating the full moon. There were always a ton of different sensations, depending on how many people were in your group and how ambitious you were. I'd just had an amazing experience with two different groups of men, but it also felt very different, even if the end result was the same.

I was exhausted and a little sore, but after I'd gotten proper snuggles from Azren and Church and caught my breath, I had plans for West and Drake.

WEST

That was utterly divine to watch. Hopefully, that cemented any of my boyfriends-in-law knocking my orgy playbook again. Because that shit was gold. I *loved* dodgeball. I breathed dodgeball during the season. I had a ton of rituals before a dodgeball game. I was a terrible dodgeball player, so no one was ever going to pay me to coach dodgeball and write dodgeball playbooks.

But like, I was *really* good at pleasing women. My pops might have barely graduated high school, but he made a decent living anyway and nabbed himself several lionesses. My pops and my moms made damned sure I wasn't going to be some selfish asshole when I met my mate.

Yeah, I wrote *really* good orgy playbooks, but I probably watched her just as much as Church did so I could always know what she wanted before she did. I just wasn't creeping in trees to do it. *I* didn't want to have sex with Church, but I'd named him Dildo Face from our first moon orgy because the boy could turn himself into a vibrator with his vampire speed.

And I didn't know for *sure* Azren could get kinky with their smoke, but I had a pretty good idea. Azren was older than the universe and they enjoyed figuring out the mysteries of how shit worked. I had Azren pegged. They'd figured out the kinky stuff, too. Like, I had to learn how to give women orgasms from books and experimenting. This motherfucker just shapeshifted into a woman and took out all that guesswork.

Which like, props to that because there were a lot of dudes that weren't even trying to be good at sex and Azren might have fucked some of them during that particular phase of their experimentations.

So, basically, I figured if Azren had figured out a bunch of god stuff the other gods didn't know and learned all the mysteries of women's bodies by becoming one for a little while, they'd probably figured out how to pinch our girl-friend's nipples with that portal smoke. I'd been wrong about a ton of shit in my life but I tried not to shriek for joy when I was not only right about that, Azren had used their smoke on her before and she *loved* it.

I didn't particularly like watching porn. Some of the guys I used to hang out with did. She would be screaming and crying in pleasure and the men weren't doing anything to deserve those cries. I found the whole thing fake and didn't enjoy it.

But I *loved* watching my girlfriend have sex with the other guys because I knew they were doing it right and she enjoyed it. George was stunning even when she was crabby because she didn't have her morning latte yet. She was fierce covered in dirt, sweat, and blood on the dodge-ball field. I also loved her with that blush on her breasts while she was getting railed by one of her other boyfriends.

George just reading her notes and studying was also the most fascinating thing I'd ever seen, but I'd never tell anyone that because I gave Church a hard time about that shit.

George finally stirred and beckoned Drake and me to her. I tried not to look like some kind of eager puppy running to her because I was a lion. A lot of people used us as symbols for royalty and some of my smaller brethren were revered as gods during certain time periods. They still were because *everyone* loved cat memes.

Fuck it. I'd been in love with this girl since Zion Skinner told me to spar with her in magical combat on the first day of class and she managed to zap my ass with magic. I didn't care if I looked overeager. Baby Drake, who learned his resting bitch face from Azren, the queen of resting bitch face, did the eager puppy thing when she asked for us.

I'd already trotted out a page from my orgy playbook. I'd had sex with George several times and knew how enjoyable it was. I wasn't planning these groupings for *us*. I was working my big, beautiful lion brain, planning all the ways we could please *her*.

But I also wasn't the orgy dictator. No one liked it if someone tried to Bogart the foursomes and order everyone around. And I wasn't *about* to tell a woman what to do. My mommas would have had big opinions on that. I *suggested* that page out of my playbook because she asked and let her decide if she wanted to do it.

"How do you want us?" I asked.

"*I* want you to hold her down again while I do things to her," Drake growled.

"Fuck, Baby Drake."

Yeah, Drake was kind of intense. And he grew up around the big, scary god I'd just watched suck the essence of another big, scary god into a little jar like one of his powers was being a sentient God Roomba. Drake wasn't scared to call Azren a dumbass to their face and totally dominate our girlfriend. I was pretty sure George liked getting held down while he bit and licked her a *lot* more than Azren liked being called a dumbass, but I wasn't going to kink shame Azren if that was a thing.

"You know how much I *love* it when you do that, but I want to try something, too. It's something I haven't done yet. I want you *both* to take my pussy at the same time."

Fuck. My mouth went dry. I hadn't done that before either. The lion in me got a little exuberant and pounced on our girlfriend. I hauled her into my lap and held her down for Drake. I had no idea if Drake kept roping me into holding George down while he ravaged her because he knew damned well felines like to play with the prey, but I loved everything about it.

Yeah, she struggled just right as Drake tortured her with his fangs and forked tongue and I kept her pinned down so he could do exactly what he wanted to her. I was fully aware our girlfriend could stop this at any time and beat both our asses if Drake crossed a line and I was his coconspirator. But so far, we hadn't met George's line when it came to sex.

I think we all had our reasons for liking the fact that George was this badass god. I was fairly certain at least one of Drake's reasons had something to do with the fact that if he had been doing *any* of the shit he liked to do naked with anyone other than another Basilisk or god, they would have been in agonizing pain. Yeah, Drake was just as much of a biter as Church was.

I was helping Drake out by growling in her ear what a good little girl she was because I was a good boyfriend like that. I had to strain to keep holding her when her back arched after she came all over Drake's tongue and fingers. That was a big one, and she'd already had several big orgasms tonight.

Drake was a lot more demanding than I'd ever be. Like, she'd had a foursome, a threesome, and that whole thing with his snakey tongue, so I probably would have engaged in the snuggle time before we double dicked her. Drake plucked her out of my arms and laid her on the blankets. My girlfriend was pretty vocal about her needs, so if she needed a break, she would have told us.

Drake settled in front of her and I took my spot behind her. George lifted her leg for us to support and give us access. The reason all the boyfriends-in-law worked was because we *communicated* in all things. If we needed to cheer our woman up, we discussed how. If our girlfriend wanted us both in her pussy, we didn't both try to shove it in at once. Because if your girlfriend was a god, you only wanted to destroy her vagina in ways she liked because her revenge would be epic. And if she wasn't, it was just fucking rude.

Drake told me to go first, so I did. Fuck. She was even hotter and wetter than usual because Baldur and Church had already been there. I groaned and nuzzled her neck with my nose so I could also scent her.

Drake worked his way in once I was settled. We started fucking her and it felt amazing. I had zero desire to touch another man's cock under most situations. It was totally straight to rub your dicks together if you were both buried inside your girlfriend. And it felt fucking fantastic.

George was reaching behind her and clutching my neck

with one arm to pull me closer and grabbing at Drake with the other. We were both gripping her under her knee, but I passed her leg off to Drake and shifted my position so I could show her clit the love and attention it deserved.

We just kept fucking her while I massaged her clit and Drake was doing the biting thing again. Yeah, maybe I was also getting off on the friction of Drake's cock rubbing against mine, but in the straightest way possible.

I didn't know if George came that hard because her vagina was celestially blessed, but every time she did, she'd clamp down on my cock so hard and flutter around it until I came myself. Drake wasn't that far behind me. We pinned George between us as we were all wracked with pleasure.

Everyone joined us on the blankets and pillows for the post-coital puppy pile. There were still a few more hours until the moon went back to sleep, but there were a lot of us and only one of George. The rest of the night might be spent sleeping and snuggling, but crystals weren't the only thing that recharged under the full moon. It was one of the reasons moon orgies were held outside no matter what the weather.

I wasn't a student at the Academy of the Profane. The next four years would be me signing in Oscar's classes and maybe picking up some things in his classes shifters could use since I technically *had* to pay attention. My people here who *were* students could just focus on classes now that Hedylogus was chilling in some creepy jar somewhere in the Netherworld.

We were all a supportive group, so it wouldn't be just George helping Baldur and Drake heal from what Hedylogus did to them. We would all be doing that. Azren was the smartest person any of us knew. Reading lips was hard and not everyone managed it. Oscar had been struggling with it as long as I'd been trying to teach him. Azren might know something that would help him master that.

Oscar told us Azren had tried to heal the damage that had made him deaf and wasn't able to do it. I didn't know if Oscar had figured this out yet, but I had. I was pretty sure Azren not being able to heal him had been the Fates fucking with Oscar to correct a mistake they made a long time ago. Oscar was the hero in this whole Hedylogus mess *because* Azren couldn't heal him.

Eventually, I would tell him that. For now, there were a lot of people reeling from the whole situation that needed to heal from it. When we got back to our realm, we'd all be doing just that in between classes, dodgeball, and moon orgies.

And if another fucking god decided to creep on campus and get stupid, we deal with them, too.

GEORGE

EPILOGUE

The Academy of the Profane was stressful for the next four years, but it wasn't 'rogue serial killer god who could take away free will' stressful. It was stressful in the way that I had to figure out my mimic powers for actual grades instead of the way the other gods figured out theirs and I really liked winning dodgeball games.

Everyone close to me helped me figure out the trigger for my mimic gifts. By the time I graduated, I could go running with Matilda, West, or Mags as any shifter I wanted. I figured out how to bite Church back and make it feel good like he did. Several of my guys requested the bite. Drake eventually told me Basilisk venom is extremely painful for anyone other than other Basilisks. If a Basilisk bit another Basilisk, it was supposed to be an aphrodisiac, so I figured that out, too.

I learned to tap into the whole Kitsune thing like Ren, but the same rules applied to me with tails as every other Kitsune. I'd only get more than one tail if I earned it, so Ren and I raised a bit of Hell to see if I could. Oscar was able to teach me his magic so I could cast it like a Bruja if I was near him.

Azren and Baldur stayed closed to the Academy of the Profane until we all graduated. Azren taught history and my dad roped Baldur into teaching sculpture as part of the magical art program. The dwarves who taught Baldur how to work a forge didn't just make weapons. They made art and jewelry and Baldur loved working with his hands and creating things.

Odin took us all to Asgard so Baldur's new family could meet his old one. They were all wary of me at first because of his ex-wife, which I got, but they soon warmed up to me. Baldur's mother, Frigg, was a god of marriage and mother-hood. It barely took her five minutes of being around us for her to decide we were all better for Baldur than his ex-wife.

Baldur's half-brother, Thor became my new idiot big brother. He made me arm wrestle him to prove how much I loved Baldur. Thor was even bigger than Baldur, which I didn't think was possible, so he beat me, but I gave him a good fight. Apparently, Thor preferred Asgard and rarely left now, but when Baldur told him about dodgeball and that a good bit of his new family played, he came here to watch one of our games. It only took one game for Thor to be just as obsessed with dodgeball as West was. It was seri-ously adorable.

A lot of our dodgeball team had pro offers when we graduated. My idiot brother and Dexter got recruited for the same team because they worked well together. They took the offer. Drake turned his down. He loved dodgeball and was an amazing goalie, but it was music that made him whole.

The league came sniffing around Oscar again when he proved he was still a badass player, despite losing his hearing. Oscar was good at dodgeball, but he loved art. My dad might not have been teaching art, but he had enough connections to get Oscar's name out and Bram had done what he promised with his shop. Oscar's flash was out there for people who liked tattoos and all that was left was Oscar learning how to put it on people himself. Oscar told the dodgeball league to sincerely eat his ass for not standing by him the first time.

The same team that recruited Michael and Dexter tried to nab me too because they needed a new team witch and Michael and I could do amazing things. I didn't particularly want to go pro. I *loved* playing dodgeball, but it wasn't what I wanted to do with my life. I was a god, and I was pretty sure I was given mimic powers to help people.

So, I made a little deal with Michael's new team. Their team witch could do what I did with Michael with witchcraft and a lot of spunk. I negotiated a nice little sum to train their team witch so that my signature move with my brother wouldn't die when he went pro and I didn't.

I used the money to buy us a house in California near Ren, West, and Oscar's family. I already had a house in Profane. Freya left me her estate when she was Minerva Krauss. So, we had properties on the East and West Coast, Azren's home in the Netherworld, and Frigg and Odin had a house built for Baldur in Asgard as they were modernizing it. We had houses near all our families.

Matilda did an additional four years of schooling in Hell with other Hellhounds and demons. Mags, Mina, and Belladonna went with her. Just like the Academy of the

Profane opened their doors to an angel and a god, even though there wasn't technically a curriculum for us, the colleges in Hell did the same for Mags, Mina, and Belladonna. They were grad students, so they were learning politics and humanitarian stuff because my twin planned on taking over the world with her girlfriends one day.

Azren dropped something on me that I had been worried about, but thought it was a problem for the future. They'd already told my parents and my aunt. Everything died and people had been trying to cheat Death for a very long time. But Azren said there were loopholes, and I had made one loving so many people.

Gods stopped aging after a certain point and could only be killed by their one weakness. But love was a powerful force that could do amazing things. Azren thought the Fates created certain loopholes because of how they created gods. Mortals outnumbered us and we weren't always going to fall in love with other gods. It would have been insanely cruel to have a being that hard to kill fall in love with mortals with short lifespans. It would be a long life of constant loss.

Azren said they only told me this because they knew my feelings were real. If a god *truly* loved a mortal, like a pure love and not infatuation, their lifespan matched the gods. They still had weaknesses, but they wouldn't die of old age. That went for children and any mortal family members that god had a certain kind of love for.

Azren's gift for essences could see that everyone I cared about was safe, barring some kind of fatal accident that one of the many gods in our family couldn't get to in time to heal. It was a *huge* relief.

And Freya got her answers, too. She was back in her godly vessel, but the only reason she was back on this realm was because Azren asked for help. Freya had done a *lot* for witches, but now it was time for her to be selfish. Each time she was born into a mortal body, she'd meet the same three men. Sometimes, they were brothers and sometimes, they'd never met each other before they met her. They'd been a variety of races, but it was always the same three essences that were getting reborn the same time Freya was entering a mortal baby.

Azren confirmed it because they reaped them, but couldn't figure it out either. It usually took much longer for any essence to be reborn.

I grew up in a giant family and I knew I wanted one, too. We eventually settled down and had lots of babies. Multiples were common in my family. It was usually twins, but I had triplets. They had different fathers like Matilda and me, but they took after me and ended up gods. One was a jokester who very much took after Ren, his brother loved to study like Azren, and the other was the spitting image of Baldur.

The rest of my kids definitely took after their daddies. I might not be able to change that the Basilisks and energy vampires nearly got wiped out, but we definitely made sure there would be at least one more of each of them in this world. I had a little lioness with West and he would not let anyone touch her hair but him. Oscar and I had an amazing Bruja we named after his Abuela who looked just like her.

My triplets were the oldest, and it was when they turned eighteen Freya got her answers. She'd been in and out of our homes, mostly traveling around looking for answers about those three men she kept meeting and falling in love with each lifetime. She didn't realize when she went back to her godly vessel, they had also been reborn as gods...as my sons until they were *much* older.

She was horribly uncomfortable about it and thought we were all going to be furious with her, but we all *deeply* believed in Fate and didn't try to tell our kids who to love. If the Fates wanted them to be together, they would be. We sent the triplets off to college and told her to get to know them the same way she did before.

And Azren was right. I always thought my parents, aunt, and uncles looked so young because my mom and aunt were witches and good at potions. It was because after a certain point, they stopped aging just like my husbands did.

My parents raised me to think that even though I was a god, I couldn't have everything I wanted because the world didn't work like that. I knew damned well that was true, but I also wasn't greedy. I *did* have everything I wanted and my life was close to perfect.

My husbands were all working jobs they were passionate about. Baldur, Azren, and I had a small clinic where we pooled our powers to help people. My dad and Loki joined us sometimes and so did my sons when they were older. Yeah, and we were all there when Fate did her thing and Freya and my triplets were hand fasted.

My kids who weren't gods were also amazing and powerful supernaturals. They were going to make amazing adults one day and since they had so many gods who loved them and considered them theirs, I was never going to have to lose them.

Yeah, I might not get every little thing I wanted, but I had everything I needed and my life was about as close to perfect as I could imagine.

AFTERWORD

Thank you for sticking it out with George's story. This is going to wrap up the Profane shared world. I might come back and do a massive Yule story to raise money for the rescue most of my pets are from with all of the characters, but this is it. If you've stuck it out the entire time, I'm sorry for some of the cliffhangers, but I'm not sorry for the dick jokes and fuckery.

If the Academy of the Profane is your first time in the Profane world, there's more! There are three complete series and a standalone. You're going to want to start with Chaos and the Library of the Profane, move to the Museum of the Profane, head on over to The Totally True Tales of Minerva Krauss, then go to the Paranormal Investigation Bureau. You'll get George's mom, aunt, Freya, and her babysitter's stories in those series.